SPECIAL MESSAGE

THE ULVERSCROFT FOUNDATION
(registered UK charity number 264873)
was established in 1972 to provide funds for research, diagnosis and treatment of eye diseases. Examples of major projects funded by the Ulverscroft Foundation are:-

- The Children's Eye Unit at Moorfields Eye Hospital, London
- The Ulverscroft Children's Eye Unit at Great Ormond Street Hospital for Sick Children
- Funding research into eye diseases and treatment at the Department of Ophthalmology, University of Leicester
- The Ulverscroft Vision Research Group, Institute of Child Health
- Twin operating theatres at the Western Ophthalmic Hospital, London
- The Chair of Ophthalmology at the Royal Australian College of Ophthalmologists

You can help further the work of the Foundation by making a donation or leaving a legacy. Every contribution is gratefully received. If you would like to help support the Foundation or require further information, please contact:

THE ULVERSCROFT FOUNDATION
The Green, Bradgate Road, Anstey
Leicester LE7 7FU, England
Tel: (0116) 236 4325

website: www.foundation.ulverscroft.com

THE WALL

The Wall is the concrete heart of the town of Amarias. You can only cross it at one checkpoint, where armed soldiers stand guard. One day, thirteen-year-old Joshua discovers a pitch-black tunnel that leads underneath The Wall. He's heard plenty of stories about the other side, and knows that a boy like him shouldn't venture into this forbidden territory. But he is compelled to go — and his world is about to be turned upside down . . . A searing fable about a divided city, *The Wall* is one boy's shocking and powerful journey to find his own sense of right and wrong.

WILLIAM SUTCLIFFE

---◆---

THE WALL

a modern fable

Complete and Unabridged

CHARNWOOD
Leicester

First published in Great Britain in 2013 by
Bloomsbury Publishing Plc
London

First Charnwood Edition
published 2014
by arrangement with
Bloomsbury Publishing Plc
London

The moral right of the author has been asserted

A catalogue record for this book is available
from the British Library.

ISBN 978–1–4448–1808–6

Published by
F. A. Thorpe (Publishing)
Anstey, Leicestershire

Set by Words & Graphics Ltd.
Anstey, Leicestershire
Printed and bound in Great Britain by
T. J. International Ltd., Padstow, Cornwall

This book is printed on acid-free paper

For Saul

Part One

We sprint for the ball, shoulder to shoulder, our backpacks thumping from side to side. I get in front, but David grabs my schoolbag and pulls me back, like a rider stopping a horse.

'Oi!' I shout. 'That's a foul!'

'There's no such thing.'

'Yes there is!'

'Not when there's no ref.'

David gets to the ball first and shields it with his body. 'Watch this,' he says, and jumps on the spot with a jerk of his heels, trying to flick the ball over his head. It dribbles out sideways and rolls into the gutter. David thinks he's a good footballer, even though he's so uncoordinated he only knows where his feet are when he's looking at them.

I wedge the ball between my ankles and leap, with a sharp knee-bend, then swivel. The sphere of leather sits up in the air perfectly, as if it's waiting for my foot, and I execute what can only be described as an incredible volley, right on the sweet spot. The ball flies away, faster and further than I could ever have hoped.

Life, as you probably know, is full of ups and downs. There is always a price to pay for perfection.

At exactly the moment my trainer whacks into the football, the empty road where we're playing stops being empty. The security car comes round the corner, but my ball is already in the air, and there's nothing I can do to get it back again.

The driver can't be looking very carefully, because he only slams on the brakes after the ball thumps into his windscreen. David runs for it. I sprint for the ball, getting to it just as the security guard climbs out of his car.

'Was that you?' he shouts.

'No,' I say, as I'm picking up the ball.

'Do you think I'm stupid?'

I'm very, very close to saying 'yes'. If I did, I think it might be the funniest thing I've ever said, especially since he probably is a bit stupid. Imagine just driving round and round all day, patrolling streets where nothing ever happens. Even if you were clever when you started, your brain would eventually turn to mush. He's got a gun, but you can't shoot someone just for calling you stupid.

I keep my mouth shut and run off with the ball, to where David's waiting for me, half hiding behind a parked car. I tell him what I almost said and he finds it so funny he punches me on the arm, which is actually quite annoying, so I punch him back, then he shoves me so I grab him round the waist and we begin to wrestle.

When the security car drives past us, David's sitting on my head, and I see the driver tutting at us as if he thinks we're idiots, but I know it's him that's the idiot.

We go back to football tricks after that, until David tries to copy my volley and the ball sails up, across the street, above the bus stop, and over the hoardings around a building site. This

4

isn't one of the normal building sites around the edge of town, either; this is the strange one opposite the medical centre, where nothing ever gets built, and you never see a single person go in or out.

'I don't believe it,' he says, which is what I knew he was going to say.

'That's a new ball!'

'It bobbled,' he says. I knew he was going to say that, too.

He's trying not to look at me, and I can see him thinking about walking away, so I step in front of him and block his path. 'You'll have to go over and get it,' I say.

We look up at the hoarding. It's more like a wall: solid wood, with nowhere to see in, and more than twice my height. It was originally painted blue, but over the years it's faded to a dish-water grey, with the paint bubbling up in cracked oval blisters. This building site is pretty much the only place in Amarias that's not spanking new. The rest of the town feels like it's just been unwrapped from cellophane.

One section of the fence is a hinged opening, wide enough for a truck, but it's locked shut with a thick chain which is rusted dark as chocolate. Thinking about my ball, lost over the hoarding, it occurs to me for the first time how strange it is that everyone calls this place a building site, when no one ever builds anything there.

'You have to climb in and get it,' I repeat.

'We can't go in there,' he snaps.

'I didn't say we, I said you.'

'There's no way in.'

'You'll have to climb over. It's a new ball. It was a present.'

'There's no way I'm going in there.'

'So you'll get me a new ball?'

'I don't know. I have to go.'

'You have to get me a ball, or go in there and get that one back.'

David looks at me with heavy, reluctant eyes. I can see on his face that he's given up on the ball, and now he just wants to get away from my nagging. 'I'm late,' he says. 'My uncle's visiting.'

'You have to help me get the ball back.'

'I'm late. It's just a ball.'

'It's the only one I've got.'

'No it isn't.'

'The only leather one.'

'Don't be such a baby.'

'I'm not being a baby.'

'Baby.'

'*You're* being a baby.'

'Baby.'

'Saying 'baby baby baby' over and over makes you a baby, not me,' I say. I'm embarrassed to be even having this conversation, but with David there's sometimes no way out. He drags people down to his level.

'Then why can't you stop whining about the ball?'

'Because I want it back.'

'*Because I want it back*,' he says, in a baby voice.

I'm not the kind of guy who hits people, but if I were, this is when I'd do it. Smack on the nose.

His backpack is dangling off one shoulder. If I

6

grab his bag and toss it over the fence, he'll have to climb in. I lunge for it, but he's too quick. Not that David is ever quick, but I'm just too slow. He's read my thoughts, and in a second he's running away, laughing a fake laugh.

David is my best friend in Amarias, even though he's extremely annoying. Amarias is a strange place. If I were living somewhere normal, I don't think David would be my friend at all.

'You owe me a ball!' I shout after him.

'*You owe me a ball!*' he says, slowing to a walk, knowing he's out of reach.

I watch him go. Even the way he walks is irritating, lolloping from leg to leg as if his shoes are made of lead. He thinks he's going to be a fighter pilot; I think he's too clumsy to control any machine more complicated than a bicycle pump.

The most frustrating thing of all is that I know in a day or two I'll have to forget about the ball and make friends again. I used to have lots of people to choose from, but out here, there's only David. The other boys in Amarias don't like me, and I don't like them. They think I'm a weirdo and I think they're weirdos. In this town, weird is normal and normal is weird.

I look up at the fence. It's unclimbable. I walk alongside it, blackening my fingertips against the rough wood, bursting a couple of paint blisters with my thumb, until I get to a corner and turn into an alley. I pause to examine the neat ovals of filth at the end of each finger, then place them back on the wooden surface and head down the narrow corridor of cool, shady air. Soon, I come

7

up against a metal dumpster. It's higher than my hand stretched above my head, but if I can climb on to its lid, it might work as a step that could get me over. If I want my ball back, this is the way.

I take off my schoolbag, hide it in the gap between the dumpster and the fence, then take a few steps back. A short run-up and a good leap is enough to get a decent grip on the hinge. With a swing and a kick, I hook a leg on to the lid, and after an awkward wriggle, which rubs more of me against the bin than I'd really like, I'm up. A tricky manoeuvre, perfectly executed. Climbing isn't a proper sport, but if it were, it would be the sport I'm best at. I can't explain why, but whenever I look at a high thing, I want to go up it.

There's a man who climbs skyscrapers. He just turns up and does it, and by the time he's off the ground, no one can stop him. When he gets to the top he always gets arrested, but he doesn't care. I bet that even the policemen doing the arrest secretly wish they were his friend. Sometimes, when I'm bored, I look at things and figure out where the best handholds and footholds would be. The best climbers can lift their whole body weight with one finger.

I look around from the top of the dumpster. There isn't anything to see — only the alley — but just viewing the world from double my normal height feels good. Sour, fishy wafts are coming up from under my feet. The lid sags under my weight, bending inwards with each step. If it breaks, I can picture how I'd look. I've seen it in cartoons a hundred times. The angry face smeared in red and brown goo, a fried egg on one shoulder, a fish skeleton on the other, spaghetti on top of the head. There's always spaghetti. If you add in the stink and imagine it actually happening, it isn't funny any more.

From the lid of the bin I can't see over the fence, but I can now see that the site goes right up to The Wall. If this place does have a secret purpose, this position has to be the key. I pull myself up on to the splintery top of the fence, and with one leg dangling on either side, look down into the site for the first time. There is a house. Just a house and a garden, but I've never seen anything like it in my life.

The whole place has been flattened. Squashed. Pushed over. One wall is still intact, at a forty-five-degree angle, and the rest has just shattered and crumbled underneath it, into not much more than a heap of rubble. Sticking out from the mound of stones and mortar, I can see half a faded pink dressing table; blocks of splayed and crinkled paper, still bound together, but no longer really books; a telephone with no receiver, trailing a wire that snakes away as if it is still expecting a call; a toy pram; a yellow dress hanging halfway out of a collapsed window frame; a DVD player bent in half; a toilet seat with an embroidered cover.

Two voices spark up in my head. One of them is excited, telling me this is the best adventure playground, the best climbing frame, the best secret hideout I've ever seen. It wants me to jump straight down and explore the ruin. The other one holds me back. This voice is quieter

9

— it doesn't even seem to have any words — but it's more powerful and keeps me motionless on top of the fence. It's a feeling I can't quite understand, something to do with the stuff spilling out of the demolished house, something to do with the obvious suddenness with which this place was transformed from a home into a heap of junk. An eerie chill seems to be rising up from the rubble. It's as if an aftertaste of violence is hanging in the air, like a bad smell.

All the houses in Amarias are the same. You see new ones going up all the time: first the concrete, sprouting metal bars like a dodgy haircut, then the red roof and the windows, and finally the cladding of stone slapped on like a paint job. This one's different. There's no concrete. Just proper lumps of solid stone.

I want to jump in and romp around and climb to the top, and at the same time I have an urge to run away and forget what I've seen. I sense that just for looking over this fence, just for knowing what the so-called building site contains, I'm in trouble.

Holding tight to the top of the fence, I look more closely over the site. Though the garden has mostly gone wild, or disappeared under rubble, from up high I can make out a pattern of paths and beds. A huge rose bush has covered a toppled wall in crimson blooms. In the corner are six old-looking fruit trees, planted in a perfect circle, forming what would once have been a shady grove. The trees are dead, with a scattering of dried-up leaves still clinging to the branches, but they surround a metal swing seat which looks as if it might work, as if it might be the only thing untouched by the carnage all around. Beyond the fruit trees, the ground is bare, flat, grooved with neat rows of bulldozer tracks, right up to The Wall.

My mouth is suddenly dry and sticky. I feel as if I've accidentally glimpsed one of my friends' mothers, naked. It seems almost shameful to be sitting here, staring at this smashed-up home that is the absolute opposite of everything my town is supposed to be. But I can't look away.

I know it's wrong to climb over these ruins, in the same way it would be wrong to play football in a graveyard, but I can't just turn and leave. I need to know more. I need to touch and feel this place, walk around in it, look for clues as to what happened. And I still want my ball.

I glance down, between my knees. The inside of the hoarding is slatted, much easier to climb than the smooth exterior. I can go in and out as quickly as I want. No one needs to know what I've done, except maybe David. He probably won't believe me, but I decide my mission can be to find a souvenir that will prove I really jumped in and explored. It won't be difficult to pick out something good. Even from up here, I can see that the possessions spilling out of the house never belonged to people like us. This was the home of people from the other side. The mystery isn't what happened to them, it's how they found themselves on the wrong side of The Wall in the first place, and why the site hasn't been cleared and built on.

I climb down the slats, and turn to face the

demolished house. Inside the site, behind the hoardings, there's an eerie silence. I could scamper up the toppled wall in a few seconds if I wanted to, but the graveyard feeling is even stronger in here, shielded from the outside world.

I shuffle along the fence, heading towards the back of the building, pulled by a strange urge to sit on the swing seat, see if it still works, hear what noise it makes. A pair of old-fashioned patio doors comes into view, a white-painted wooden frame and lots of small square panes of glass, one in each corner tinted blue. The nearer door is crushed and shattered; the other is untouched, still upright, half filling a doorway from nothing to nothing.

I find a garden path made of red tiles, which leads me in a smooth arc to the swing seat. It's furry with rust, like a sunken ship. I give it a gentle push, expecting it to squeak, but instead I hear a bang from the far side of the garden which makes me jump backwards.

A flash of movement around the side of the house catches my eye, and I see a small cloud of dust rising from the earth. As the dust clears, a square sheet of metal becomes visible.

I crouch motionless behind the swing seat, ready to run and hide if anyone appears.

Nothing moves. Minutes pass, and everything remains still and silent. If anyone was here when I arrived, they've now gone. I see my ball, nestled in a dusty channel between two clumps of stone, sitting on a mouldering scrap of red cloth that looks like the remains of a cushion cover.

I wait a little longer, until I'm sure that I'm

alone, then I fetch my ball and slowly approach the metal sheet. It has a greasy, ridged surface, which I kneel and touch. My hand jumps back at me. The metal is hot, glinting in the bright sunlight.

There are footprints in the dust around me, leading towards and away from where I'm squatting. Along the path of these footprints, I see something odd: something not dusty or old or broken. It's small, but new, and still working. A dim gleam, barely visible in the daylight, is coming from one end. It's a torch. A working torch, still on.

I pick it up. I switch it off and switch it on. It can't have been there long; the batteries are still fresh. I turn and look again at the metal sheet. The bang; the footprints; the torch — these three things connect. There's something under that metal.

I scour the wasteland around me, checking I'm still alone. I wonder for a moment if I should get help. Tell an adult, maybe. But what would I say, and why on earth would they believe me or be interested? I found a torch that works. Something moved and went bang. In fact, what were the chances of me even getting to the interesting part of the story before being told off and punished for climbing into the building site? Besides, even if they did believe me, and I had uncovered something important, would I be allowed to see it? Would I ever be told the truth about what was discovered? Probably not.

If I want to find out what's under there, I have to do it myself, and I have to do it straight away.

13

I bend my knees and heave at the metal, revealing a glimpse of a dark hole. I push again, the hot, sharp edge digging into my skin, but with a firm shove, it slides aside. I drop the sheet, and immediately realise this hole is no ordinary hole. There's a rope tied to a metal pin that has been hammered into the soil just under the surface. The rope is knotted at regular intervals, each gap the length of my forearm. I can make out four knots, then nothing: just a black void. The hole is the size of a manhole, but an irregularity to the shape gives the feeling it has been dug without machines. This is the entrance to something.

I kneel at the edge and shine the torch downwards, with my arm stretched out as far as it will go. In the weak, thin beam, I trace the rope to where it ends in a tangled white blob, sitting on a dark surface that looks like soil. But it's hard to be sure.

I can't look at a high thing without wanting to go up it. Now I'm staring down this hole — a hole like nothing I've ever seen before — and the same voice is piping up, telling me I have to go down, I have to take a look, I have to know what it's for and where it goes.

I have a hunch as to what this might be, and I know how dangerous it is to get involved with anything like it, but on the other hand, stumbling across this mystery, in the middle of my boring, boring town with nothing to do and nowhere to go, is like finding buried treasure. I can't just leave it there and walk away.

Maybe I ought to work out the risks, remind

myself of everything I've been warned about, take stock of what I have to lose. I know that's what David would do if he was here with me, but that's not the kind of person I am, and it's not who I want to be, either. Mysteries are for solving, walls are for climbing, secret hideouts are for exploring. That's just how things are.

I pocket the torch and slide myself into the hole. The first knot is just beyond the reach of my feet, so I squeeze the rope with my knees and edge myself downwards, hand over hand, until I have a knot to stand on. After that it's easy to shunt myself lower, knot by knot, to the bottom. I'm just beginning to enjoy the climb when I hit the soil, and find myself wishing the hole was deeper.

The earth at the bottom is softer and darker than on the surface, cool against the palm of my hand. There's a musty smell, like a bag of football kit you've forgotten about for a few days. I switch on the torch and immediately see that my suspicion was correct. The hole is more than a hole. It's a tunnel, held up with props of rough wood and thin planks that look like they've come from packing crates. Mostly, though, it's just a thin but seemingly endless tube of soil, disappearing ahead into darkness, in the direction of The Wall.

Now I have a choice. I can go back up, collect my football, and head home; or I can go through. I know what I ought to do. I know what every other boy in Amarias would do. But as I see it, those are the two best reasons there could possibly be for doing the opposite.

I've lived in Amarias since I was nine, and in those four years I've never once been to the other side. The Wall is taller than the tallest house in town. If I wanted to see over it, I'd have to stand on the shoulders of a man who was standing on another man who was standing on another man who was standing on another man. Depending on how tall they were, you might need one more. This opportunity has not yet arisen.

The Wall was put up to stop the people who live on the other side setting off bombs, and everyone says it has done an excellent job. Most of the people who work on the building sites in Amarias are from the other side, and if you drive to the city you see lots of people who look like they come from those towns, but other than that, even though they're living right next door, it feels like they aren't really there. Actually, that's not right. You know they're there, because The Wall and the checkpoints and the soldiers who are all over the place are a constant reminder, but it's as if they are almost invisible.

I thought I'd never see into a town beyond The Wall until my military service, but now, looking down this column of musty air, I realise that within five minutes I could be poking my head up, seeing what's there. The alternative is to wait five more years, until my conscription.

16

People say hysterical things about what's on the other side, but adults can't help exaggerating. They're always trying to make you believe that one cigarette will kill you, that crossing the road is as lethal as juggling with knives, that cycling without a helmet is bordering on suicide, and none of it ever turns out to be true. How dangerous could it really be just to pop through and take a quick look? And how frustrated will I feel tomorrow if I just climb back out now and go home?

It sounds crazy, but I'm not even scared when I decide to go for it. Frankly, it's the only logical course of action. If you have the chance to uncover a secret and you walk away without looking, there's something wrong with you.

The torch lights a few metres of tunnel ahead of me, but no more. I look upwards one last time and see, as if through a telescope, a disc of blue sky with one tiny puff of cloud drifting across it.

I crouch on to my hands and knees, waving the torch in front of me, trying to get used to the way it produces only a narrow beam of visibility enclosed on all sides by dense, velvety blackness. At first, it seems almost like a magic trick, the way objects disappear the instant you move the torch away from them. Then I think how odd it is, when you live in a town, that you can get through your whole life without ever seeing real darkness. Amarias is constantly illuminated, with orange streetlights that stay on all night, and floodlights at the checkpoint.

One last worry pops into my head. I take the phone from my pocket and squeeze it to light up

17

the screen. Down in my hole, there's only one bar of signal. I put the torch down and write a quick text to my mum: 'Playing football with David. Back later.'

Clutching the torch in my right fist, with my other hand flat on the damp earth, I begin to edge forwards. The sound in the tunnel is both oddly loud and unsettlingly quiet. I can't hear any outside noises at all, but every movement I make seems to bounce back at me off the walls, as if amplified. The scrape of my hand and the torch against the soil; the drag of my shoes behind me; the panting of my own breath; all these seem to boom around me like a static echo which only quietens when I stop moving. Even then, I feel as if I can hear myself swallow and blink.

Fear seems to seep out of the soil, into my body, like coffee soaking through a sugar lump. As tension closes round my heart and squeezes my lungs, I try to imagine that the real me is somewhere else, up above in the daylight, safe and calm. I pretend there are two versions of me, one in the tunnel, another one encouraging me on from above. The more I think of this, the easier it becomes to picture, like a cross-section through the earth: me on my knees going through a horizontal tunnel, then above that a layer of soil, then above that another me, matching my movements, walking through the gardens of the demolished house, getting closer and closer to The Wall, and at any moment simply ghosting through it to the unknown place on the other side.

It's a strange idea: not just passing through The Wall, but also the above-and-belowness of it. Usually the world just feels like a flat skin you walk around on, then sometimes you remember that every place is more than just one patch of land, because there's also the air above it and the ground below it. Each spot is actually a column, going right down to the magma at the centre of the earth, and up, into the sky and beyond, for ever. People forget that when you go upstairs, you are actually standing right on top of the people who are downstairs. Think about it hard enough and it's properly freaky. If floors and ceilings had to be made of glass, people would go crazy. They wouldn't be able to take it, and everyone would end up living in bungalows.

It's useful to have things like this to think about when you're doing something scary, because I have no idea how long I've been crawling, or how far I've gone, at the moment when my torch picks up a patch of something greyish-white. I stop and extend the torch in front of me, peering into the gloom, squinting to try and form the shifting blob of colour into a recognisable shape.

Another metre of crawling gives me my answer. It's a coil of rope. I've got to the end of the tunnel. I'm on the other side.

'You've done it!' I think to myself, in a booming military voice. 'A daring and risky mission executed with determination, courage and skill.' If I believed in medals, I'd award myself one right there and then. In fact, I hate medals. They gave one to my dad. Mum has hidden it somewhere and I don't even care where.

All I need is a quick look outside. After that, I can head home. I grip the rope and give it a tug, checking it's firmly attached, then switch the torch off and put it in my back pocket. In pitch darkness, one knot at a time, I begin to climb.

The cover over the opening wobbles with just a gentle touch. It's made of metal, but is thinner and lighter than the one at the entrance. Or maybe this is the entrance. That all depends on who the tunnel was built for, and why.

I gently slide the cover to one side, creating an opening big enough for my head, then work my feet up to the next knot. All I have to do now is straighten my legs, and my head will be poking out, giving me my first view of the other side.

I come up in an alleyway between a ragged concrete building with bricked-over windows and The Wall, which on this side looks unrecognisable. It is the same size, of course, and the same concrete, but unlike the bare grey surface I'm used to, this side is entirely covered for the first two metres of its height with graffiti: a mixture of drawings, slogans and random scrawls. None of it is in my language, so I can't read a word. One image, of a huge, old-fashioned key, is repeated in a long line above the text, twenty or thirty times, so high it must have needed a ladder to do it.

At one end of the alley, a high chain-link fence blocks the way through to what looks like either wasteland or an abandoned garden. In the other direction my view is obscured by a pair of large rubbish bins, but I can see a few passing feet and a glimpse of the odd car. This is the way to the town, but the tunnel exit (or entrance) is set up so you can get in and out without being visible from the street. I check again that no one can see me, swivelling my head in all directions, then push aside the tunnel door and haul myself out. As soon as I'm up, I push the cover back over the tunnel with my feet.

I stand dead still, not daring to move. Through a gap between the bins I can see a sliver of what looks like normal life: cars, motorbikes, pedestrians, people going here and there doing the things that people do, carrying plastic bags, pushing children in buggies, chatting, standing around. But even within this little slice, I can see that something is fundamentally different from what I'm used to. Perhaps it's the bustle, the noise, the crowds; perhaps it's the way people look and walk, how they talk to one another and what they're wearing; perhaps it's the oddity of knowing that the freakishness of this place is only in my head, in its unfamiliarity to me. These are ordinary people having an ordinary day in what for them is an ordinary town, but it feels as if my short journey through the tunnel has transported me further away from home than I've ever been, and this small glimpse, this tiny sliver of a view, is simply not enough.

I edge towards the bins and squeeze myself through the gap, just far enough to see out of the alley. It leads to the street through a narrow opening between two tall concrete buildings, the walls streaked with green and brown stains. I stare, pressing myself into the shadows, watching and listening, slowly creeping forwards to widen my view. I know I ought to turn and head straight back to safety, but what I'm seeing holds me there, watching. This place is bursting with something I can't quite put my finger on, a feeling of bustle and life which seems like the very essence of what the quiet, clean, just-built streets of Amarias lack.

Eventually I reach the corner, and allow myself a quick look in each direction — two speedy snapshots of this close-but-distant world. Rows of shops and stalls line the road, everything jumbled together. In front of me, a man in a tracksuit is standing alongside a wooden cart piled high with cigarettes. Behind him is a grocery store, with sacks of beans, lentils, chickpeas, couscous and rice laid out on the pavement, underneath boxes of aubergines, green peppers, potatoes, cauliflowers and lemons. Further down the street, an old woman in a black headscarf is sitting on a plastic crate behind a waist-high stack of eggs, but her pavement space is shared with an array of car seats, springs, cogs and axles which have spilled out from a garage. Further on, there are more rows of old men and women sitting behind small stacks of vegetables, mixed in with younger guys selling mobile phones and phone accessories encrusted with fake jewels.

Opposite the alley is a bakery with a large hand-painted sign, showing a slice of green cake with wings flying through an electric-blue sky. In the window, there's a heap of oval loops of bread, like stretched bagels, and bright yellow star-shaped pastries.

In the other direction, there's a butcher with three whole carcasses almost as big as me hanging from hooks, outside which two middle-aged guys are sitting behind a wooden tray on a low stand, displaying bracelets, hair clips and baby shoes. Further down are fruit stalls and sweet stalls, blocking the entrance to a noisy workshop in which two men, obscured by clouds of dust, are operating a circular saw surrounded by stacks of doors. As I watch, two teenage boys pass by, dragging an enormous canister of cooking gas. A wooden cart piled with a teetering pyramid of oranges follows closely behind them. The mournful wail of a solo voice backed by violins is drifting down the street from one direction, clashing with a hectoring speech blaring from the distorted speakers of a badly tuned radio.

Next door to the bakery, an old man in a crocheted white cap is sitting on a plastic stool in a narrow doorway, opening and closing a cigarette lighter, watching everything, looking neither bored nor interested.

Nothing, on its own, is particularly weird, but taken all together, it's the most astonishing street I've ever seen, both enticingly alive and strangely depressing. There's no paving on the pavement and the tarmac on the road is old, cracked, and dotted with stagnant puddles. The buildings don't look properly built, with cables and pipes hanging off them in strange places. Many seem unfinished, sprouting tufts of iron bars from their roofs. Hardly anything is painted, and the shops all spill out on to the street as if there's no clear difference between inside and outside. Not one of the passing pedestrians seems to find any of this even slightly strange.

Staring at this mysterious vision of strangeness and normality, I lose track of my intention to snatch a glance and leave. Even when a couple of people notice me, staring momentarily then walking on, my feet are still slow to turn me round and take me back. Then I spot a group of four boys crossing the street in my direction, heading straight towards me, at speed. They're big, at least a year or two older than me, and their eyes seem to be glowing with a strange intensity, twinkling with excitement as they bear down on me.

I spin on my heel and sprint down the alley. I hear their footsteps accelerate as they give chase, then angry shouts boom out, echoing down the column of dank air. I can't understand the words, but this obviously isn't a friendly greeting.

With my heart beating so hard it seems to be battering against my rib cage, I push through the gap between the bins. I can see that I'll get to the tunnel before the boys, but if they follow me down, and through, what then?

My feet drive hard against the dusty ground as I accelerate away from the bins, hurling myself towards my escape route, but suddenly I see I'm not alone. There's a boy standing on top of the tunnel entrance. His arms are folded across his chest and his feet are planted firmly on the trapdoor. He's the same height as me, and looks thin but tough. Even though he's neatly dressed, in a clean school uniform, just the way he's standing makes him look like the kind of kid who knows how to throw a punch.

I pause, only a few steps away from the tunnel. He stares at me, his gaze hard and sad, as if he understands exactly who I am and what I want, and with an almost regretful look on his face he gives his head a small shake. He isn't going to move. He isn't going to let me into the tunnel.

I could try to push him away, but if he fights back I'll be done for. The four guys chasing me are already pushing between the bins. They'll be on me in a matter of seconds.

There's only one direction left to run: onwards past the tunnel, towards the chain-link fence. The boy stares at me impassively as I take off again, running the only way I can, further down the alley, towards who knows what? If I can't get over that fence, I have no idea what those boys will do to me. It will be bad, but how bad? I've never even been in a proper fight before, and now I know I'm about to be beaten up — punched and kicked at the very least — by a gang of boys bigger and older and tougher than me, who hate me just for being who I am, for coming from the other side of The Wall.

Even if I do get away from the boys, I'll need to find a way back to the tunnel. If I get lost, I'm in serious danger. There might be adults here who wish even more harm on me than these boys. As my hands crash into the wire of the fence, juddering me to a dead stop, it strikes me that I might never get home.

I grip hard and begin to climb. At the first two attempts, I slip back down having barely cleared the ground. Only the very tips of my trainers will fit into the tilted squares of wire that make up the fence, and my fingers alone aren't strong enough to hold my weight.

The gang is closer now, running past the boy standing on the trapdoor, sprinting towards me, still shouting. There's an edge of triumph in whatever it is they're saying. They know they have me cornered.

In desperation, I kick off my trainers and begin to climb again. I can now get my big toes into the fence holes. The wire bites into my skin, but I spider up the fence using all my strength, just as the boys catch up with me. They jump up at my ankles, one of them catching hold and pulling me down towards him. His pull jerks my other toe out of its foothold, and for a moment I'm hanging only by my hands. I have scarcely a second's more strength to support myself, but my half-fall causes the boy to lose his grip on my ankle. I shove my toes back into the fence and continue to climb, as fast as I can, the fence clacking and swaying under my weight.

It seems like only a moment later that I'm up, over and letting myself drop down on the other side. I land heavily, skidding on the stony ground and falling on to my back. Above me, I see that

27

two of the four boys are following me over the fence, but their size makes it harder for them, and they're slower than me, still only halfway up the other side.

As I stand again, I'm now close enough to reach out and touch the two boys who have given up on the climb. The hate in their eyes shines furiously out at me through the fence. I try to think what I could say to make them realise that I'm not worth hating — that I have nothing against them — that I'm just a boy who's never done anything bad to anyone — but no words form in my head. It seems for a moment as if one of them is about to speak, then a frothy, white globule flies from his mouth, towards my face. I have time to blink before it hits, time to glimpse its stringy form rotating through the air, but not to get out of the way.

I turn and run, wiping the warm, viscous saliva from my face as I go. The small patch of open ground, which I now see is planted with abandoned, dried-out vines, leads me to a T-junction. I head blindly to the right, running down a narrow street of low concrete houses, dodging between clusters of children and weaving between low-slung washing lines. Everyone stops what they're doing and stares as I run past.

I can feel the rough, stony ground cutting into the soles of my feet with every step, but there isn't time to slow down or pick level ground for each footfall. I zigzag left and right as much as I can, turning at every junction, but whenever I slow, thinking I might be getting away, I hear

28

again the shouts of the boys who are chasing me.

My thighs soon screech at me for a rest, the muscles seeming to harden and thicken around my bones. My throat tightens to a narrow, burning pipe, delivering only feeble threads of air to my gasping lungs.

I press on and on, as far as I can go, until, eventually, I realise my legs can carry me no further. I stagger to a halt and listen. For an instant: silence. My pulse seems to be hammering throughout my body, in my fingertips, my neck, my temples, as if every part of me is expanding and contracting to pump blood. I hear no shouts, no running footsteps, but they can't be far behind. My last hope is to hide, and I have only moments to get myself out of sight.

I look around the narrow street, and see a black motorbike parked against a wall, with a corner of space half concealed behind it. This is hardly a perfect hiding place, but it's my only option.

I jump into the gap and squash my body into itself, curling up like a foetus. When I have found the best position, I hold myself absolutely still, and breathe as steadily and quietly as I can, fighting to rein in the insistent rasp of my lungs.

A sudden beep from my pocket pierces the air. I pull out my phone. There's a text on the screen. 'OK. Have fun. Mum xxx.'

My phone! Is there someone I could summon to help me? Who could I contact? How could I describe where I am, when I don't even know? Whatever might be possible, at this moment I can't make a sound, let alone a call, or even risk

29

another beep. With my thumb muffling the speaker, I switch it off.

It seems bizarre that these words can beam out from a mast somewhere on the other side of The Wall and find me here, crouched behind a motorbike. The thought of my mum, probably standing at the stove, typing out this message, makes my throat tighten and my eyes sting. I can see it: the pans bubbling in front of her, the curve of her neck, the slight frown as she struggles with the tiny buttons. It's possible that I'll never again find myself in that kitchen, that at this very moment she's cooking the last meal she'll ever make for me, and I won't even taste it.

As I twist to put the phone in my pocket, I see something astonishing and terrifying, directly above me. There's a girl, leaning out of a raised ground-floor window, and her large brown eyes are looking straight down at me. If I'd seen her before, I would have written off this hiding place immediately, but now it's too late to change. She's wearing a grey and purple school uniform, and looks no older than me, but her hair is plaited on either side of her head in the style of someone much younger. Her eyebrows are puckered together, forming an expression of amused puzzlement.

For a strangely drawn-out moment, we look at one another: the girl leaning out into the street, me crouched down behind the motorbike. With my eyes, I beg her not to give me away. I put a finger to my lips, just as I hear the sound of four sprinting footsteps run past me, so close that particles of dust clatter against the spokes of the motorbike wheel. I flinch and press myself against the ground, willing the boys to keep on running.

They pass by without spotting me, but before the footsteps go out of earshot, I hear them falter, then stop. The road just ahead of the motorbike forks in two. I hear them exchange a few words then turn and head back in my direction. I feel something inside me give way, an internal collapse of courage and hope which feels like the ground caving in under my hiding place, dropping me into a helpless freefall.

The boys speak again, in louder voices, their feet now less than a metre away, but their language incomprehensible. Then I hear another voice: the girl. From the gestures and intonation, it's clear what is being said. They want to know if she saw me, and where I have gone.

Without looking down at me, she points up one of the roads, sounding enthusiastic and bloodthirsty, wiggling her finger fast as if to encourage them to hurry. They don't even wait for her to finish speaking before they run off.

She watches them go without even glancing downwards. After the sound of their footsteps has receded to nothing, she lowers her eyes and gives me what is almost a smile. I look up at her, too shattered and confused to smile back.

She beckons me upwards and I slowly uncurl myself, crouching for a moment behind the saddle to check with my own eyes that the boys have gone. My legs feel stiff and sore as I straighten and look at her through the open window. She has a pretty, friendly face, with wide, full lips and prominent front teeth, as if her mouth was intended for a slightly bigger head. Her eyes have a ring of black flecks at the perimeter of large, brown irises, like the site of a minuscule explosion. They are the eyes of someone who thinks fast.

She says something to me, but I can't understand. My mouth seems incapable of shaping a smile or uttering any words of thanks. Then, without any warning, she shuts the window in my face and disappears.

I look around me. I'm totally lost. I have no idea how I've got to this place, or how to get away from it. It won't be long before the boys, realising they've been sent the wrong way, return. I wonder for a moment if I should crouch down behind the motorbike again, or if it's futile to put off the inevitable any longer. Perhaps I should just stand there and let them find me.

A door clatters open and the girl appears again, on her front step. She barks more words at me, urgently this time, but I still can't understand. I shrug, and she takes a deep breath. Forming each syllable carefully, she speaks once more, this time in my language.

'Come inside,' she says.

I look at her blankly.

'Quickly,' she says. 'They might come back.'

I squeeze out from behind the motorbike, almost knocking it over, and follow her into the house. As soon as we are in, she closes and bolts the door behind us.

I try to thank her, but when I open my jaw, my chin begins to wobble, and this sensation causes my knees to decide that they, too, have forgotten how to behave. Jelly-legged, I realise I can't remain upright for much longer. I lean my back against the door and slide downwards until the floor comes up to meet me. Without any real idea of how it happened, I find myself sitting on the tiles of this girl's hallway.

She indicates with her hands that I should stay put, and walks away, returning a few moments later with a glass of water. I'm not sure if it's safe to drink the water on this side of The Wall, but I don't want to seem ungrateful and I'm desperately thirsty, so I down the whole thing in one gulp. As I hand her the empty glass, I realise I've got back the ability to voluntarily move my face, and I stretch my lips into a smile of gratitude, worrying, as I do so, that my expression might bear more resemblance to a grimace of pain. I feel like I need a mirror to check that my features are doing what I think they're doing.

She takes the glass from me, our fingers brushing as she does so. Mine are black with filth, hers are clean and slender, with nails immaculately painted a dark shade of blood red. It's a strange mismatch: these adult hands and that childish hairstyle. Her bare feet move soundlessly across the tiles as she walks away, then returns with a refilled glass. I swallow this one, again, in a single slug.

With nothing more than a raise of one eyebrow, she offers me another glass. I smile and nod, more confident this time that my smile really is a smile.

This third glass I drink more slowly. I even manage a thank you.

'It's OK,' she says.

'For saving me, I mean.'

'That's OK, too,' she says. Her voice is deeper than you'd expect from a girl her size, her accent strong and throaty but easy to understand. She leaves a gap between every word, pronouncing each one as if it's a jigsaw piece being slotted into place.

'It is very kind of you,' I say. 'I mean, more than kind. I don't know what the word is. They were going to . . . I don't know . . . ' I can't finish the sentence. I don't want to imagine what they would have done to me.

'I hate those boys. They're bullies. They beat up my cousin.' Her forehead wrinkles with anger, her lips pursing into a resentful pout.

'Do you think they'll come back?' I ask.

'I don't know.'

'I want to . . . I want . . . ' I can't get the next word out. The feel of it moving from my brain to my tongue sets my chin spasming again. I stop myself, take a deep breath, then try to get through the whole sentence in one quick gabble. 'I want to go home.'

I stare down into my drink and sip. A swirling green pattern covers the glass; the rim is painted gold. A worm of sweat slides down my spine. I shiver, momentarily unsure if I am hot or cold. It strikes me that I can smell a sour, meaty waft coming from the residue of the boy's spit on my cheek. The stink of it brings back the look on his face as he spat — a pure hatred I've never seen

34

before, let alone had directed straight at me — as if without that fence between us, he would have reached out and ripped me open.

I dip my fingers into the glass and dab at my cheek and eyelid. My mother might have phoned David's mother by now, and found out that I'm not with him. She could have phoned the school, too, to check that I left on time. It's probably dawning on her that something has gone wrong, that I'm missing, but even her worst nightmares didn't contain the possibility of me being here.

I'm not, in truth, very far away at all. Probably only a few hundred metres. But I'm in another world.

'I'll try and help you,' she says, 'but we have to be fast. Before my father gets home.'

'OK,' I say, pulling the phone from my trousers. 'Thank you. Can I phone?'

'Phone who?'

'Home. They can send someone to get me. I need an address.'

'Send who?'

'I don't know. Soldiers, I suppose.'

'The army?'

'Yes.'

'Here?'

'Yes. Just to get me.'

'No! No no no! Not here.'

'Why?'

'Put it away! Put it away!'

I return the phone to my pocket. 'But . . . '

'Can you stand?' she says.

I push against the ground and heave myself up. My legs feel achy and weak, barely strong enough to support my weight. The girl has turned away and is looking through a cupboard. This room, with its cracked tile floor covered in one place by a small threadbare rug, seems to be the whole apartment. There is a cooking area in the corner, a wooden table surrounded by five flimsy chairs, one small sofa that looks like it has almost fallen to bits. The whole cramped, dark space isn't much bigger than my bedroom.

The walls are decorated with an array of photographs, some framed, some just stuck to the wall; some recent, some old and faded. Even at a glance, you can recognise the same faces at different stages of life — feel a family swelling over time. The most ornate frame is around an old black-and-white portrait of a severe-looking couple seated in front of a large, elegant house, with four smartly dressed children posing stiffly around them. The youngest child has a blurred head which is facing both forwards and to the side.

As the girl turns back from the cupboard, holding an intricately patterned black-and-white scarf, I notice a pile of bed-rolls stacked under the window. 'You sleep here?' I say, realising as soon as the words come out that the surprise in my voice has been badly concealed.

'Over there,' she replies, pointing to a patch of floor, apparently not offended by the question or even noticing my tone of voice. Then I think perhaps she did understand, because she eyes me closely for a reaction as she adds, 'and my mother and my father and my brothers.'

I try not to move any muscles in my face, but just nod. 'Where are they all?'

'Out. But they'll be back soon, so we must be fast. This is my father's,' she says, handing me the scarf. 'Be careful with it.'

I take the scarf, unsure what she wants me to do with it. I stand there for a moment, smelling stale cigarette smoke rising from the soft cotton. She steps towards me and wraps it around my head and shoulders.

'Where are your shoes?' she asks.
'I had to take them off to get over a fence.'
'Are your feet OK?'
'I don't know. I don't want to look.'
'Do they hurt?'
'They sting, but it's fine.' Just thinking about them sends needles of fresh pain darting up through my legs.
'Maybe I can lend you some sandals.'

Her voice sounds reluctant. I know I ought to refuse, but the idea of heading outside again on the bare, raw soles of my feet is too awful. I shrug and she walks away, returning with a worn pair of plastic and foam flip-flops, several sizes too big, which she places in front of me. The insides of the soles are flattened and smoothed to the exact outline of her brother's feet, including each toe.

Now I've seen them, I almost want to change my mind and refuse, but I know I can't. I slip my feet reluctantly in.

'Now you look OK,' she says. 'Not too strange.'
'Thank you.'

She smiles at me, and I find myself smiling back. I'm not sure why. I feel sick with nerves at the idea of leaving her home.

'How did you get here?'
'Through a tunnel,' I say, wondering as soon as the words are out of my mouth if this is something I should admit.
'Where?'
'I don't know.'
'You don't know?'
'I know where it is from the other side, but on

38

this side it's a blur. I came up, then I was chased away. I just ran for it. I can't remember the route. It's a long way.'

'I can't take you to the checkpoint. I'm not allowed near the checkpoint.'

'Can you tell me where it is?'

'It's closed now. There's no point.'

'They'd let me through.'

'You won't get close enough.'

'What do you mean?'

'Have you never seen a checkpoint?'

'Of course I have.'

'Have you never been through one?'

'Of course. They just wave us through.'

'Well, not on this side.'

'But they'll see who I am. Where I'm from.'

'They won't. They won't see you and you won't see them. When it's shut, it's shut. Just barbed wire and fences. There's no one to speak to, and if you think you can just walk up to one of their bunkers on foot then you really are crazy.'

I almost ask her what would happen, but I realise I don't have to. Then, in a flash, I remember something. 'The tunnel! It's near a bakery with a picture of a flying slice of cake.'

'I know where you mean. It's close. You must have run in a circle.'

'If you can find me the bakery, I can get to the tunnel.'

'OK. Let's go.'

In an instant, she's out of the door. I struggle to catch up and match her fast but unhurried stride.

'Behind me,' she snaps. 'We're not together.'

I let myself fall back, and trail her from a few steps behind, tracking her movements out of the corner of my eye so I don't seem to be following her. Partially concealed by the scarf, and without anyone chasing me, I realise it's actually quite easy to walk along these streets without anyone giving me a second glance. I look a little different, but not too much, and it seems that even if people can tell I'm from the other side of The Wall, nobody is particularly interested. A couple of people throw me a second glance, registering faint surprise to see someone like me, wrapped in a scarf, walking these streets where I don't belong, but no one speaks to me or tries to get in my way.

After a couple of turns from the girl's house, we find ourselves on a busy street, jostling our way down a crowded pavement. The shops are all lit up now, mostly with bare bulbs hanging from naked electrical flex, and there is a bustling atmosphere of people heading home from work, buying things for the evening meal: women squeezing and sniffing vegetables, haggling over prices, gossiping with friends and shopkeepers. It all feels strangely normal yet exotic, and odd to think this place has always been here, so busy and alive; so close, but invisible. I'm struck again by the buzz in the air here, a hum of activity that you never find on the quiet, spacious streets my side of The Wall.

The girl stops walking and points across the street. I follow her finger towards the sign of the flying cake.

'You know where to go?' she asks.

I look opposite the bakery, and there is the alleyway where I stood, looking out at this street, only a short while ago.

I nod. 'Thank you,' I say. 'I . . . I think you saved my life.'

She nods back, holding me with a brief but forceful stare, as if there's something she's on the brink of saying, then she turns on her heel to walk away. Without thinking, I reach out and grab her arm. I can't let her disappear so suddenly.

'Wait,' I say. 'I want to give you something. I owe you.'

She gazes at me with her mesmeric, glistening eyes, a stare that fizzes into me with such force it's hard not to look away. For a long time, she seems poised to speak, but still no words come out of her mouth. She twists her arm free of my grip.

'What? What is it?' I say.

She looks as if she's battling against an idea, then her eyes drop to the ground. 'Do you have food?' she says, not looking at me.

The way she says it makes me look at her more closely, and I notice for the first time how thin she is, registering with a jolt how, when I took her arm, I felt my fingers looping around the bone.

I can't think what to say. As my shoulders lift into a helpless shrug, her eyes dart past me, as if she's seen something, or someone, that has alarmed her. Before I've even thought to ask her for an address, before I've had time to check my

41

pockets for money, she has spun away and rushed off in the direction we came. I watch her skinny form dodge left and right through the crowds, then slip out of sight.

The sounds of the street recede as I hurry down the alley. Every few steps I turn to check behind me, but no one is following. I squeeze between the bins and run for the tunnel.

After pushing the trapdoor aside, I reach into my back pocket for the torch. It's empty. I hurriedly check all my clothes, but the torch is gone. At some point in the chase it must have fallen out.

A sour waft rises up from the black void below me. The sight of that dark, chilly hole fills me with dread, but as I stand there, hesitating, I remember the gang of boys who chased me. Two of them didn't follow, and are probably still close by. They could be watching right now. Every second I stay there, looking down into the hole, wishing I had a torch, is a second I could be spotted. It's a terrifying idea to go down that tunnel alone, in the pitch dark, but being chased down it would be unimaginably worse. If someone did catch me down there, someone who wanted to hurt me, under the ground they'd be able to do whatever they liked with no one to see and no one to stop them. And no one to find the evidence afterwards.

With my clenched stomach sending acid squirts into my throat, I lower myself down. While I can still reach, I pull the trapdoor closed behind me, in case anyone comes past and sees that it is out of place.

As it booms shut, I find myself plunged into a darkness more intense than any I have ever experienced. It doesn't seem like just an absence of light, but is a powerful, sinister presence that crawls over me, smothering my face with something thick and heavy.

The thin, high gasps ratcheting through my mouth are the only sound. My hands, gripping the rope right in front of my nose, are invisible. They feel like faraway objects over which I could easily lose control. I'm no longer sure I can trust them to lower me down.

I hang there, clinging to the moist, hairy rope, trying to get used to the dark, dangling in this vertical shaft of cold, velvety blackness. The mouldy smell of the tunnel creeps into my nostrils as the dank air slips under my clothes and across my skin. I stay there so long the muscles in my legs begin to tremble. I force my hands to listen to me, sending nervous-system screams towards my fingers, mentally prising them loose from the rope and compelling them to take me down to the tunnel floor.

I blink and blink, until I realise there's no question of getting accustomed to this level of light, because there simply is no light. There's nothing to see. Down here, my eyes are useless.

Crouched on all fours, I stretch an arm ahead of me, then circle it up, right, down and left to feel the ceiling, walls and floor of the tunnel. In this way I get a sense of where I am, and which direction I have to crawl.

The tunnel, which felt so quiet as I travelled in

the other direction, now seems inhabited by eerie sounds. I can make out a low thrum, which rises and falls; possibly the sound of a street above, possibly something else mysterious and unknowable. There is a quiet clicking sound that might be the sound of drops hitting soil, or not. I also notice, for the first time, an acrid, sulphurous smell in the air — an odour of rot, or poison, or, perhaps, explosives. I wonder momentarily if this is definitely just a tunnel, or also some kind of underground storage facility.

I begin to crawl. Hand knee hand knee. Hand knee hand knee. I don't need light, and I can't get lost. I'm in a tunnel. I just have to close off all the voices in my head that are telling me to be afraid and concentrate on this simple task: hand knee hand knee. If I can do this straightforward thing, I can get home.

I have no idea how long the tunnel is, or how far a single crawl takes me, but I decide to set myself a target of 250 crawls. I'll count down. I'll parcel the distance up into these clear units and count down, backwards, filling my head with numbers, blotting out all other thoughts.

Hand knee hand knee. 249.

Hand knee hand knee. 248.

Hand knee hand knee. 247.

I'm somewhere in the 150s when I feel something slippery under my hand. A thin squeal fills the air. I freeze, and hear a scamper of tiny feet running away ahead of me.

A rat. I have put my hand on its back. I look at my hand to see if anything has come off the rodent on to me, and to examine myself for a bite, but of course I can see nothing. I can feel nothing, either, other than a faint greasy smear, so I can't have been bitten. If you are bitten by something, you know, but in this darkness, it seems hard to know anything for sure. The messages arriving in my brain from outposts of my own body seem jumbled, confusing, and not entirely trustworthy. I feel strange about my hand, now, as if I don't want to touch it, but you can't not touch your own hand. It's your hand.

That rat, I realise, is still up ahead of me. And where there is one, there might be hundreds. I don't know much about rats, but I know they don't live alone.

I stop and think, listening to my fast, shallow breaths bouncing back at me off the tunnel walls, trying to figure out what I can do about the rats, but soon I realise I'm not actually thinking anything. There is nothing to think, no alternative plan to search for. I just have to carry on.

Hand knee hand knee. 150.

Hand knee hand knee. 149.

Hand knee hand knee. 148.

I decide to stop every five to listen out for rats. With each stop, I shout and clap three times, trying to scare away any rats that might be near, trying to make myself sound and feel big.

Hand knee hand knee. 103.

Hand knee hand knee. 102.

Hand knee hand knee. 101.

Hand knee hand knee. 100.

I stop, shout, clap. One hundred more to go.

I'm more than halfway. I'm going to make it. I will get home.

Hand knee hand knee. 5.

Hand knee hand knee. 4.

Hand knee hand knee. 3.

Hand knee hand knee. 2.

Hand knee hand knee. 1.

Hand knee hand knee. 0.

I stop again. I reach out in front of me. Nothing. I should be at the end! I've got to zero, but there's only emptiness ahead of me. Where's the end of the tunnel? Could there have been a fork I didn't notice? Have I taken a wrong turn? Might I now be heading down another tunnel of unknowable length, perhaps miles of it, leading me who knows where — perhaps even back to the other side of The Wall? Should I turn round and check that I'm heading the right way?

A judder surges through my body, rattling me from the inside, taking over my limbs and torso. I slump forwards and lie on the cold soil, trying to quieten the barrage of panicked questions racing through my mind. I tell myself to concentrate on slowing my breathing, to calm myself, to stop shaking. I remind myself that I chose the number 250 at random. There is no reason to be more frightened now than one minute earlier, when I was still moving forwards through the darkness. I don't know how long the tunnel is. I was only guessing.

I've been down it once already, though, and I feel certain I got through much faster in the other direction. I wasn't hurrying when I had the torch; now I'm going as fast as I can, but the tunnel seems to go on and on without end.

Perhaps I'm not going to get home, after all. Perhaps I'm now in a maze of tunnels, trapped, stuck here until I die and am eaten by rats. Or would the rats start on me before I'm even dead?

Maybe the only thing to do is to lie here a little longer until I have more strength. A little rest might do me good. I'm so tired and afraid that for a moment it seems as if, whatever I decide, an irresistible wave of sleep is going to wash over me. But if I sleep, will the rats crawl on me? Will they take experimental nibbles at me to see if I'm done for? Are they looking at me right now, assessing whether or not it's time to move in?

I decide to allow myself just a minute more to gather my strength. I close my eyes and think of my old house, by the sea, and as an image of it comes into my head, the shudders in my body begin to recede. I picture its smooth concrete walls, white as a new tooth, crisp against a blue sky. I imagine myself looking out of our wide bay window, which was like the prow of a ship. If you stood in the middle with your nose pressed to the glass, you could see nothing but water.

This window formed one end of the big open space that more or less made up the whole house. It was mostly empty, furnished with not much more than a cracked leather sofa, a round wooden dining table, and a bright red kitchen in the corner. They were three separate rooms when we moved in, but Dad bought a sledgehammer and took all the walls out. My earliest memory is me clinging to Mum, listening to a thumping wall, scared but excited, then the plaster cracks and shatters, cascading to the floor, and, as the air clears, Dad appears in the hole with white dust all over his face and a huge grin, looking like a happy ghost.

Sometimes I'd lie on my back and look at the scribbles of sea-bounced light that jiggled on the ceiling. In the afternoons, the room was cool and shady. We had curtains, but only the seagulls could see in, so we never drew them except on the very hottest days, when the thin white cotton would flutter and dance in front of the open windows.

I was tiny when we first moved there, and my favourite toy was an orange wooden trike. When I see the house, I usually picture myself in that huge, bright room, wheeling this way and that through a scattering of toys, bumping into the furniture, dismounting and remounting, lost in elaborate fantasy tasks and journeys.

That was about ten years ago, so I don't know if I remember it from my memory, or from the home videos I've watched. We've got one DVD made up of short, shaky little snatches of our old life. There are only a few glimpses of Dad, because he was usually doing the filming. In one, he's pretending that he wants to pick me up, but he can't because I'm too heavy. I'm no taller than his knee, but he grunts and groans with the effort, bulging his cheeks and making the tendons in his neck stick out, then he goes into spasms and acts like he's having a heart attack. I laugh so much that I fall over, and the picture shakes crazily as Mum runs to stop me banging my head. I went

49

through a phase of watching this DVD every day, until the time Liev burst in and ejected the disc, accusing me of selfishness and cruelty. He ended up telling me it was 'time to move on', then walked out with the DVD.

I've looked everywhere in the house, right up to the attic, but without any luck. I don't think Mum would have let him throw it away, but I can't be sure.

In that house by the sea nobody ever prayed, except for on the morning we all dreaded, which came once a year, when Dad had to go off on his army reservist duty. Last thing before he left, he always took an old leather-bound book from a high shelf, and stood there for a minute or so, mumbling something to himself. Then he turned and went.

Once, after he'd gone, I asked Mum to get the book down for me. She showed me my grandfather's name written in curly old-fashioned handwriting on the title page, then flicked it to the bookmarked page, the prayer for travellers.

I can't remember the exact wording of the prayer, but I remember the point of it. I remember that you ask God to help you reach your destination in peace. I remember that you ask Him to save you from any enemies you might encounter. I remember that you ask for kindness and mercy, from God and from anyone you meet on your travels. And I remember how it ends: 'Blessed are you, Eternal One, who responds to prayer.'

None of those things happened. My father

wasn't saved from his enemies. Five years ago he said goodbye, walked out of the house, and never came back. I've been told it was a sniper, but not where, or how, or why. I'm not sure if Mum knows any more, or wants to know more, or would tell me if she did.

I can see it, just like with the home videos, always the same, a scrap of looped footage stored in my brain that I can't delete or change. I never see the moment he is hit, just him lying there in his uniform, bleeding into the street, surrounded by people shouting and shooting, but silently. There's never any sound. I can see the noise, but I can't hear it.

It's the only image I have of him in uniform, and I know I've made it up. He let me touch the rough green cotton pressed and folded in his kit bag, but he never allowed me to see him wear it. Even on the day he went, he always left the house in T-shirt and flip-flops. Before reporting for duty, he must have stopped on the way and changed. He didn't want to fight, but he had to, and they killed him.

Liev thinks he's become my father, but he hasn't.

Lying here in the dark, parts of that prayer come back to me, short phrases asking God to lead me safely home. If Dad was still alive I might say them aloud, but I know for a fact it doesn't work. It didn't work for him, so it won't work for me. There is no one up there who will ever help you. Liev prays and prays and prays, but I know he's just talking to himself. If I want to get home, I have to do it on my own.

51

I force myself back up on to my hands and knees and begin to crawl. This time I'll count upwards. If I get past a hundred I'll think again, but until then I'll just crawl and count, crawl and count.

Hand knee hand knee. 42.

Hand knee hand knee. 43.

Hand knee hand knee. 44.

Then a gentle bump — a tickle, almost — against the crown of my head sends my hands scrambling ahead of me to feel the obstruction. The first touch makes me leap backwards in horror. It's something hairy, and it twitches when I touch it.

I fall on my back and wait for the sensation of teeth sinking into my flesh. There's nowhere to run or hide. I lie frozen, with my legs and arms sticking up into the air, but the teeth never come, and silence fills the tunnel. I roll over, reach out and feel once more.

It's the rope. I look up and see what looks like a triangle — just the shape, a triangle — hanging there in the fathomless darkness. My eyelids flutter up and down, trying to blink meaning into this strange sight, but I can't make any sense out of it. All I see is a grey, abstract shape, floating in space, impossible to compute as something small or large, close or far away, until the distances and dimensions snap into place, and I realise it is a patch of evening sky. I didn't close the cover at this end. This is the gap I came through on the way in.

I grip the rope as hard as I can, and for a moment it seems as if I don't have enough strength in my arms to haul me upwards, but I push on, refusing to allow my muscles to give up on me, and at the moment when my fingers begin to feel like locked, burning claws over which I no longer have any control, a breeze ruffles my hair, and I find myself rolling up and out into the dust of the building site.

A little light is spilling in from the street lamps, and this shadowy landscape of dust, gravel, stone and shattered furniture at that instant looks like the most beautiful thing I have ever seen. Just to see again at all — to have the use of my eyes back — feels exquisite. I flop on to my back and look upwards, relishing the sensation of vision, awestruck by the magnificence of the vast, star-speckled sky.

Slowly, strength trickles back into my limbs. I'm safe, but I'm still not home. I have to get home.

I stand, raising myself on weak, juddery legs, and notice something round and white by my feet. The football. It looks like some distant relic you might see in a museum, from a time long ago — the time when I kicked it happily through the streets with David.

I pick it up, not because I really want it, more as a souvenir of something, of the person I was a few hours ago, who I feel might no longer exist.

I walk to the place where I entered the building site and toss the ball over, listening to it bounce, roll and settle on the other side. The climb out looks splintery and difficult, but I know I can do it. Now I'm through the tunnel, back on my side of The Wall, nothing will stop me getting home.

As I reach up to begin the climb, a knot at my throat slips loose. Something slides from my shoulders and flutters downwards. At first I can't think what it might be, but as its cool softness brushes my hand, I realise with a stomach-wrenching plunge of guilt what I have done. It is the scarf. The scarf lent by the girl who saved me, and even though she asked for the simplest thing in return, I gave her nothing. Worse than that, I now see I have stolen from her, both her father's scarf and her brother's flip-flops, which I am also still wearing.

In an apartment as stark and bare as hers, these items will be missed. She'll have to think of an explanation. The truth, I sense, won't do.

I knot the scarf across my chest and begin to climb.

When I appear at the door, Mum's hands go up to her cheeks and her mouth opens as if she's letting rip with an almighty howl, but only a strangulated rasp comes out: half scream, half sigh. Her eyes, which are red and wide, gape at me as if I'm returning from the dead. Before I've even stepped into the house, she reaches out and pulls me towards her, clutching so tightly I can barely breathe.

'I thought you were gone,' she says, whisper-singing into my ear, her lips hot against my skin. 'I thought you were gone. I thought you were gone.'

Again and again she says it, squeezing me into her and rocking us to and fro as if we are clasped in some joint prayer. I squeeze back, breathing in the smell of her — a unique mingling of her sweet fruity perfume, with a hint of washing powder and the faintest waft of body, of pure her. I inhale as much of her as I can take in, snuffling myself into her without shame or embarrassment. I am home. I'm safe. I'm not gone.

Enfolded in the powerful clench of her arms, snuggled into the intimate cloud of her scent, I wonder if it was almost worth going through the tunnel, experiencing that terror, to get this reaction from my mother. I can hardly remember the last time she touched me. This woman, wrapped around me, embracing me with this fierce affection, feels like my old mother, my real mother, a person who slipped away when Dad died, walled herself in with her grief, then hid deeper still, behind Liev.

'I thought *you* were gone,' I almost say, but I wouldn't be able to explain, so I just pull her tighter towards me, feeling her body convulse with waves of sobs. I'm crying, too, happy-sad tears, not just with relief to be home, but triggered by everything else that seems to be in the air around my mother; something to do with this moment taking us back to the day we never discuss, when our old life ended. That day is with us, inside our hug. I can feel it.

She usually pretends he is forgotten, but in this instant I feel for the first time as if she understands what I understand: that you cannot, after all, bury the dead. Even if you run away, and look in the other direction, and never talk about it, a person — a dead person — will not disappear. An absence can be as vivid as a presence, and to me, Dad's absence is almost like a pair of glasses I never take off — it is something I look through, rather than at, changing everything I see, always visible yet invisible.

Eventually we let one another go, and she pulls me into the house.

'Where were you? What happened?' she gasps.

I have my story ready. I tell her a football went into the building site, but having climbed in and jumped down to retrieve the ball, I realised I couldn't climb out again. I tell her I shouted for help, but no one heard me, and I only escaped by using my bare hands to build a platform out of bricks and junk.

57

'Why did you climb in there?'

'To get my ball,' I say.

'But . . . you can't do that! You mustn't do things like that!' She's trying to be severe, but her voice is still filled with hugs, and one hand is stroking my neck.

'I'm sorry,' I say, smiling up at her. A strand of hair is stuck to her left cheek, glued into place by tears. I push it free with my index finger and tuck it behind her ear. I can't remember the last time I touched her hair, which is so dark that is shines. When Dad was alive and we lived by the sea, her hair was short and spiky. Or sometimes it was. Every time she got it cut, she came back with something different. Now it's long, and she never seems to go to a hairdresser, and whenever we leave the house she covers it up.

'It's just a football,' she says. 'We'd get you another one. I was so worried. You scared me!'

'I won't do it again.' Her fingers are tickling me now, and I step back.

'Well, just wait till Liev gets home,' she snaps, but there's still more honey than venom in her voice, and we both know it's a weak threat.

I smile at her, sort of kissing her with my eyes. She smiles back, then a thought seems to stop her. She puts a hand on each of my shoulders and shakes me, a jolt of tender aggression. 'This isn't an ordinary town,' she says, with a pointed and direct stare. 'Things happen here. We have lots of protection, but no amount is enough. There are people living very, very close who want to get us. They want us out.' She's holding me at arm's length now, her forehead clenched into a

58

frown. For the first time, she looks plausibly angry. She pokes me in the chest with her index finger. 'If I worry when you disappear, it's not because I'm some stupid, anxious mother; it's because you hear stories all the time about people who find themselves in the wrong place, without anyone to defend them, and they never come back.'

The jab of her finger and the sudden coldness in her voice jolt me upright, as if she's dropped a sliver of ice down my back. My father-mother has slipped away again. She has disappeared in front of my eyes, and I don't know when I'll see her again. This is my Liev-mother, my Amarias mother, back again until some other crisis briefly pushes her aside.

'Who? Which people?' I say, stepping beyond the range of her poke.

I can see her jaw muscles twitch as she clenches her mouth. 'Don't be smart with me.'

'You said you hear stories all the time.'

'Don't talk back!'

She has her poking finger ready again, but I'm poised to dodge away. 'If it's so awful here, why don't we go back home. If it's not safe, let's go.'

'This is home. I'm not getting sucked into that conversation.' She turns and walks towards the kitchen.

'I hate it here!'

In the doorway she stops, swivels and stares at me, her head cocked on one side, as if she's trying to decide how angry to be. 'Well, we're here,' she says eventually. 'And if you stop trying to hate it, you might discover it's not half as bad as you make out. Do you think we could afford a comfy house like this anywhere else?'

'Oh, it's about money now, is it? Is that why we're here?'

'I'm not having this conversation.'

'Is it God or money? You keep changing your mind.'

'What happened to your trainers?' she snaps, pointing at the filthy flip-flops I'm still wearing.

I prepared a story for this, too, but it isn't a good one. The girl's scarf is hidden in my bag, but there's nothing I could do about my missing shoes. 'It was some boys at school. They played a trick on me.'

'What kind of trick?'

I'm cornered. I've run out of excuses. It's time to go on the attack. 'Why are you hassling me? I thought you'd be pleased I'm safe!'

'I am pl — '

'Well leave me alone, then!'

'Do you know how much those shoes cost? Are you going to get them back?'

I run upstairs, dodge into my room and slam the door. For a long time I stand there, waiting for her to burst in, turning over possibilities in my head for how I might have lost the shoes. I could say some boys were picking on me. I could say they threw my trainers over The Wall. If she makes me say who did it, there are plenty of names to choose from. But the door doesn't move, and after a while I flop on to my bed.

Liev can say whatever he likes when he gets back, I don't care. He's not my father. He's my anti-father.

By the time Liev arrives home, I've washed and changed, and I'm curled up on the sofa in a nest of cushions, watching a cartoon. It's about a dog who keeps on trying to leave his house to get the bone he's left outside, but whenever he does he's smacked in the face with a plank by another, bigger dog, who hides in wait for him. The smaller dog never gives up, and keeps on looking for new routes to his bone, but every time he gets close, the bigger dog appears with his plank and whacks him over the head. It's quite funny.

Liev does what he usually does when he walks in. He goes to the kitchen. Mum is there, cooking, and I can tell by the tense gabble of her voice that she's telling Liev what I've done — or what she thinks I've done — and is asking him to tell me off. From the suck and slap of the fridge door, I can hear that Liev is snacking as she talks.

I feel him appear in the doorway, but don't look up.

'Your mother tells me you did something stupid today,' he says.

I shrug, contemplating my options. I could ignore him, putting off the conflict, but that would just make him angrier. I could be sarcastic, calling Mum 'your wife' to match his 'your mother', which might be briefly satisfying, but would ultimately make everything worse. It's never worth getting Liev angry. Most conversations I have with him, I'm thinking ahead like a chess player, figuring out my best moves to give away as little ground as possible without pushing him into one of his rages.

I glance up and see that although he's facing towards me, his neck is turned, and his eyes are on the cartoon. This is a good sign. If he was in the mood for an argument he'd have switched the TV off before speaking, to get my attention. He would have positioned himself in front of me, with his hot breath on my face. Having other people's attention is a big thing for Liev. Few things make him crosser than the idea that you might not be listening to him.

The way he's standing and his weary tone of voice give the impression he's ticking me off only to satisfy my mother. She clearly hasn't succeeded in communicating the level of her panic. Everything looks calm now. No one is missing; no one has been harmed. It seems as if he just doesn't believe anything bad really happened. He's going through the disciplinary motions as a domestic chore. I just have to play along.

'I lost a ball in the building site. It wasn't even me that kicked it there.'

'You gave your mother a terrible fright.'

'I know. I said sorry.'

'Well, that's good,' he says. 'But if you ever . . . ' His voice tails away, distracted. The small dog is climbing up the chimney, but the big one has seen what he's doing through the window, and is hiding behind a chimney pot with his plank. The small dog's head appears. He looks around and smiles, thinking the coast is clear. He jumps out and is all ready to leap down from the roof, when the big dog stands up with his plank and swings it like a baseball bat. WHACK! With the sound of a long, descending whistle, the small dog flies into the far distance while the bigger dog runs around the four corners of the roof like he's scored a home run, acknowledging the cheers of an imaginary crowd. Liev gives a tiny, comma-sized smile, and turns back to me. 'If you . . . ever . . . you know, lose something in there again, you have to promise me you won't go in.'

'OK,' I say.

That seems to be it. Easy. If he knew what I'd really done . . . where I'd been . . .

He's already on his way out when curiosity gets the better of me. 'Why?' I say.

He stops and turns, his face now blank and puzzled, as if he's already forgotten what we were talking about. 'What?' he says.

'What's in there that's so forbidden?'

'Nothing. It's just private property.'

'Whose is it?'

'Well . . . it's private, but I suppose it belongs to all of us.'

'So it's public?'

'It's . . . disputed.'

'By who?'

'The people who used to live there.'

'Who used to live there?'

'No one.'

'No one? So who's disputing what?'

'You know what I mean, smart guy,' he says, with a sneer. 'They abandon their houses then they act like it's our fault.'

'I saw it. I was in there,' I say. 'I saw the house.'

He stares at me, not blinking, a cold, level gaze.

'Have you seen it, too?' I ask.

He shrugs. 'They're bad people. They build without permits. They don't listen to the government, they don't listen to the army, they only understand violence.'

'What happened to the people who lived there? Where are they now?'

'Gone.'

'Gone where?'

'Somewhere they belong. Why are you asking all these stupid questions?'

'I just . . . it was weird. The house. It's smashed up, but everything is still there, as if they didn't even pack — as if something just fell out of the sky in the middle of an ordinary day and crushed the place. It felt spooky.'

'You don't have to worry. Nothing fell out of the sky. It can't happen to us.'

'That's not what I mean. I felt something bad.'

'You *felt* something?'

'Did anyone die?'

I sense him begin to lose his patience. 'When these things happen every care is taken to save lives, but some people don't want to be saved. And people die everywhere all the time. It's normal. What's crazy is that we have to fight so hard for every square inch of land we want to live on. What's crazy is that there are traitors who help those people fight for land that ought to be ours. What's crazy is that some people won't stay where they are put, and just go on and on and on trying to stop us living normal, peaceful lives. And if you're having *feelings* and worrying about things that don't concern you, then I suggest you concentrate a bit harder on your studies, and spend less time speculating about things you can't possibly understand. Do you hear me?'

He's now looming over me, and above his beard I can see his face is flushed, with tiny deltas of purple veins lit up around the rims of his nostrils. I shrug and turn back to the TV. The big dog is now hammering the smaller dog into the ground like a fence post.

Liev stands over me a short while longer, slightly out of breath from his rant, then slips away, back to the kitchen.

I don't want to risk talking to him again before dinner so I flick off the TV and retreat to my bedroom, picking up my schoolbag as I go. I have to find a hiding place for that scarf.

In the middle of the night, the red digits of my bedside clock seem bright enough to illuminate the whole room. It is 3:31. The numbers are solid, but the colon between them flashes once a second. I don't know what woke me, it might have been a dream, but now I'm wide awake, watching the two flashing dots.

However hard you stare, however much you promise yourself you're not going to look away for even an instant, it's almost impossible to catch the numbers changing. They somehow do it without you seeing the moment it happens. There's something pleasing about 3:33, and I decide it will be a special achievement if I see it come up.

I manage to catch 3:31 turning into 3:32, which is like a neat little dance step — the bottom half of the 1 skips to the left, exactly as all three horizontal lines fill in — but 3:33 seems to take ages and ages to arrive, and next thing I know it's there and I missed it. Different minutes are different lengths. I know that's not actually true, but that's how it feels.

I flick on my bedside light, sit on the edge of the mattress for a while, then lift up the frilly cotton skirt that hides the space under my bed. I've had the same thing under there for years, and no one ever sees it except me. If David found it, I'd die.

I pull it out. I haven't looked under there for months, and the whole thing is covered in a film of dust. I can't really explain what it is, or why anyone of my age would be interested in it, except to say that when you're an only child you spend a lot of time on your own, and the best way to avoid boredom is to make things up. When you spend long enough on the same made-up thing, it sometimes ends up being impossible to explain to anyone else.

To the untrained eye, it's a wooden board roughly half the size of the bed, with houses and people on it. That's all. The houses are made of Lego, cardboard, plastic and wood, assembled from all sorts of different places according to some scheme I can no longer remember. None of the buildings match, and half of them are totally the wrong scale. There's also a random mish-mash of figurines from various board games and model kits and wherever else plastic people turn up. A couple of dogs and cats are in there some-where, but no other animals and certainly no dinosaurs or anything stupid like that.

It's hard to explain what I do with it, but an hour or two can easily slip by on my hands and knees, moving the people around, making up stories. When I know no one is watching, I can lose myself in this fantasy town as if I'm somehow all of the people who live in it at once. It's like being God, except that God doesn't exist and I do. None of the people in the town correspond to real people, but if one of them was Liev, and he was praying to me, and I was God, I'd totally ignore him. In fact, I'd do the opposite of everything he asked for.

When I've finished I always shove it right under the bed, hidden where it can't be seen by anyone who visits my room.

I stand over the fantasy town, gazing down at it. Along one edge is a wall, the same height as the tallest house. It's made from a cut-up cereal box, taped to itself and to the board it is built on. I remember the afternoon I added in the wall, years ago, taking hours over getting it to the right height and making it solid. There's even a watch-tower in one corner, made from the inner tube of a toilet roll topped with a yoghurt pot which is usually filled with soldiers. Now, for the first time, it strikes me as strange that I put this wall at the edge, with nothing on the other side of it.

I stare and stare, motionless. In the middle of the night, time feels different. During the day it's a river, always flowing. Now it's like a pond, just sitting there, and I'm floating in it, suspended, looking down at this child's game which suddenly feels infinitely familiar and totally alien, like everything I am and everything I'm not, all at once.

It's not a stamp, and I don't feel angry or destructive as I'm doing it, but slowly and delib-erately, I lift a leg and step on to a cardboard house at the heart of the town. With the sole of my foot, I feel the tiny structure resist for a fraction of a second, before it crumples under my weight. One by one, I calmly crush all the others that are made of cardboard. Two are made of balsa wood. Those I pluck from where they're glued into place, and squeeze in my hands until they shatter. The feeble wood pops and snaps easily in my grasp. I carefully flatten the wall, then pick out and dismantle the Lego houses, brick by brick. There's also a police station, taken from something for much younger kids, which is just one moulded piece of plastic. At first it doesn't want to come apart, but with the help of a chair leg I manage to prise the roof off, and once I've done that, the rest of it comes apart quickly. Then there's the school and the park and the shops to think about.

Next time I look at the clock it's 4:21, and I'm standing over a mound of rubbish. My heart is beating fast, and I know I'm not going to get to sleep, but I also know I've finished. I shove most of the loose bits on to the board and push the whole thing back under my bed. A few bricks, figurines, shreds of cardboard and pieces of broken plastic are still strewn over the floor. One by one, leaving no evidence, I pick them up and dump them in the bin.

As I pull the sheet over me and feel the coolness of the pillow against my cheek, it feels good to know the smashed-up town is right underneath me. I'm pleased I've dealt with it. I just have to get it bagged and into the outside bin before Mum finds the mess and starts asking questions.

I watch the flashing dots on my clock, and decide that I'll wait for 4:44. That will be a good switchover to see, then I'll be able to sleep.

The 4 on digital clocks isn't really a proper 4 at all. It's an upside-down 'h'. Whoever convinced everyone this could count as a 4 was very clever.

Part Two

I take my usual route to school and call on David, holding my football prominently under one arm as he comes to the door. I see him clock it, but he doesn't comment.

I tell him I climbed in and got it myself. He just shrugs.

'You won't believe what's in there,' I say.

He doesn't answer, so I let the silence hang. I can see he still wants to act indifferent, but I know I've aroused his curiosity.

'What?' he says, after a long pause.

'A house,' I say. 'The weirdest house I've ever seen.'

We're kicking my ball along the street, taking turns, but now I pick it up. I want his full attention.

'Weird how?' he says.

'Smashed up. Demolished.'

'What's so weird about that?'

'The feel of it. There are clothes everywhere, and furniture still inside, and books, as if people are still living there. Except it's totally flattened.'

'And?'

'And what?'

'I thought you said it was weird.'

'That is weird. You don't think it's weird?'

He shrugs. 'They have to do it.'

'Who has to do what?'

'The army. Imagine how cool that is. Just

flattening a house. Imagine being the driver. Dooosh!' He barges into me for emphasis, almost knocking me over, as if he's the bulldozer and I'm the house.

I barge back, but he jabs out his arm and gets me in the bicep with an elbow. I don't rub it, or give away that he's hurt me. A second later, despite intending to keep quiet about it, despite knowing I shouldn't, I hear myself tell him that I found a tunnel.

'A tunnel?'

'Yeah, but you mustn't tell anyone.'

'What kind of tunnel?'

'There was just a hole in the ground, and when I went down to see what it was I found a tunnel, going under The Wall.'

He stops walking and fixes me with a suspicious stare.

'A tunnel! And you went down it?'

I know I'll be in dire trouble if any adult finds out what I did, but I can feel my secret wanting to be told in the way an ice cream wants to be eaten. David is the closest thing I have to a best friend in Amarias. If I can't tell him, I can't tell anyone. But immediately, seeing the horrified look on his face, I sense that I've miscalculated.

I imagine myself telling him about the girl on the other side, and how she saved me, but I couldn't do anything to help her. I imagine describing the tiny home she lives in; her request for food and her skinny arms and proud, sad eyes. I imagine trying to explain the guilt that needles into me every time I think of her, and it is somehow obvious that he'll never understand what I want him to understand, and he'll never keep my story quiet. He's lived in Amarias all his life. His parents were among the town's pioneers. David, I know, never doubts for a moment that Amarias is the place it pretends to be. My uncertainty, to him, would be incomprehensible, subversive, disgusting.

I realise at once that I have to stop talking before giving anything else away. In fact, I have to think of a way to unsay what I've already said. I force out a laugh and punch him on the arm. 'You believed me!'

For a moment, the wary glint stays in his eye, then he punches me back. 'I didn't.'

'Yes, you did.'

'Well, it's possible,' he says. 'I bet there are tunnels. They'll do anything to blow us up. They're crazy.' He reaches out and pulls the ball from under my arm, bouncing it as he talks. 'Sometimes I look at the soldiers,' he goes on, 'and I can't wait.'

'For what?'

'Until it's our turn. Can you imagine what that's going to feel like? Wearing the uniform. Carrying a gun. Going over to the other side and having all those people, everywhere, scared of you, doing everything you tell them.'

I turn away. I can't imagine. Even trying at that moment to picture it, I can't make it seem real or plausible. The first face that comes to mind is the girl. As an image begins to form in my mind of her at the point of a gun — at the point of my gun — David banishes it with his squeaky, excited voice. 'And if anyone crosses you or messes you around . . . ' He tosses me the football, lifts an imaginary rifle to his shoulder and fires three invisible rounds. 'DOOF! DOOF! DOOF!'

His eyes are scary, now. Alight with enthusiasm.

'It's the best army in the world,' he says. 'And in a few years we're going to be in it. You know how lucky we are?'

I can't think of an answer, so I just stretch out an arm and shove him in the chest, pushing him into a wall. I run off, laughing a forced laugh, knowing he'll chase me, knowing he's faster and rougher, and will have me on the ground in no time. His retaliation is bound to double what I did to him, but I don't care. I just keep running and laughing.

★ ★ ★

All morning, I struggle to concentrate. Every page I look at seems to morph into the image David has conjured up, of me in uniform, holding a gun to that girl's head. When I try to banish this vision, another pops up to replace it, of the boys who chased me, and what they would have done if they'd found me behind the motorbike. I imagine them laughing at my cowering body, kicking the bike over, then setting to work on me. When I try to shut off this sickening avenue of thought, my brain just takes me back to the girl, and the look of sudden fear on her face as she turned away, without even a goodbye.

I gobble my lunch as fast as I can, forcing myself to think of anything other than the girl, struggling, as I have done all morning, to get my thoughts back to my own life, to my own world on this side of The Wall. As soon as the food is inside me, I hurry to the playground and force my way into a game of football, chasing the ball frantically wherever it goes, not waiting for a pass, or picking a position, but just running as hard and fast as I can, using the game as a way to obliterate the poisonous thoughts that have invaded my head. I'm usually timid in the tackle but in this game I feel no fear, and slide in on people, taking pleasure in the crunch of their legs against mine as I compete for the ball.

I begin to sense people looking at me strangely. I see a gaggle of boys at the far end of the pitch muttering to one another and staring in my direction, but I don't stop. For the first time since going into the tunnel, the knot of tension inside me feels as if it is loosening. The other boys in the game, usually my sort-of friends, today seem distant, unimportant, not entirely real.

When I score a goal, barging between two defenders and whacking a shot into the bottom right-hand corner, I run the whole length of the pitch as a celebration, but no one on my team joins in. If anything, they shrink away from me, but I don't mind, and after kick-off I just redouble my efforts, running even faster after the ball, tackling even harder, until I become aware that my heart and legs are screaming at me to stop, and my stomach is tightening, moments away from throwing up.

I stop, walk to the sideline, and sit on the ground. Nobody comes with me or asks if I'm OK.

While my nausea subsides I watch the football, a little dizzily. The other boys seem further away than ever, their shouts muffled and hollow, their excitement at the game strange and not quite comprehensible.

As I begin to feel more normal, a wayward shot flies out of nowhere, straight towards my face. The only way to avoid a broken nose is to flatten myself against the tarmac, which I do just in time to feel the ball skim millimetres above my hair. When I sit up again, the boy who kicked it is staring at me, smirking. Several other boys have similar expressions on their faces, and I realise this wasn't an accident at all, but a well-aimed missile. I look away, pretending not to have noticed. I decide to give myself another minute or two before I leave, so they won't think they got me.

Just as I'm getting ready to stand, David appears with his friend Seth, a chubby boy with a droopy bottom lip which always glistens with saliva. Seth hates me. They stand so close I have to crane my neck to see their faces.

'Seth wants to hear about the tunnel,' says David.

I blink into the sunlight, which is forming a shimmering halo above their heads. 'What tunnel?'

'The tunnel you found in the building site.'

I stare at David, fixing my mouth into a rigid,

secretive slot. 'What are you talking about?'

The two boys gaze at me for a few seconds, then, as if to some invisible cue, they burst out laughing and walk away.

I've told David too much. I can't trust him.

A hand on my shoulder sends my body lurching upwards. My throat emits a strangled gasp that is almost a scream. Half my face is numb.

For an instant, my brain scrabbles and flails, not understanding where I am or what is happening. A person is standing over me, a woman, her brow creased with an anxious frown. It's my mother. This place, all around me, is not where I was a moment earlier.

I'm in my room. I'm at my desk. In front of me is my homework. I must have fallen asleep with my head on an exercise book.

'Dinner's ready,' says Mum. 'I've been calling and calling.'

'Sorry,' I say, the word emerging as a dry croak.

'Are you all right?'

'I'm fine.'

'You look awful.'

'I . . . I think I had a bad dream.'

'What was it?'

'Nothing. I don't know. It's gone.'

'Come and eat.'

'OK.'

She tries to help me out of my chair, but I shrug her off.

'I'll come in a minute.'

'OK. But quickly. And wash your hands. It's getting cold.'

'I'll come,' I snap. 'Just give me a minute.'

She retreats, leaving the door half open behind her. I close my eyes again, groping after the receding threads of my nightmare. I was in the tunnel again, but it was wet at the bottom, a layer of water thinly covering everything, but it wasn't cold, and it was OK to be crawling there, until I notice the smell, and become aware that the liquid under my hands and legs is more viscous than water. I lift a hand and turn it over, but can't see anything until a trapdoor opens above me, and a shaft of light shines down. My palms, fingers and wrists are red. Then something grabs my shoulder, and I spin round, knowing it's the hand of the boy who spat on me, knowing he'll be holding a gun, but he vanishes before he appears, and the tunnel suddenly isn't the tunnel, and the hand is the hand of my mother, waking me up to call me for dinner.

* * *

Mum and Liev watch me wordlessly as I walk into the dining room. It's at times like this that I most miss having a sibling, these moments when there are two sets of eyes on you, watching everything you do, analysing every twitch of your face, with no one else to divert or distract them.

Most of the other families in Amarias are huge. If Dad hadn't been shot, I know I'd have brothers and sisters. It sometimes seems as if he isn't the only person missing from the family, as if they killed more than just my father.

81

I sometimes wonder if there's something wrong with Liev, and sense that the smallness of our family is part of the reason people are suspicious of us. It isn't normal, round here, to have just one child.

If Liev did have a proper son — one who was really his — I know he'd treat him differently. The idea of a mini-Liev in the house, who'd believe what Liev said and would want to be like him when he grew up, makes me want to puke. Better no brother at all than one like that. Except, perhaps, at times like this, when there's nothing I want more than for there to be another human being in the room, doing something, anything, to get those four beady eyes turned away from me.

'I made your favourite,' says Mum, as soon as Liev has finished the blessing. 'Roast chicken.'

'Thanks,' I mutter.

'I thought — after what happened yesterday . . . '

'After what you did,' interrupts Liev.

'I just thought,' Mum carries on, trying to pretend Liev hasn't spoken, 'you've had a nasty fright, and you deserve a treat.'

I nod. I'm not going to thank her twice.

'Your mother's too nice,' says Liev. 'You don't deserve her.'

'And I deserve you?' I think, but hold it in. The truth is, I don't deserve Liev, and neither does Mum. He worked his way into the family without anyone noticing what he was doing, and now he's in charge.

Mum was pretty crazy after Dad died. She

tried to hold herself together, but for months she seemed like a pane of glass riddled with cracks that was still somehow sitting there in the frame. You couldn't look at her without thinking the slightest tap would shatter her into a thousand pieces. I tried to help, but I felt pretty shaky myself, and you couldn't speak to her for longer than a minute without her lips beginning to tremble and her eyes glazing over. When I had the choice, I often just tried to keep out of her way.

That's when Liev started appearing. At first it was a relief. Mum needed sympathy when she went quiet, and she needed someone to act as if they were listening when her mood shifted and she started to talk. Even when she was saying the same thing for the hundredth time, Liev never seemed bored or impatient or eager to leave. Before long, he was with us every evening. It felt strange that he was religious, but religion takes up a lot of time, and Mum seemed to like that — having days, weeks and months punctuated by rituals that Liev gradually sneaked into our routine. Mum was lost, and he was like a compass, always pointing north, always leading her in one direction.

For a while, I was grateful to him. I wanted to be kind, I wanted to look after her, but I couldn't do it. I was too angry and upset to have anything to spare for anyone else. Liev was tender with her in the way I wished I could have been. She was a fragile object I didn't trust myself to carry, and I was pleased to be able to hand her over to someone else.

He's still gentle with her now, still treats her as if the slightest upset might break her, except these days the thing he's usually trying to protect her from is me. He thinks I'm selfish and inconsiderate, and he never stops trying to squeeze between us and police the way I talk to her. If he wasn't around everything would be fine, but he just can't resist stepping in and trying to make everything fit his stupid rules.

If I'd resisted him from the start, I might have been able to keep him at bay, but by the time I realised what he was up to — that he was working his way in for good, and he was going to change everything and never leave — it was too late. I still remember the moment when I realised what was going to happen, and that he had beaten me.

I was only nine when he first started visiting, and was always desperate for someone to play board games with me. There were weekends when we sat at the dining table for whole afternoons, rolling dice and moving counters, while Mum drifted around, keeping her distance and encouraging us to 'bond'. It felt good to have someone else in the house other than just me and Mum. He was someone to hide behind, someone to handle her mood swings, someone to turn us round and make us look forwards rather than backwards.

He tried his best to be nice to me, and I tried to like him, but the day when he suggested a 'family outing', I realised for the first time what he was trying to do. He was all smiles when he asked me where I wanted to go, and Mum was right there, too, grinning down at me, and I saw, in a flash, that they were both in on it — they were working together — lining up a replacement father.

I stood there, speechless, overwhelmed by the horror of this idea — by the idea that *anyone* might think they could do that, let alone this old, bearded, dreary stranger — while they gazed at me, waiting to hear my choice of outing. I opted for the swimming pool, not because I like swimming, but because I thought it was the best choice to expose the ridiculous gulf between Liev and my dad. I thought the sight of him in a pair of trunks might wake my mother up and force her to see what she was doing.

When he walked out of his cubicle, tiptoeing on the wet tiles as if he didn't want them to touch his feet, I thought for a moment my plan might work. I already knew he was no athlete, but the way he looked in his old-fashioned trunks (which were not much bigger than a pair of women's knickers) was creepier than I had dared imagine. His body was fat-but-thin, skinny and also saggy, with flesh the colour and texture of dough, so soft it looked as if a firm poke would leave a lasting dent. And even his toes were hairy.

'So, let's swim!' he said, rubbing his hands together, struggling to act as if the outing was anything other than a grim duty. He didn't seem to have any idea of how awful he looked.

Mum didn't react to the sight of him in the way I'd hoped. She somehow stifled her instinctive response, which must have been to run screaming from the building, and didn't even flinch when we emerged from the changing rooms. Perhaps this was tact; perhaps she'd seen it all before. This wasn't a thought I wanted to dwell on.

I made sure to splash him a lot, and to be as irritating as possible within the bounds of what I could pass off as playfulness, but nothing riled him. I could tell I was getting on his nerves, and that he didn't find chlorinated water in the eyes even one-tenth as amusing as he pretended to, but he took it all with annoyingly good humour.

Eventually I resorted to asking him if he liked diving. We were at the pool with the high boards, and straight away he was suspicious.

'Sometimes,' he replied, smiling warily, his eyes flicking towards Mum to see if she was listening.

I drew closer to her. 'Let's do some. Will you teach me?' I said.

He shrugged a reluctant yes, so I swam to the edge of the pool, checked that he was following, then went ahead to the diving tower and waited for him at the bottom step. I could see Mum at the far end of the pool, watching. I gave her a wave, and as soon as Liev was near, began to climb.

Up I went, past the low board, then past the medium board, hearing the metallic echo of Liev's footsteps behind me, feeling his weight judder the frame of the ladder. I didn't stop or look down until I'd made it all the way to the ten-metre platform. I'd never been up to this level before. A glance between my legs showed the swimmers looking miniature and foreshortened, their screams and yelps blending into a continuous shrill drone. The drop had always looked high from the pool, but it seemed enormous when viewed from above. The idea of walking to the end and throwing yourself off was sickening. I shuffled from the top of the ladder to the railing that ran along the edge of the platform, my knees feeling loose and unreliable as I lurched for the metal bar, which I gripped with all my strength while I waited for Liev.

I knew he was on a mission to prove himself to Mum, so he wouldn't be able to dive from a lower board or turn back. It was a long time before he appeared at the top, and when he did his face was pale, his lips puckered into a hard white ring. The saggy muscles of his arms juddered as he hauled himself up.

Trying to hide my smirk, I turned back to Mum, picking her out far below and giving her an enthusiastic wave with my right hand while holding on tight with my left. I couldn't make out her expression as she waved back.

Liev clambered on to the platform, clumsily heaving himself from his knees to his feet, then inching towards the railing, which he clutched with knuckle-whitening force. For a while, he stood with his head bowed, catching his breath.

When he looked up, every scrap of friendliness had vanished from his eyes. 'I know what you're doing,' he said, his voice cold and flat.

'Did I go too high?' I replied, all innocence and smiles.

'I know exactly what you're doing.'

'My dad was a really good diver,' I said. 'He wasn't afraid of anything.'

He held my gaze, breathing slowly through his nostrils, as he lifted his index finger and gave me a sharp jab in the ribs, just below my heart. 'Do you think you're smarter than me?' he asked.

I tightened my grip on the railing, feeling suddenly vulnerable, higher up than was safe, more naked than I wanted to be. It struck me that I'd never been alone with him before, out of earshot of my mother. His body was positioned to conceal me from her view.

'Don't play me,' he said. 'Don't ever think you can play me. You won't win.'

He reached out, and with one finger raised my chin, forcing me to look at him. His mouth was stretched into an affectionate a friendly smile that was somehow also the opposite.

'So are we going to be friends?' he said.

I shrugged, staring at a single droplet that was clinging to the tip of his beard.

'Friends?'

I still didn't answer, but he carried on as if I had.

'Then let's shake on it,' he said, as if we were now, at this moment, meeting for the first time, on a high diving board. In a way, we were. This, I realised, was the real Liev.

There was nothing to do but raise my limp, soggy hand and shake. His fingers were puffy, soft and warm. He pumped my forearm up and down, as if I was a lever-operated machine. This gesture seemed to satisfy him, and he took a single contented breath.

'Good boy,' he said, 'good boy,' repeating it twice with a sing-song intonation, like a trainer rewarding an obedient dog.

With that, he tilted his head back and rolled his neck through one slow circle, then turned and walked towards the end of the diving board. He tried to appear confident, but his walk was hunched and uncertain, his knees never quite straightening, his hand hovering, ready to grab the railing. No one had been up here for a while: other than his footsteps, the surface was dry. Soon, there was no concrete ahead of him, only air.

He curled his toes over the lip of the platform, spread his arms, and stood there, swaying slightly. The gusset of his trunks had sagged away from his body, releasing droplets of water which splashed between his ankles.

With his chin raised, he slowly bent his knees and leapt forwards, flying through the air with his back arched, a perfect, graceful swallow dive. For half a second, it was beautiful. Then, as his head speared towards the water, the flaw in his technique became apparent. With several more metres to fall, he was still rotating. His legs and arms began to flail in a futile attempt to correct his trajectory, before the skin of his back hit the water with the sound of a whipcrack. A circular wave spread out from his point of impact, causing concentric rings of swimmers to bob in the water. A ripple of laughter echoed upwards as the sound of the splash faded.

He resurfaced and swam towards my mother. I couldn't make out the expression on either of their faces, but I could see that before he said a word, he kissed her on the lips. It was the first time I ever saw him touch her. The sight of that kiss stabbed into my chest like another poke. That was the moment when I knew he'd beaten me.

I climbed down the ladder, struggling on the slippery rungs, my body heavy with foreboding. Liev had taken charge. I didn't know where he'd lead us, but I sensed that everything was going to change, and I was powerless to stop it.

'Too high for you?' he said, as I swam into earshot.

'Is your back OK?' I asked.

'Fine.'

'Must be sore.'

'Not really.'

'Can I see it?'

'Nothing to see,' he said, splashing me playfully-but-not-playfully in the face.

Not until we were in the changing rooms did I get a look at his injured skin. A livid rash spread across his back as if someone had strapped him to a table and sandpapered him, the redness interrupted only by a thin white line, like a streak of lightning, that divided the wound. You could see the whole area would be hot to the touch. It seemed amazing that he hadn't wept, hadn't given away even a hint of discomfort. A slight flinch as he put on his shirt was the only sign he was in any pain.

On the way home, he clutched the steering

wheel with both hands, holding his body upright so his back didn't touch the seat. He told me my swimming needed work and offered to take me back to the pool, just the two of us, 'for a few lessons'.

Mum swivelled in her seat and smiled at me. 'Isn't that kind?' she said.

I didn't answer.

Within two months they were married, and Liev had moved us out here, to the Occupied Zone, into a brand new house at the edge of Amarias.

★　★　★

'Are you OK?' says Mum, leaning towards me and stroking my cheek.

I lean back, out of reach, and stare down at the untouched chicken on my plate. Liev is already halfway through his portion. 'I'm fine,' I say. 'Just tired.'

'You had a big fright.'

'I'm just tired,' I snap.

'OK,' she says, raising her hands in a fake mini-surrender. 'You're just tired.'

'Of course he is,' says Liev, squeezing out his sarcasm through a mouthful of rice. 'Falling asleep over his school-work. You think that's how to get good grades?'

'He's doing fine,' says Mum.

'I know he is. Fine is fine, but fine isn't good. Fine isn't excellent.'

'Let him eat,' says Mum.

'Am I stopping him? Am I?'

Mum shrugs.

'He's thirteen years old. You can't tiptoe round him all the time.'

I put my head down and try to make a start on my meal, wondering how long the two of them will be capable of carrying on this conversation without any input from me. Except that I can't eat. The chicken on my fork looks succulent, dripping with a thick, glistening sauce, but in my mouth it tastes stringy and dry. I chew and chew, wishing there was some way to spit it out, but those four eyes are on me more attentively than ever, so I keep going and make myself swallow.

I can feel my hungry stomach crying out for sustenance, but the idea of actual food entering my body feels nauseating and strange.

Silence fills the room as I force down five or six mouthfuls, before cutting and mixing the rest into a careful array designed to conceal how much food I'm leaving.

'Are you sure you're OK?' Mum asks.

I nod.

'You want some dessert?'

I shake my head.

'Ice cream? We've got some lemon sorbet.'

'No thanks.'

She reaches out to put a hand on my forehead. I let her slender fingers rest, warm and gentle, against my brow.

'You don't feel hot,' she says.

'I'm just tired. I said already.'

'Of course you are.'

'Can I go to bed?'

Mum and Liev exchange anxious looks. She tries to help me up from my chair, but I shrug her off and walk away, muttering that I'll be fine in the morning.

★ ★ ★

I stand in the middle of my room for a while, not getting undressed, not even really thinking anything, just standing there. I only notice I'm doing it when Mum walks in, closing the door in her special, quiet way, not lifting the handle until the door is fully shut.

She sits me down on the bed and squeezes herself next to me, up close so our thighs are pressed together.

'Has something happened?' she says. 'Something else.'

Her face is so close, I have to blink to focus. It's the face I know best in the world. Every wrinkle and freckle, every blemish, every expression is familiar to me. Even when she seems far away, lost in her mysterious, private struggle to make sense of what has happened to her, she also feels like part of me, like the only person in the world I actually know.

I want to tell her about the tunnel. For a moment it seems as if I have to tell her about the tunnel, as if what I've done and where I've been is a toxin, bottled up inside me, that will leak into my bloodstream and poison me if I don't find a way to get it out.

With her sitting next to me on the bed, concerned and attentive, waiting for me to

93

speak, I sense I might never get a better opportunity to explain what I did, where I went, how I escaped, and who saved me. I know I have to find a way to share the burden of the feeling which is throttling me, a sense that I owe my life to someone I have wronged.

I take a deep breath and look up, ahead of me, at the wardrobe. Behind which is hidden the scarf. Belonging to the girl. Who lives in that small, dark, cramped room. Impossibly distant, yet not far away at all. All she asked for was something to eat, but I gave her nothing and walked away, stealing her scarf and her brother's footwear.

Why was she hungry? No one goes hungry on this side of The Wall. My portion of roast chicken, still warm, would now be in our kitchen bin, slowly cooling, slithering downwards amongst a mass of uneaten, discarded food.

I feel a hand on my back, rubbing from one shoulder blade to the other, across my spine. My mother's soft, low voice rises up. 'You can tell me. Whatever it is, you can tell me.' Her top lip is red, her bottom lip pale.

Something yields in my chest, and I sense a reservoir of tears begin to fill, somewhere behind the bridge of my nose.

'We can help you,' she says.

We. Anything I say to her, she will pass on to Liev. If I tell her the truth, a chain of events will begin that will move immediately out of my control. Liev will tell the police, the police will tell the army, the army will go over The Wall and get to work. There will be an investigation, cross-examinations, imprisonments. An angry, vengeful machine is primed to leap into action, just as soon as I open my mouth. If I don't want to start up that machine, I can't say anything to anyone.

I sit up straight and breathe in sharply. 'It's nothing,' I say.

She lowers her chin and gives me a jokey-angry stare, with an attempt at a comedy frown. She's trying different tactics. Giving humour a go.

I stand up, turning away from her.

'You're sitting on my pyjamas,' I say.

'If you . . . if it's something . . . '

'What?'

She looks up at me, her hands folded neatly in her lap. 'I just mean . . . I can keep a secret.'

'From who?' I want to hear her say it: from Liev.

'From . . . anyone. Everyone.'

'About what?'

'I want to know what's wrong. What's happened to you.'

'I've told you what's wrong.'

'When?'

'Just now.'

'What is it?'

'It's that you're sitting on my pyjamas. And I want to go to bed.'

She flinches. I concentrate on keeping my facial muscles as still as I can, while Mum stares at me. Her dark eyes look sadder and tireder and more disappointed them ever. She presses her hands into her knees, and raises herself heavily, then steps back and watches me retrieve the T-shirt I sleep in.

Without saying anything more, or looking back, she slips out of the room and closes the door.

I stop playing football at lunchtime. Instead, I go to the library to do my homework, or, at least, to pretend to do my homework. That's what I lay out in front of me, but I usually just sit there, thinking, daydreaming, drawing.

I never let myself draw the tunnel, in case anyone sees and asks awkward questions, but I do draw the buildings and people I saw on the other side. I want to help myself remember. Or forget. Or perhaps a mixture of the two. I don't honestly know why I keep on drawing these things, but it's what always seems to come out of my pen — the ragged streets, the puddles, the water tanks on every roof, the wires everywhere, a few faces. And that girl. Again and again. Her thin, serious features; her stick-like arms; her blazing eyes.

Just how thin was she? I draw and draw, but I can't get it right. I'm not sure I remember her correctly. The more versions I produce, the less accurate they seem. The harder I struggle to grasp it, the more elusive her image becomes.

One day after school, I realise my feet aren't walking me home. They are leading me in the other direction, out of town, along a road I've never before taken alone, and never on foot. I don't know why it happens, but on a quite ordinary Wednesday afternoon, I find myself walking to the checkpoint.

The town stops abruptly. The last house, which is the same as mine, right down to the pale stone driveway spotted with engine oil and neat rectangle of lawn, sits next to an expanse of rocky emptiness. The road carries on as before, a wide stretch of smooth, fresh tarmac, with a crisply painted white line down the centre; just the same through the neat, polite little streets as now, beyond this invisible border into barren scrubland dotted with low, thorny bushes and the occasional cactus. A few plots are laid out alongside the road with string pulled taut across metal pegs, but no building work seems to have started. I can't tell if these are just speculative markings, or if the land has been bought and a house is on the way. Buildings appear fast here. Nothing happens for long stretches of time, then you find yourself walking down a street of houses you've never seen before, filled with families you've never met.

I walk on, squinting in the harsh sunlight. There's no shade anywhere, and my shirt is soon soaked with sweat. The sun seems to bounce up off the tarmac, attacking my face from above and below. The horizon bubbles in the heat haze, as if the land itself is close to boiling point.

A round concrete building, like a squat, armoured air traffic control tower, is the first part of the checkpoint to come into view. Of course I've seen it hundreds of times before, but only while passing through by car, never like this, on foot, with time to notice how tall it is, how forbidding. I can't see any soldiers looking down, but the angle of the concrete parapet looks as if it would conceal whatever or whoever is up there.

Under the tower is a tangled thatch of razor wire, trailing over the whole area where The Wall expands out into a zone of warehouse-like corrugated-iron huts, metal fencing, steel gates, and dense, seemingly random scatterings of concrete roadblocks.

As I get closer, I see the road where cars from my side cross The Wall. One bored-looking soldier is waving everyone through unimpeded. Just the colour of your number plate is enough to get you through with only a brief pause. Everyone in Amarias has yellow number plates, and if you are yellow, you can get through any checkpoint or roadblock without being held up. Number plates of cars from the other side are white with green text, and those are pulled over and searched. I can see one family seated silently on a rock beside their car, whose doors, boot and bonnet are open, while a pair of soldiers — young-looking guys, eighteen or nineteen — examine the upholstery and the engine.

Through a separate gateway, I see the traffic moving in the other direction, a trickle of vehicles, mainly lorries and old cars, one at a time, like drops leaking from a tap. A fenced pedestrian pathway emerges next to this gate, carrying a steady stream of people. Most of them seem to have similar expressions on their faces — distant, weary — as they hurry out and walk towards a concourse where swarms of minibuses gather and leave, rapidly and efficiently sweeping people away from the looming wall. All the buses seem to start in this one place; none come through the checkpoint.

I know from maps how The Wall follows a looping, circuitous route that makes no apparent sense. I'd heard rumours that people from the other side often had to cross over just to get from place to place within their own territory. It certainly looks that way from the movements I see here, with everyone who comes through seeming immediately to set off elsewhere. No one walks up the road where I am standing, towards Amarias.

Behind me I notice a rocky outcrop, as high as The Wall. I climb it, scampering up the hot, crumbly surface on all fours, in the hope that I might get a view of the other side. A cascade of tiny stones skitters down in my wake.

From the top I can't see much more than a jumbled tangle of rooftops, covered with those familiar water tanks, but from one vantage point, an angle through the gateway in The Wall gives me a glimpse of something I've never seen before — the approach to the other side of the checkpoint, an area shielded from the view of passing cars by a large 'Welcome to Amarias' hoarding.

My view isn't much more than a narrow slice, but it's enough to make out a network of metal cages, like something for funnelling livestock. Each cage is as wide as one person, with thick metal bars left and right and above. A long snake of men, women and children fills each cage, shuffling slowly forwards in single file, held back by remotely operated turnstiles which seem to be allowing them through, one at a time. Above these cages are raised gantries, with soldiers pacing up and down, watching over the caged people, rifles clutched in both hands. I can make out a low bunker made of the thickest concrete I have ever seen, which looks as if it contains more soldiers, presumably the ones operating the turnstiles.

The front of the queue leads into a building with a metal roof. I can't see what happens in there, or guess how long people are stopped before being allowed through The Wall, but I can see that the queue is lengthy and slow-moving.

Looking again at the faces of people hurrying out and making for their buses, I see something else, something I haven't noticed before: an expression poised between patience and rage, weariness and defiance, pride and helplessness.

I sit and watch, unobserved. I think again of the boy who spat on me, remembering the feel of his clammy saliva splatting into my cheek and eyelid — a memory still nauseating and repugnant, but now not quite so baffling.

I'm not sure if this is what I expected to see. I haven't particularly thought about the check-point before, about how people get from one side of The Wall to the other, so I don't really have an alternative vision in mind that this could either confirm or contradict. But as I watch, I feel a curdling, clenching sensation in my stomach. It's strange enough just to sit and observe, knowing how often I've driven through without the

slightest hindrance. More bizarre is the knowl-
edge that soon I won't be just a spectator. It isn't
long before I'll be a soldier, possibly one of those
soldiers, sitting in a bomb-proof bunker and
operating an electric turnstile, or walking that
gantry with a rifle pointed down at a caged line
of people. If you refuse, you're sent to prison.

I want to leave the outcrop, but feel paralysed
by what I'm seeing, transfixed by the faces
coming through the checkpoint. Only as the light
begins to fade do I climb down and head home,
walking fast yet mindlessly through the town,
barely seeing the streets around me, the row after
row of identical houses, the neat little buildings
with their neat little windows and red-tiled roofs
like something flown in from an American TV
show and randomly plonked here, thousands of
miles away, on a barren hilltop.

Everything in Amarias is so new, so fresh, it's
almost as if a magic spell has conjured it up out
of thin air. And no one seems to find this
strange. No one seems to worry that there might
be some other spell somewhere that could make
the place disappear as quickly as it appeared.

At the doorstep I delay putting in my key, and
stand in a daze, staring at our tiny patch of grass.
The sprinkler is spitting an arc of water across
the lawn, whirring round and round, chk chk chk
chk chk.

I look at the car in the driveway, our little
Japanese saloon, my eye drawn to the number
plate. The yellow number plate. This was our key
to The Wall. With a yellow number plate, you are
not checked at a checkpoint, so The Wall isn't

really a wall. We can go where we want, on new roads specially built to take us to other new towns populated by other people with the same yellow number plates. With a white number plate, you are on a different map, subject to different rules.

Wherever we chose to live, wherever we built our towns, people like me got these yellow checkpoint-opening plates. Everyone else, living all around us, could only get white ones. With this yellow rectangle on your car, the army was your friend and you could move freely. With a white one, The Wall, the barbed wire, the soldiers, the watchtowers, the guns had another meaning entirely.

I turn away from the car, not wanting to look at it any longer, but confronted by my front door I freeze, like an actor with no lines in his head, scared to go on stage. I feel as if I have a part to play, a role I have been assigned, but I can no longer remember what it is.

Mum opens the door.

'What are you doing?'

I work my tongue around my mouth, looking for words. 'I couldn't find my key.'

'It's in your hand.'

'I got it just now. It was in the wrong pocket.'

She frowns, and I can see the next question forming on her lips, so I put my head down and walk in, heading straight for my room. I can hear her voice behind me, asking what happened to my face, bleating about sunburn, but the sound of it gets pleasingly quieter as I walk away, and is reduced to almost nothing when I close my door.

I feel strange, later, as I sit down for dinner — as if I'm not quite myself, and the room around me isn't the room I'm used to. I think of how the rows of identical houses seemed vaguely unreal after what I saw at the checkpoint, and now the inside of my own living room has a strange, glossy quality to it, like something up on a stage. It feels like a room pretending to be a room, with possessions placed in it to keep up the act. I look around at the bookcases, and the jaunty paintings on the red walls, the plump sofas, the mauve light fittings, the plasma TV, and not one thing I can see feels like it is mine.

A man speaks, and it's Liev — the man who pretends to be my father, sitting at the table that pretends to be a dining table in the house that pretends to be my house. He rushes through the blessing and carves our skeleton-like rack of lamb. Putting down the knife, he turns to me and examines my sunburn. It's unusual for Liev to look at me like this — as if he's really looking.

'So what happened to your face?' he says, smirking.

'What happened to yours?' is the obvious answer, but you can't say things like that to Liev. He'd get so angry his head would explode. Pieces of beard would fly everywhere, a storm of hairy spiders. Instead of brain, millions of prayers would fly out on tiny bits of paper, like confetti. I can picture it. Cheeky comment — red nose — bulging eyes — pulsating veins — BOOM — flying spiders — prayer confetti.

104

I just shrug.

'You have to be more careful,' says Mum. 'Skin cancer's not a joke.'

'Knock knock,' I say.

'What?'

'Who's there? Skin cancer.'

'Stop it!' she snaps.

'You're right,' I say. 'It's not a joke.'

'What's he talking about?' says Liev, to Mum. She shakes her head and cuts her meat.

'So where did you go?' says Liev. 'Your mother says you were late again.'

I chew and chew and chew, the lamb turning leathery and dry in my mouth. If you magnify a virus a hundred thousand times, you get a big fluffy ball that looks like a mouthful of chewed lamb. For a while, I think through the lies or excuses I could use, then decide not to bother. I feel weird — almost weightless — as I say, casually, 'The checkpoint.'

Liev's knife clangs against his plate. 'Is this another joke?' he says.

'What, like skin cancer?'

'Such a smart guy! Always the smart guy!'

I lever a hunk of lamb away from the bone, not looking at him. The fat stretches into transparent, stringy gunge before it snaps and gives way.

'I just hope you're joking,' he says.

'You didn't!' says Mum. 'Why would you do that? It's not safe!'

'How can it not be safe? It's crawling with soldiers.'

'Ignore him,' says Liev. 'He thinks he knows everything, and we'll see where that gets him.'

105

'Did you go there?' says Mum.

'He's just trying to shock us,' says Liev. 'Don't give him the oxygen.'

'I'm warning you . . . ' says Mum. We lock eyes, and I can see that she doesn't know what she's warning me against, or what she's threatening me with, or who I am or what I want. It's as if we're looking at each other through a pane of glass, like you see in prison movies, when your visitor's right in front of you but you have to talk on the phone. For an instant I feel sorry for her, and I can see her reading my thought. I'm not sure which one of us is the prisoner, which one the visitor.

I give her a little half-smile, and she half-smiles back, but there's something so pleading and desperate in her expression that I have to look away and turn back to my food.

Eventually I escape the table, having forced down half a plateful of main course and refused dessert. It's only the excuse of a homework backlog that gets me away.

All evening I stare at my schoolbooks, but the text swims incomprehensibly in front of my eyes. I can't focus. My thoughts just slide, again and again, back to the checkpoint, to the cages and guns and razor wire, to the checkpoint and the girl.

I have two homework deadlines the next day, but I can't write a word. As the time reaches nine, then ten o'clock, and I realise I'm never going to finish, or even start, it occurs to me that tomorrow I will be punished. But this idea seems ridiculous. The word 'punished' feels like a joke.

In bed with the light off, long into the night, the same thing, on and on. The checkpoint. The cages. The guns. The razor wire. The Wall. The lines of people and their clenched, bitter faces. The girl.

Saturdays are quiet in Amarias. All the shops shut. Barely a car moves on the streets. Liev doesn't even like me going outside with a ball, in case the neighbours, or God, are watching.

Liev always turns his armchair, which usually faces the TV, towards the patio doors. He unlocks the glass-fronted cabinet which looms over the dining table, takes out one of his big leather-bound texts, and sits there for hours on end. The book stays open on that chair all day, and no one is allowed to touch it, even when Liev is doing something else. If someone visits, the chair still stays like that, facing away from the room, so people know they are interrupting.

Liev knows I'm never going to be like him, and he gave up trying to fix me years ago. My job, on Saturday, is to catch up on my homework while trying to avoid expiring with boredom. As long as Liev doesn't see me working, he doesn't mind. And since his chair is always pointing outwards, he doesn't see anything. Perhaps that's the point. As long as I don't touch the TV, he isn't too bothered what I do.

At the end of the day, the book goes back on the shelf, the cabinet doors are locked, the chair is turned back towards the room, and we eat.

It's the slowest day of the week, with every hour, every minute, dragging on as if someone's filled all the clocks with treacle, but this Saturday seems to crawl past at its usual speed and also somehow vanish in a flash. I spend the whole day in my room, and at the end of it all, none of my homework has been finished. I don't know what I've done or where the time went. I've drawn a perfect spiral on a page of maths paper just by colouring in the tiny squares; I've done an exhaustive study of which coins can stand on their edges for the longest times on a variety of surfaces; and I have peeled an invisible shiny layer off a history textbook without making a single tear, so it still looks the same, just not shiny any more. As for my actual work: nothing.

We eat dinner in near silence, with a strange tension hovering over the table. Mum clears the meal, clucking disapprovingly at my half-full plate. She goes backwards and forwards from the kitchen, taking away the plates, glasses and cutlery, then the water jug, napkins, candlestick, and even the place mats. Each time, she returns from the kitchen empty-handed. Liev watches, not moving from his chair, breathing noisily through his nose. I hear the scrape and clatter of leftovers going into the bin, a splash as the water jug is emptied into the sink. Eventually, she returns and sits. There's no dessert. The table is bare. She looks at me, looks at Liev, looks at her hands, leans forwards. Suddenly this feels less like a meal, more like a business meeting.

There's an awkward silence before she clears her throat and says, cheerily, 'We've been looking into child psychologists. Not that you're a child any more, but . . . there are some very good ones in the city.'

'What?'

'We think it's a good idea.'

'What are you talking about?'

'We'd like to help you.'

I stand, wanting to run away from the table, away from my mother and Liev, out of the house, out of Amarias. I see, like a minuscule dream as long as a blink, a vision of myself running through rocky scrubland, up a hill, with nothing around me.

'You think I'm mad? Is that what you're saying?'

'No! You just seem troubled, and you don't want to talk to us about it, so I thought maybe we should find someone else.'

I can think of no answer so I just stare at her, thrown by a sudden onrush of conflicting emotion, a queasy stew of fury and gratitude. I can't tell if her suggestion is a dire insult or a lifeline.

'Why don't you have any friends?' says Liev.

'I've got friends!'

'What's wrong with you?' he continues.

I turn to face my stepfather. 'Everything's wrong with me,' I say, half sarcastic, half sincere.

He gazes at me, baffled, then swats the air between us. 'Ach!' he says, directing an I-give-up shrug at Mum.

'Maybe you should try it,' she says, looking up at me, her face frozen into a ludicrously false attempt at encouragement and optimism.

'Maybe *you* should try it. Maybe you're the crazy one,' I bark, my voice springing up to a little boy's squeak then back down again.

Liev stands, his chair legs screeching against the floor tiles. 'Don't you dare speak to your mother like that!'

Mum gets up, too, and edges between us. 'It's OK,' she says. 'He's just upset.'

I stare at Liev, blinking but not looking away or stepping back. He's still taller than me, but not by much, and not for much longer.

'Why did you bring us here?' I say.

'Because it's where we belong,' says Liev. 'Right here.'

'Says who? God?'

'I won't have you talking like that in my house! Like these things are some kind of joke!'

I tilt my head back and roll my eyes. Trying to look bored rather than afraid, I turn and walk to my bedroom, ignoring the sound of Liev yelling at me to come back, to learn some respect, to grow up.

A while later, Mum knocks, opens my bedroom door a crack, pushes through a bowl of strawberries, and closes it again: a peace offering.

I know how my mother works. Today it was a suggestion; next week it will be a demand; in time, she'll force me. Unless I can find a way to appear normal and happy, they will send me to a shrink. I have no idea what those people do, but I can guess. If they are experts in anything, it's wheedling out information people don't want to give. It will be like an interrogation, and I don't know if I'm strong enough to hold in my secret.

★ ★ ★

111

Much later, after the house has gone silent, I slip out of bed and reach behind my wardrobe. The scarf feels smooth and slippery against my skin, worn down to a perfect softness through years of use. I bundle it up and sniff. It smells not of the girl, but of her house. It smells of the other side — of spicy food and alien soap and cigarettes and foreign sweat. I take it to bed with me, inhaling the scents of these unknowable people, with their strange homes and mysteriously constricted lives, as if studying these smells might unravel the mystery.

All the time I've lived here, I've been told stories about 'the enemy' and what they want to do to us, and how only our army can stop them. Everything about Amarias, about the way it's built, where it's built, The Wall, the soldiers, the checkpoints, springs from this story. If you doubt this, your whole world dissolves. In Amarias, if you don't know who your enemy is, you don't know anything at all.

I twist the scarf around my hand, watching my fingers redden, then slowly go purple. The skin under the nails fades to a ghostly white, and my pulse begins to tingle in my fingertips. That girl — this girl — who saved my life using this scarf — was she the enemy? Was she my enemy?

I release the twist on the scarf and feel the blood pressure in my hand equalise, my sausagey fingers quickly returning to normal. I think of my father, and how he wouldn't allow me to see him in uniform. I never understood why, and I'm still not sure, but this memory seems like a droplet of sanity within a drenching storm of confusion. And as I think of him, heading off for his military service in his T-shirt and shorts, with his huge green army bag slung across his shoulders, it strikes me for the first time — a thought as crisp as the chime of a bell — that unless I do something, myself, to fight the shame and guilt that's haunting me, I might be crushed by it.

Like the sensation of blood flooding back into my whitened fingers, I feel some strangled, starved essence of myself refill and revive, as I realise what I have to do.

My bag is packed and ready.

1) Two bags of rice, two bags of pasta, one bag each of lentils, chickpeas, walnuts, hazelnuts and pine nuts. A packet of ginger biscuits, two bars of chocolate, three tins of soup, two each of chopped tomatoes, tuna and sardines. A jar of honey. One bag of flour, one of sugar.

Most of it I have taken gradually, over a fortnight or so, from Mum's larder — picking out spares and doubles that were hidden underneath things, never taking more than a couple of items at any given time. The rice, pasta, flour and sugar I have bought partly with my savings, partly with a banknote I found inside Mum's purse. I picked them up on the way home from school, and during homework time transferred them from my schoolbag to a hiding place, underneath the winter clothes in the bottom drawer of my wardrobe.

This amount of food is as much as I can hide, and probably as much as I can carry.

2) Change of clothes.

Bought from a charity shop during a visit to see my aunt in the city. Now I've seen what people wear on the other side, it wasn't hard to find something that will allow me to blend in. It's not radically different — just old jeans, scruffy shoes and a baggy T-shirt — but the clothes I already own all look too pristine, and somehow stamped with where I'm from. A baseball cap is the key element. I noticed a couple of people wearing them, so I think a big one, pulled down low, will conceal my face without making it look like I'm trying to hide.

3) Torch.

The size of a marker pen, doctored with a few strips of packing tape around the middle, like a belt with a dangling end. The idea is that I'll be able to put the loose flap of packing tape in my mouth and cast some light ahead of me, but still have both hands free for crawling.

4) Map.

It's easy enough to find one on the web and print it out. Not so easy to locate my start or end point. After studying it night after night, rehearsing in my mind the route the girl took to walk me back to the tunnel, I draw on, in pencil, an educated guess as to where I think I might emerge, where I expect to find the flying cake bakery, my path along the main shopping street, and the three turns that should take me to the girl's house.

The map is only a safety net. I've committed as much of it as I can to memory, and plan not to look at it anywhere in the open. I can't risk being seen reading a map.

The last thing I do before putting it in the bag is to rub out my route.

5) The scarf.

6) The flip-flops.

7) Four plastic bags.

Plain, with no writing or logos.

8) Football kit.

To be placed over the top of numbers 1 to 7, in case Mum glances in the bag before I can get out of the house.

I don't feel any fear until the moment I find myself standing on top of the dumpster, about to climb into the building site. The fringe of splinters sticking up from the top of the hoarding is the first thing to remind me that this isn't just an adventure, a lark. The feel of that jagged wood sticking into my flesh comes sharply back to me, sparking off a chain of half-forgotten memories: the sour, eggy smell; the enveloping darkness; the clammy soil against my palms; my breathless gasps echoing ahead of me like water slithering down a plughole.

I thought I'd remembered my fear, but it's clear that the truth about going under The Wall has slid away. The memories I've been carrying around are like an outline, a dot-to-dot of the real thing, and only now, near the entrance to the actual tunnel, about to go through, do I feel the image filling itself in. Up close, the sheen of excitement evaporates, giving way to a sickening sensation in my throat and belly. This was fear: dark, fierce and chilling.

★　★　★

I knew my resolve was bound to falter at some point, and I prepared myself for this moment with a short loop of invented footage, staged like an interview: my father, looking out at me, telling me to be brave and carry on, telling me I'm doing the right thing, reminding me how much I owe the girl and what it would mean to ignore this debt. I stand there on the dumpster with my eyes closed and watch it once, twice, three times. When my eyelids pop open, I'm ready to carry on.

Seeing how high it is from the dumpster to the top, I realise I can't get over the fence carrying the bag on my back. With the added weight, I won't be strong enough to pull myself up using just my fingertips.

I lower the bag off my shoulders and swing it like a pendulum, back and forth, until each swing is up to shoulder height, then with all my might I toss it upwards. It hits the top, teeters, then clatters down noisily on the other side. I didn't design the package for such a long fall, and it seems unlikely it will have landed undamaged. I should have chosen better. The jar of honey was a bad idea.

I hoist myself up on to the fence and, without pausing to look at the demolished house, climb down to examine my bag. I yank the zip open, pull out the decoy football kit and chuck it aside. As I feared, the honey jar has smashed. The only other breakage I can spot is the bag of sugar, which has split.

There's no time now to worry about the honey, or to clear up the mess. I quickly strip, toss my clothes to the ground, and put on the outfit I bought at the charity shop. A sticky streak is smeared across one thigh, but I look OK. I look ready for the other side.

I lift the bag on to my shoulders and hurry towards the tunnel, grabbing a quick glance at the demolished house. It's still there, just how I remembered. I knew it would be, but I have to check. Even when something's real, and right in front of you, it can still be hard to believe.

The hatch is squarely in place over the hole. Was that how I left it? Did I move it back into position after I climbed out? I can't remember. Footsteps criss-cross the area — people have come and gone — but when, I have no idea.

I shunt the metal aside with two hands and lie on my belly, staring down into the darkness. There's nothing to see, and nothing to hear. If anyone is down there, they are still and silent. My nostrils take in a dank, sour waft. I haul the bag towards me, lower it as far as I can into the column of black air and let it drop. I can hear the glass of the honey jar shattering further. The sound of it reminds me of the torch, which I have stupidly left in the bag.

I hurry, knot by knot, down the rope to the bottom of the hole, and scrabble through the bag in search of the torch. If it is broken, the whole thing's off. I can't go through the tunnel again in the dark. Not for anything or anyone.

As soon as my fingers find the ridged metal in its packing-tape wrapper, I grip and twist. A beam of light springs into my face, dazzling me, and for an instant I am disappointed. My last chance to back out has gone.

Moving as fast as I can, I take up the position I practised in my bedroom, on all fours, with the bag hanging down under my stomach, the straps across the backs of my shoulders. This way it won't snag on the roof of the tunnel as I crawl. I put the torch in my mouth, gripped by its home-made handle, and look at the narrow void ahead of me. Twinkles of dust swirl in the feeble beam of yellow light. The tape in my mouth is bitter, rough against the tip of my tongue.

It occurs to me that if I hadn't found this tunnel, I'd never be under the ground like this, surrounded by soil, until I died. This is where you go when your life is over. This is where they put my father.

A memory spirals into my mind of his funeral, of picking up the spade from a conical pile of soil; tossing in my three spadefuls; the *thunk, thunk, thunk* as the sods of earth landed on the coffin, each one a little less woody than the last; planting the spade back in the soil for the next person; only my mother ahead of me, a long queue of mourners behind; to one side, a row of soldiers in full uniform, heads bowed, armed.

It strikes me that it's cold down here — pleasantly so at first, a relief from the sun — but if I stop moving, or get stuck, this temperature won't seem so kind. I don't know if I'm more afraid of the tunnel or of the place on the other side, but as I begin to crawl, I sense a new kind of fear settle into me, fear like a bite of lemon, sour but also sweet, repellent but delicious. I feel this fear embrace me, focus me, calm me. It tells me not to worry or speculate or count or guess at my progress. I just crawl, without a thought in my head other than the act of crawling.

I have a torch. If anything creeps towards me, this time I'll see it. I still hear occasional chirrups and squeaks, the odd fluttering of tiny feet, but nothing comes into view.

The idea of The Wall, somewhere above, makes me tingle with excitement. All that concrete is right on top of me, as solid and impenetrable as ever, yet I'm almost magically passing through to the other side with nothing to stop me.

As I shunt myself forwards, the tins of food swaying and clanking under my belly, I notice a new thing about the tunnel. The smell isn't constant. For one puzzling instant I get a waft of coffee, then, later, cinnamon.

A splintery scrape against my shoulder gives me an explanation. The ceiling props are made from packing crates: planks of wood, buried deep underground, still clinging to a trace memory of their previous life.

Sooner than seems possible — I feel as if I'm barely halfway through — I see the knotted rope looming into the pool of light ahead of me. I accelerate and reach out, needing to confirm with my hands, in this strange, untrustworthy light, that the rope really is the rope.

I slip the bag from my shoulders and unzip it. The honey jar is shattered into several pieces, the lid still neatly screwed into a jagged ring of glass. Sticky, golden goo has filled one corner of the bag and smeared itself over several of the tins and both bags of pasta. Roughly half the sugar has leaked away through the split, but the rest is salvageable.

I take out my four plastic bags and pack the food into them, smearing off the worst of the honey with my hands. I put the flip-flops into the least sticky bag and, using my cleanest fingertips, wrap the girl's scarf around my neck.

Using a wooden ceiling prop I try to scrape my hands clean, making a row of honey stalactites, then I reach for the rope. I climb as quickly as I can, leaving everything at the bottom, and push the trapdoor aside. I've decided that if anyone is in sight, I'll close the lid, sit tight for a while, then try again. I'll give it three tries — maybe half an hour or so — then I'll give up. This is the plan. These are the limits of courage I have set myself. If I do turn back, I can just lift the food out of the tunnel and leave it there. Someone will find it; someone will eat it.

But now, thinking of the boys who tried to attack me, who might be up there looking out for me again, I remember that the tunnel seemed in some way to be theirs. If I leave any food in or near the tunnel, these are the people who will get it. Maybe even the boy who spat on me, the boy who looked like he was ready to kill me. Did I really want to leave a present for him?

Perhaps he'd see the text on the labels and know where it was from, and wonder if someone from the other side had come to help. Perhaps . . . no, I couldn't imagine my way into their heads. I will never know what those boys think, beyond that they despise me and would be happy to watch me die. *They* know who their enemy is: me, and everyone like me.

Under the bins I can see distant feet walking along the high street, but the alley is empty. I drop down and hoist up the four bags, one at a time. Before my last climb, I switch off the torch and stash it at the honey-free end of the bag.

Crouching at the tunnel entrance, I push the hatch back into place. Before standing upright I look in each direction once more — towards the street; towards the chain-link fence; up at the apartment windows above me; along the spray-painted edifice of The Wall — then I loop my sticky hands into the plastic bags and set off.

With the cap pulled low and my chin angled downwards, my face is obscured from the view of anyone taller than me. I choose my pace carefully, fast enough to make quick progress, slow enough to appear unhurried. I look around casually and infrequently, as if I'm familiar with my surroundings and know where I'm going.

At the alley exit I glance up at the flying cake bakery. This is my lighthouse, the only landmark I know, the beacon I'll be relying on to get me home. The same old man, sitting on the same plastic stool, is positioned in his doorway, still fiddling with the same cigarette lighter. He catches my eye for a moment, but doesn't seem surprised or interested.

I turn right and walk, struggling under the weight of my bags. The plastic handles cut into my fingers, but with the load distributed evenly on both sides, there's no relief to be gained by swapping hands. The muscles across the top of my shoulders feel like taut cables pulled almost to snapping point.

I decide to allow myself a quick pause every couple of minutes, and to use these rests as the moment to look up and gauge my position. While on the move, I just force myself onwards with my head down.

First rest: still on the main street. On my left, a man with no front teeth standing behind a cart arrayed with soaps, wallets, toothpaste, batteries and a heap of cellophane-wrapped remote controls. Distorted music blares from tinny speakers behind his head — a high, mournful, slippery voice. I vaguely remember the look of the stall. Still on course.

Second rest: same street, in a gap between a woman selling small, gnarled aubergines from a wooden box, and a shop festooned with brightly coloured ankle-length coats. I avoid looking at the aubergine woman, sensing that I'm being watched. Up ahead is the first turn-off to the right. This is the one marked on the map, but it feels too close to the tunnel, and doesn't look right. I decide to keep going.

Third rest: the next junction. There's a food shop on the corner selling cheese, milk and yoghurt from a glass-fronted fridge out on the street. I think I remember this, turning here, with the girl. A man hovering in the doorway wearing tight, pale jeans says something in my direction and takes a few steps towards me, so without looking up I gather in my bags and hurry down the side street.

Fourth rest: dusty crossroads in the residential quarter. This is different from my pencilled route, which involved a quick left-right at a T-junction, then a fork. Two men shove past carrying a long bundle of copper pipes. They almost knock me over, but I duck out of the way just in time. My cap falls off, but I get it back on fast. Bad idea to stop here. I take the left turn.

Fifth rest: my mental map has dissolved now, bearing no relation to the place around me. Is this the second of the two quick turns? I allow myself only enough time to get some sensation back in my fingers, then take a right, plunging blindly on.

Sixth rest: my shoulder muscles are trembling, my fingers stinging. This feels like the correct distance, but nothing looks right. I'm searching for a green front door with a square iron knocker. I remember it clearly. Or there's the black motorbike I hid behind, which should be parked in front of the house. Now I've strayed from my route I'm as good as lost, except for a mental thread I'm clinging on to: the route back to the main road, and towards the bakery. I decide to keep going until I feel this thread weakening. The second I think I might be losing track of the way home, I'll just dump the bags and turn back.

Seventh rest: close to giving up. I know this street is wrong. In front of me is a yellow-painted building set back from the street, which I'm sure I've never seen before. No one seems to be around, so I give myself a longer rest, then turn round. I hang on to the bags, but head back to the main street.

Eighth rest: a green door! But no square knocker. No shutters on the window. I remember shutters above me when I looked up at the girl from my hiding place. Looking around, I see a whole street of green doors. This feels right. I pick up the bags and carry on.

Ninth rest: an iron knocker, but not square. Round. Shutters, but no motorbike. Could I have misremembered the knocker? I step

125

towards the window and look at the ground, which is scattered with square indentations. The bike stand. I remember, inches from my nose as I hid, the motorbike was supported by a metal stand. Stepping closer I see a few small black circles, just visible on the grey ground. Oil stains. I look again at the door. Three steps up from the street. Yes, that's the door.

With the bags at my feet, I look at the house. This is it! My scheme has worked! But as I stand there with my heart pounding, I realise I now have no idea what to do.

My plan ends here, as if I were making an ordinary delivery to an ordinary family, but staring up at this doorway, I'm struck by the risks involved in knocking. Quite aside from the possibility this might be the wrong house, it's clear that someone other than the girl is likely to answer the door. What then? How will I explain myself? And if the girl isn't at home, what reception will I get? What would they do to me: a boy from the other side with the missing scarf and flip-flops, a few bags of food, and no language to explain anything? I'd be at their mercy. The girl helped me, but the rest of her family might hate me on sight, like the spitting boy and his friends.

Every muscle and tendon in my body seems to slacken as I feel all confidence drain out of me. My plan suddenly looks stupid, foolhardy, lethal. But I've come this far. I can't just drop everything and run for it. Not now.

The urge to flee, to get myself back to the tunnel and home, tugs me away from the green door, hauling me backwards, but if I don't want my efforts to be wasted, I know I have to at least approach, and leave the bags on the girl's doorstep. They might be stolen, they might not, but either way, if I do this, I'll know I tried my best.

I inch towards the threshold and put the bags down as quietly as I can. Knock and run?

No. No running. I mustn't do anything that could attract attention.

The scarf, I decide, can go through the letterbox, then I'll be able to return home confident I'm no longer a thief. It's a message the girl will understand. If she gets that, she'll know who delivered the food. I don't want praise, or thanks, but I want her to know.

The letterbox is small, with stiff springs, but the scarf fits through if I stretch it out and feed it in little by little. I do this as fast as I can, working the cotton in lumps from my thumbs to my fingers and poking at the narrow slot. I've almost finished when the door springs open, giving way in front of me, toppling me forwards.

I straighten up as fast as I can and find myself looking into the angry, bearded face of a man who looks a little older than Liev. This has to be the girl's father, the owner of the scarf which is now hanging from his letterbox. He says something to me, a string of harsh, guttural words I can't understand, and I realise that given the choice between attempting to explain myself and running away, there's no contest. I promised myself I wouldn't run on this side of The Wall, but this man — the look on his face — changes everything. It's time to run.

I turn on my heel and bend my knees, poised to jump down to the street. My toe is pressed against the lip of the top step to launch me off, but before I'm airborne something bites down hard on my forearm. It feels like a machine, an iron clamp fixing me in place, but it's the man's hand. Darts of pain shoot up my arm. I try to break free — I wriggle, twist and pull — but it's pointless. His fingers are as strong as handcuffs.

Before I can speak, the man yanks me inside and slams the door.

With its broken tiles and threadbare, greying rug, the hall of the house is instantly familiar. I am at least in the right home. But as the man continues to shout, anger gurgling in his throat, this seems like no guarantee of safety. I sense from the set of his jaw and a slight quiver in his arm that if I continue to give no answer, within a matter of seconds, he'll hit me.

He pulls my cap off and tosses it on the ground. A jolt seems to rip through his body as he realises who I am, as he notices, only now, that I'm from the other side.

I know this will probably be the trigger for a beating, and I flinch under his grip, but he doesn't move. Cautiously examining his face, I see that his expression has shifted, as if his anger is now tempered by confusion and even a hint of fear.

'I'm a friend,' I stutter.

He seems to understand me, but it's a while before he speaks.

'Are you from the other side?' he says, speaking my language now, fast and fluently, with a thick accent. Even though we're inside the house, his grip still hasn't loosened on my arm.

'Yes,' I say. There's no point attempting to deny it.

'What are you doing here?'

'I'm a friend.'

'Who are you working for?'

'No one.'

'*Who are you working for?*' He shakes me, jolting my shoulder so hard I can feel the bone shift in its socket.

'No one. I came on my own.'

'Who sent you?'

'I came on my own. No one knows I'm here.'

'Who is it?'

'Nobody.'

'What are you doing here?'

'I'm a friend.'

'A friend of who?'

'Your daughter.'

'My daughter!?' His eyes, the whites zigzagged with tiny jags of red lightning, bulge in their sockets. 'How do you know my daughter?'

'She helped me. I was outside your house, and I was lost, and some boys were chasing me, and your daughter hid me.'

'Why?'

'I don't know. She helped me get home. I came back to thank her.'

'Thank her?'

'To return the scarf she lent me, and to bring her a gift. Look on the step outside.'

The man at last lets go of my arm and looks through the front door. He reaches out and brings the bags into the house, glancing inside each one.

'You brought these?'

'She asked for food but I didn't have any.'

He looks again at the bags, still suspicious, as if they are some kind of trick. A man in his late

130

teens walks in. He is tall and thin, with gelled hair and an angular face. He's wearing jeans which are slightly too short for him, ironed into immaculate creases. They begin a long conversation in hushed voices, both of them staring nervously at me as they speak.

'You met my daughter?' says the man, switching back to my language.

'Yes.'

'What is her name?'

I have no idea. I know nothing about her. If she isn't in the house, there's no way of proving my story.

'Er . . . I don't know. But I can tell you how she looks. And she lent me that.' I point at the scarf that's stuck halfway through the letterbox, dangling like the tongue of an exhausted dog. 'If you bring her here, she'll tell you I'm not lying.'

The two men have another discussion, and the teenager leaves. The older man locks the front door with a key, which he removes and puts in his pocket. He then walks to the kitchen and returns with a glass of water. I think for a moment it might be for me, and reach out my hand just at the moment he begins to sip.

'Are you thirsty?' he says.

I nod.

'Are you nervous? Frightened?'

I nod again. I can't tell if he's being friendly or is trying to trick me.

'Why are you here? What do you want?' he says.

'I told you already.'

'Who are you working for?'

'No one. I'm just a boy. I'm not working for anyone.'

'Anyone can work for anyone. You think I'm an idiot?'

'I don't know what you mean.'

'Huh! Of course you don't.'

'I don't!'

'Who sent you?'

'No one.'

'How did you get here?'

'There's a tunnel.'

'You came through a tunnel?'

'Yes.'

'What tunnel?'

'A tunnel. I found a tunnel.'

'Where?'

'In a building site.'

'Which building site?'

'It looks like a building site but it's not. It's a demolished house. It comes out in an alleyway near a bakery. The one with the flying cake.'

'How did you find it?'

'I just found it. I was looking for a football.'

'Who knows about it?'

'No one.'

'Did you tell anyone?'

'No.'

'Does anyone else know it's there?'

'No.'

'How do you know?'

'I mean I haven't told anyone.'

'Why not?'

'Because it's a secret.'

'Why?'

'Because . . . I don't know . . . I just didn't tell anyone.'

'Why should I believe you?'

'Because it's true.' I hold out my hands, showing him the soil under my fingernails. I point to my mud-stained knees. 'I crawled through. Twice. Your daughter saved my life. She said she was hungry.'

'She's not hungry.'

'I didn't want to come back, but it felt wrong. The more I thought about it, the worse it felt, living so close but giving her nothing in return.'

'That's why you came?'

'Yes.'

'Who gave you this story?'

'No one!'

'Do you think we are idiots?'

'I'm not lying!' I feel tears of helplessness begin to prick at my eyeballs. 'I'm not lying!'

The door gives a rattle. Barely taking his eyes off me, the man steps backwards and opens it with his key. The gel-haired teenager bursts in, dragging his sister behind him. It's the girl. Her face is streaked with tears. She shoots me a quick, angry look as the man begins to shout again, harshly interrogating her. I can tell by her gestures and tone of voice that she's backing up my story. For a moment I think he might be about to slap her. I can't understand why he's so angry.

The father has forgotten to relock the door, and it occurs to me in a flash that while their focus is on the girl, I might be able to make a run for it. But that brother is taller and older than me. He'd catch me in an instant. Instead, I lift the bags from the doorway and carry them to the dining table. On the pale wood, I lay out two bags of rice, two packets of pasta, bags of lentils, chickpeas, walnuts, hazelnuts and pine nuts, a packet of ginger biscuits, two bars of chocolate, three tins of soup, two of chopped tomatoes, two of tuna, two of sardines, one bag of flour and half a bag of sugar, split down the middle.

By the time I've finished, the table is covered with food, and the room is quiet. They have stopped shouting at the girl.

'Some of it is sticky,' I say. 'I'm sorry. There was a jar of honey but it smashed.'

No one speaks. A woman in a black shawl, the girl's mother, has now appeared. All four of them stare at the table, like mourners transfixed by a corpse.

'It's as much as I could carry,' I say, just to fill the silence.

The woman shuffles forwards and looks at each item, one by one, without picking anything up. She mutters something to her husband in a low voice.

'Where did you get it?' he asks.

'I brought it for you,' I reply, dodging the question. 'All of you. I wanted to say sorry.'

'Sorry?'

'I mean thank you. For saving me.' I turn to the girl. 'You said you were hungry.'

Her eyes are moist, glinting in the dim light. She opens her mouth, then closes it again, her head moving slowly from side to side, almost a nod, almost a headshake, but not quite either.

Her father has a softer expression on his face now, but it doesn't last. With his eyes darting between his daughter and me, he says, 'I don't know who is more stupid, you or her. You know who those boys are? The ones who chased you?'

'No.'

'They are very dangerous. You don't lie to them. You don't speak to them. You want to be safe, you stay out of their way. You hope they don't notice you.'

'But they'd already noticed me. They were chasing me.'

'That's your problem. Now go. I don't want to see you here again. And we don't need your food. We're not hungry.'

'But — '

'We don't want your charity.'

'It's not charity. Your daughter helped me.'

'Take it away.'

'I can't. It's too heavy.'

'You shouldn't have brought it.'

'I wanted to help.'

'Did you ask him for food?' he says, looming over the girl.

'No! I just . . . I thought he might have something in his pockets. Some sweets.'

He turns back to me.

'Why did you do this?'

'She helped me. I wanted to help her.'

'If you get caught here, it's no help. No help at all. It's very dangerous for all of us.'

'I'm sorry.'

'If you are hurt, by those boys or anyone else, it's a big problem for the whole town.'

'I'm sorry.'

'Just go. And be careful.'

A few moments ago I would have settled for this. All I wanted was to get out of this house unharmed. But now I can't move. I can't walk back out there. Not yet. I need to gather my strength, have a think, plan my route to the tunnel. The thread that was supposed to lead me to the high street has snapped. I don't know my way home.

I look across at the girl for support, but her eyes are cast down to the floor, her cheeks flushed with what looks like either anger or shame.

'No one knows you're here?' says the man.

I shake my head.

'What if something happens to you?'

I shrug.

'What would your father say if he knew what you've done?' he barks.

'He'd be proud. And I don't have a father.'

The man's eyebrows pucker together, pinched by a flicker of confusion.

'You don't have a father but he'd be proud?'

I look up and hold his gaze. 'Yes. He's dead. He was killed.'

I don't let my stare waver, and for a while we seem to be caught in some kind of contest, then he blinks and looks across at his daughter. Walking in perfect silence on her bare feet, the girl hurries out of the hallway, returning a few moments later with a glass of water, which she hands to me without speaking. I down it in one gulp.

'Thank you,' I say. 'I'll go.'

I turn to leave, but a hand on my shoulder stops me. It's the father. The skin on his fingers is tough and ridged, like bark. 'How will you get back?' he says. 'Through the checkpoint?'

'No. I can't.'

'You people can get through. It's us that can't.'

'Not on foot. Not from this side, just me, on my own. They'd ask me a thousand questions and they'd contact my home, and they'd want to know how I got here, and if my stepfather finds out that I crossed The Wall, he'll . . . he just can't know.'

'Why?'

'He'd go crazy.'

'So how are you going to get home?' he says.

'Through the tunnel.'

'Go, then. Go. And watch out. If those boys are near the tunnel, don't let them see you.'

'OK.'

'And thank you. For the food. You are brave.' He reaches out to shake my hand. As we shake, he says, 'But brave is the best friend of stupid, and you are also stupid.'

I nod, my lips curling into a reluctant smile as I step towards the door. Before I can leave, the girl lunges forwards and blocks my path. She begins to speak in her own language, furiously gesturing at me, at her mother, at the food, at the scarf, addressing the whole fountain of words to her father, who listens with his head bowed, at first not catching her eye.

Eventually he looks up, reeled in by her fervour, and quietens her with a raised hand, like a man trying to stop an oncoming car. 'OK, OK, OK,' he says, turning towards me. 'I'll take you back to the tunnel. She doesn't want you to get hurt.'

'Thank you,' I say. I know I ought to tell him it isn't necessary, but the idea of going back out there on my own fills me with dread. Without help, I might not find my way home.

'But I want something in return,' he says, turning and scrawling on a scrap of paper.

His son watches him closely. I can feel the girl's eyes on me. I turn my head and sneak her a nervous smile. She casts her eyes down to the floor, but I can see she's smiling, too.

'You shouldn't have come back,' she says, her voice so quiet I can barely hear it.

'I had to,' I say. 'You saved me.'

She shrugs. The desire to reach out and touch her soft, serious face is so strong, it seems for a moment as if I won't be able to resist, but I still haven't moved when the father turns round and hands me a piece of paper.

He's drawn a basic map of the area, with The Wall a thick black line down the centre, and just two streets sketchily drawn on my side. It's only the three hills which encircle the town, all clearly marked and correctly oriented, that make it obvious what the map is supposed to represent. There's a single dark cross outside Amarias, on my side of The Wall, etched so hard in ink it has dented the paper and made a tiny tear.

He points at the X. 'You know where that is?'

'I don't know the place, but I can understand where it is.'

'I want you to go there, once a week.'

'Once a week?'

'It's my olive grove. It was my father's and his father's, and I'm looking after it for my sons, but since The Wall was built I can't get there. I have a pass for the first Friday of each month, but no more. Just one visit a month, and sometimes even with a pass they still don't let me through. The olives are OK, but there are three terraces of lemons, and half the trees have died. At this time of year, they need water. I want you to go every week. There's a pool in the corner, which fills from a spring. There's a bucket. I want you to do every tree with one bucket. I want you to check the spring is filling the pool. Can you do that?'

'I think so.'

'You will?'

'Yes.'

'You promise? Promise and I will take you to the tunnel, safe.'

'I promise.'

'What is your address?'

'Why do you want my address? I've promised.'

'This is a separate thing. You make this promise, you are my friend, yes?'

'Yes.'

'If you are my friend, I should have your address and your name.'

'Why?'

'Because we are friends.'

'But why?'

'You don't trust me? If you don't trust me, why should I trust you? Why should I believe your promise?'

'But why do you need my address?'

'Because you never know what will happen. On this side of The Wall, anything can happen. The worst thing you can think of, something you can hardly imagine, suddenly it can happen.'

'What does that have to do with my address?'

'Because one friend on the other side of The Wall can help.'

'How?'

'Because you are free. You can get things when you need them. You can go where you want to go. No one blocks your streets or closes your shops or comes to get you in the night.'

He hands me his pen and a fresh piece of paper. I press it against a corner of the food-laden table. My hand trembles over the white sheet. I'm not sure what to do. I have no idea why he wants my address, and what he intends to do with it. I know I could make one up, but I sense that he might know, and that it's unwise to risk angering him again. I still need his help to find the tunnel.

The girl's voice rises up through the thick silence. 'We won't hurt you,' she says. 'I promise. Just one day we might need help from the other side. If we are attacked.'

'Attacked?'

'Yes.'

'By who?'

The four of them exchange a look, as if I've said something stupid. No one speaks or looks at me, and in their silence, I understand. None of them wants to say it, but two words are hovering unspoken in the air: *by you.*

'There's something coming,' says the man. 'It's like a thunderstorm. Before it arrives, you can feel it in the air.'

I press the pen on to the paper and write my name and address in capital letters. The father takes it out of my hands, holds it long-sightedly at arm's length while he reads it, then folds the paper twice and places it in a drawer.

'OK,' he says. 'Now we'll go.'

I want to say something more to the girl, I want at least to touch her hand, but no words come, and I find myself walking towards the door, away from her, looking backwards as I go.

'What's your name?' I stutter.

'Leila.'

'Leila,' I reply, testing out the two syllables in my mouth, my tongue nudging twice against the crest of my palate. 'I'm Joshua.'

'Choshua,' she says, with the smallest of smiles. 'Choshua.'

'Yes, Choshua.'

On the street, Leila's father moves quickly, faster than I can walk.

'Don't run,' he snaps, when I speed up to avoid falling behind.

'You're too fast.'

He slows a little. 'And don't speak. Not this language.'

I nod, and the man leads me onwards, a complicated, winding route through back roads that I don't recognise, until we emerge on the main street, opposite the flying cake bakery.

'This is — '

He cuts me off with a hand shoved against my chest and a sharp 'shh'.

I want to tell him he doesn't need to take me any further, but he's already accelerating into the alley, so fast I can no longer stay next to him without running.

We're halfway to the bins when I hear a raucous, scooping whistle above us. I look up and see a face in a window overlooking the alleyway. It's the boy who gave me that regretful shake of the head as he blocked the tunnel entrance, the first time I crossed over. He's waving his arms at someone behind me.

I turn and see a boy standing in a diagonal shaft of dusty sunlight between the alley and the bakery. It's one of the gang who chased me. He waves up at the face in the window and lets out a shout, whether at me, or the person in the apartment, or someone else, I have no idea. I break into a run, sprinting for the tunnel, overtaking Leila's father. He, too, is running now, but from here, if he doesn't go down the tunnel, he has no escape. His only other option would be to climb over the chain-link fence, but judging by the stiff, slow way he runs, and the speed of the boys, he doesn't stand a chance.

Almost immediately, I hear several sets of footsteps following us down the alleyway, and more angry shouts. I turn back as I squeeze between the bins and see that Leila's father has been pushed to the ground. The first boy down the alley, who now has three others following behind, kicks him in the stomach with vicious force. The sound of it, like a heavy sack dropping on to concrete, echoes down the alley towards me.

He pulls his leg back for another kick, then lifts his head and looks at me. For an instant he freezes, his eyes locked on mine. '*Run! Run!*,' I think, but I'm not running. I'm just standing there, staring at this felled man, Leila's father, this person who only minutes ago announced himself as my friend, but is now spluttering and choking, writhing on the dusty ground.

The boy abandons his half-finished kick and sets off at speed towards me. Now the message gets through to my legs. I sprint towards the tunnel and shove the hatch aside. If I jump in, rather than using the rope, I'll gain an extra few seconds. I crouch and look back down the alley one last time.

I can only see feet now, under the bins: two sets running towards me, several more landing kick after kick on the body and head of Leila's father. He's curled into a ball to protect himself. It seems unforgivable to leave him there, when he's in the alleyway to help me escape, when the whole situation is my fault, but I know I'm powerless to help, and that to turn back would be suicide.

I twist and jump into the darkness. The ground arrives sooner than I'm expecting and whacks against my feet. Something in my ankle wrenches out of place with a hot little internal twang, like a tiny bubble of boiling liquid bursting deep inside the joint.

Pain shoots up my leg in darts that feel intense, but also strangely abstract and far away, as if the wiring of my body somehow knows it has to prioritise my escape. There's no time to worry about a mere ankle. I begin to crawl, not using my knees, but squatting like a dog, touching the ground only with my hands and feet. It's the closest I can get to running. I'm some way down the tunnel, and already in pitch darkness, when I remember that the torch is still in my bag, stashed behind me near the entrance.

I stop crawling. I know it would be insane to go back, but for an instant I feel I simply can't go through the tunnel again without a light. Then I hear a voice, close and echoey. Someone is down in the tunnel with me. No — two voices: a conversation, accompanied by the sound of shuffling against the soil. They've followed me into the tunnel. I haven't got away.

I lurch into motion, resuming my dog-like sprint. I can see nothing, not even my hands pushing and scrabbling at the soil, sending me hurtling onwards into the pitch blackness. My lungs heave the thick, mushroomy air in heavy rasps, driving me onwards with all my might; but despite those two voices echoing through the space, one second seeming far behind, the next right on my heel, despite delving into myself for every last drop of energy, I soon begin to sense that my pace is slowing.

On and on I go through the soupy blackness, my hands and arms more sore and tired with every second, my throat constricting into an acid knot. The skin of my palms feels as if it is being grated. There isn't the time or the light to see if I'm drawing blood, but something feels sticky and strange in the contact my hands are making with the soil.

Part of me is praying for the end of the tunnel, part of me is dreading its arrival. It's unnatural and terrifying to be pushing on as fast as this, using every muscle and fibre for speed, knowing that ahead is a hard earthen wall, invisible in the darkness, which at any moment will smash into my head. The voices are still behind me, a little fainter perhaps, but still following, occasionally shouting bursts of what sound like threats, so I can't worry about the wall. My job is just to get away, out of the tunnel and over the building-site fence, before they catch me.

If I falter or fall, if they catch up with me, down here they'd be able to do anything, and no one would see, and no one would find out what happened to me. I'd be the boy who disappeared: the boy who went to a football match that didn't exist and never came back.

The dangling rope gives the faintest of brushes against the crown of my head as I surge forwards. I raise my arm as quickly as I can, turning my head to the side, but I can't stop in time. The soil smacks into my cheek. I reel back, my head seeming to empty itself, like a computer switching off. If I'd been standing up, I would have fallen. Even on my knees I feel a toppling sensation, as if I might be blacking out. Everything is black already, of course, so I can't even tell if my eyes are still working, but I feel a momentary sensation of weightlessness, as if I'm coming loose from my own body.

A buzz ripples through my spine, my brain reboots, and I remember where I am. I flail with both hands, searching for the rope. I have no idea if I fell unconscious, or how much time has elapsed since hitting the end wall of the tunnel, but the voices now sound closer than ever, tumbling towards me in booming, overlapping echoes.

Two dancing pinpricks of light at first seem like nothing at all, perhaps some strange underground insect flying in front of my face, then I realise it is a pair of torch beams, moving towards me.

My arms swipe at the air, my heart beating out a non-stop rhythm of incessant heavy blows, no gaps, no pairs of beats, just a constant fast thump like crazed dance music heard through a wall.

I feel a tickle at one wrist and grasp at the swaying rope, then spring to my feet and climb. With what feels like the last residue of strength in my body, I shove and shove against the heavy trapdoor, which at the third attempt shifts aside.

I reach up towards the hot whiteness, squeeze through and wriggle out into the wasteland. Sunlight forces itself against my eyeballs with overwhelming, blinding power, disabling my vision as completely as the darkness below. Contracting my eyes into tiny slits, I stagger through the building site, not sure if I'm heading in the right direction, just trying to get myself further away from the tunnel, from whoever is following me.

As the whiteout dissolves into glimpses of stony ground, I cast my eyes up towards the wooden hoarding around the building site. My legs seem to give way underneath me as I plunge against it and slump to the ground, flattening myself against the hot, dry soil.

After a while, with my eyesight restored, I crane my neck and look back at the tunnel. No one has yet emerged. I freeze and stare at the hatch, waiting and watching, my breath slowly returning to normal as I scour the area around me for a better hiding place.

I know I ought to carry on running, get up and out, over that fence into safe territory, but I feel strangely immobilised, afraid to go any further. The ground, millimetres from my nose, smells curiously sweet, wafting into me an odour of grapes and flesh.

The hatch doesn't move, and nobody climbs

out. As it begins to seem as if no one is going to follow me out of the tunnel, I notice, at first with mild curiosity, that I'm in terrible pain. My ankle is drumming out a pulse of insistent complaint, sending a signal that only now, like the return of a distant memory, seems to get through to my brain. My body's ability to keep the bad news at bay has run out. It is sprained, and the pain suddenly feels like pain: vicious and shrill.

Diagonally across the building site I see my heap of clothes. If those men had caught up with me in the tunnel, if I'd never got home, someone would eventually have found those clothes and connected them to me. From here, it looks like the scene of a suicide.

This thought sparks an image back into my mind — the last thing I saw before jumping down into the tunnel — Leila's father, curled into a ball, two men kicking at his head and back. If they figured out I was from this side, and that he was with me, they might take him for a collaborator. If that's what they thought of him, anything was possible.

I have a clear view of The Wall from where I'm lying. If I could see through it, I'd be able to see him, probably lying in a pool of blood, perhaps still under attack. Then I remember there's a mobile phone in the pocket of my trousers. Ignoring the howls of outrage from my ankle, I run across the building site, wrestle the phone from the floppy material of my empty trousers, and dial.

Their first question is the location of the incident.

My head spins, struggling to think of a response. 'I'm next to The Wall, near the building site at the edge of Amarias. I can hear something over The Wall. I think someone's being attacked. I can hear them screaming for help.'

There's a sceptical silence on the other end of the line. 'How old are you?'

'What's that got to do with anything? Someone's hurt. It's urgent.'

'Is this a prank?'

'No! You have to help!'

'They have their own ambulances. Stop wasting my time.'

'But — '

The line goes dead.

Fighting back tears of helpless rage, I hobble towards The Wall, over mounds of rubble, then smooth soil marked with bulldozer tracks.

'HELLO!' I shout, craning my neck skywards. 'HELLO? HELLO? CAN YOU HEAR ME? ARE YOU ALL RIGHT? ARE YOU ALL RIGHT?'

No sound comes back. I flatten my ear against the rough concrete. Nothing. I realise I never even asked the man his name.

'CAN YOU HEAR ME? CAN YOU HEAR ME? ARE YOU ALL RIGHT?'

Silence.

Like a tree sucking moisture from the soil, I feel a wave of remorse rise from my feet, up through my legs, stomach, chest and neck. Tears begin to leak from my eyes, slowly at first, then a surge of uncontrollable sobs gushes out, crumpling me to the ground.

I lie there, curled into a ball, weeping. My plan had backfired in the most appalling way. I tried to help the girl who helped me, but I'd done the exact opposite. Her father had taken a brutal beating, and it was my fault. I only wanted to do one small, good thing. I only wanted to give the girl what I owed her. But here, that was impossible, dangerous, stupid.

Eventually, I roll on to my knees, force myself upright, and hobble away from The Wall, limping on my stiff, swollen ankle. I look down at the trousers and shirt I chose that morning from the drawers in my bedroom, and they look like a costume, almost like fancy dress. It is as if these clothes belong to a boy who doesn't exist any more.

I peel off my muddy, honey-stained jeans and put on the clean outfit. I scuff my football kit into the soil, so it will look as if I've played, then turn and look for a hiding place where I can conceal the charity shop clothes. Seeing the tunnel, the hatch still ajar, I realise that I'll never go through again, not if my life depends on it. The clothes can stay where they are. I don't need them any more, and I don't care who finds them.

I take one last glance at the demolished house, then place my hands against the splintery hoarding and begin to climb.

Part Three

Part Three

The ankle is easy enough to pass off as a football injury, but the flayed skin on my palms is another matter. I try to convince Mum that it happened when I skidded off my feet during a warm-up on tarmac. She's sceptical, and a conversation with David's mother ends up exposing the entire football match as a ruse.

My backup excuse is feeble. I say I wanted to be on my own in the hills. I tell her I was desperate to go rock climbing, but I knew they'd never allow me, so I just set off and did it on my own. A fall scraped my hands and twisted my ankle. This isn't much more plausible than the football story, but I stick to it.

'That doesn't make sense,' says Mum. 'Why would you do that?'

I shrug.

'You can't just go off like that! There are people out there!'

I shrug.

'It's forbidden!' says Liev. 'Who do you think you are, just going off and doing these things?'

I shrug again. Later, they try a different approach.

'Look at your hands! It's both of them — the same scrapes! How did you do it?' says Mum.

'I told you.'

'We don't believe you.'

'I'm not lying,' I lie.

'We think you are,' she says.

I shrug.

'The football story was a lie! Why do you think we're going to believe this?'

I shrug.

'This insolence!' barks Liev. 'Where did you learn it? What on earth makes you think this is acceptable?'

I shrug.

'STOP SHRUGGING!'

I shrug.

'He's impossible,' says Liev, lifting his arms and slapping them down against the side of his thighs.

'Why are you doing this?' says Mum.

'He's impossible! What are we going to do with him?'

'Look at your hands!' says Mum.

'I just scraped them,' I say. 'I slipped.'

Liev's mouth opens and closes again, like a goldfish. Mum stares at me, squinting, as if I'm so far away she can't quite tell if it's really me.

It is strangely enjoyable to lie, quite consciously and deliberately, and to stick at it in the face of whatever evidence or outrage is thrown at me. Mum and Liev both know I'm lying, and I know I'm lying, but we all discover this brings us rapidly up against the limits of their power over me. They shout, but I'm not afraid; they confiscate possessions, but there's nothing I miss; they ground me, but I don't care, since I can barely walk, and there's nowhere in Amarias I want to go, and no one I want to see.

Their final punishment is to confine me to the

154

house for three weeks, outside school hours. I take it with an indifferent shrug, and make a point of never complaining or asking for a single outing. I can't help finding it funny to see them discover how many little errands I usually run for the house, which they now have to do for themselves. Liev barely even knows where to buy bread.

I leave my room only when I have to, and speak as little as I can to either of them, scuppering their attempts to ignore me by ignoring them first.

The one time we're all together is when we eat, usually in near silence. Liev scoffs away, seemingly unbothered by the tense atmosphere. Mum picks and nibbles at her food, looking tragic, as if she's the one being punished. She's thinner than she used to be. The skin under her eyes is loose and dark. The way she behaves, you'd think she was working night shifts down a coal mine or something, but she's not. She's not doing anything. I don't know how she doesn't die of boredom.

It's weird listening to Mum and Liev trying to have conversations as if I'm not there. What they talk about more often than anything else is her back. Mum's bad back is her hobby. When Liev can't think of anything to say he asks her how her back has been that day, and she often comes out with an incredibly long answer. You can see the effort in his eyes as he attempts to look interested. Sometimes I make a point of watching him listen to her, which I know annoys him, but he can't say anything.

Every month or so there'll be some new cushion to sit on, machine to stretch with, or exercise to perform, but none of them lasts long. At the moment she's into a huge inflatable football-type thing. She goes crazy if I kick it. Genuinely crazy.

Before we moved to Amarias, her back was fine. If I ever said this, she'd go even crazier than if I volleyed the ball-chair into the TV.

In the course of my three weeks at home, something under the surface of the whole family shifts. Their attempt at a punishment proves to be a liberation. In some strange way, I feel suddenly free of them: free to tell them nothing; free to live among them while at the same time remaining entirely concealed. It's as if something has been dragging me back all my life, and I didn't even know it was there, but now it's been snipped away, and I'm lighter and faster than I ever thought was possible.

I feel as if there is a new line around me: an edge, where I stop and Mum starts. Before, it was a blur. She's still my Mum — I still love her and need her and want her to be less miserable — but I realise that I have now, in some way, got rid of her. It's a delicious feeling, like putting down a heavy bag, like jumping off a high wall, like sprinting into the sea.

★　★　★

I examine the map every night. After the house goes quiet, after Liev begins to snore, I creep to the drawer where I hid the food for Leila and

156

there, under my winter clothes, is the small, cryptic diagram drawn for me by her father.

I know it by heart now, but that doesn't mean I understand it. Some elements are obvious, others — small marks I didn't even notice when he first handed it to me — are incomprehensible.

The Wall, a thick line down the centre of the map, is the starting point, but even this is odd, not quite corresponding to reality. The checkpoint is the only way around The Wall, but on Leila's father's drawing, one road simply ghosts through the concrete. On my side, this ghost road is one of only two he has drawn. The far side is criss-crossed with a network that matches the map I downloaded from the net, but this route through The Wall is a fantasy.

After looking at the map again and again, night after night, a theory occurs to me. Perhaps this layout is not an invention, but a memory. He's made the streets of Amarias disappear not because he wants them to disappear, but because he's never come here. Or, rather, he once came here often, before Amarias was built; but after the bulldozers moved in, and new streets and houses were constructed, and The Wall went up, he was never able to come again. He wouldn't even know what was here. The map in his head was the pre-Amarias map. He was old; my town was new.

His current route to the olive grove took him out to the checkpoint and around the edge of town. In the past, he, and his father, and his father's father, would have walked in a straight line, along this map's vanished road, wafting through the rows of houses they couldn't have known would ever be built here, on the edge of their town, for people like me, from far away. Perhaps they walked right here, through this house, through my bedroom.

I'm struck by the obvious but new thought that everything ever built was once not there. Every town was once a field, a forest, a desert, a nameless nowhere that grew into a named somewhere. Amarias was different, though. The not-thereness of Amarias was so recent, the thereness so sudden, that with this map in my hand the town seemed, for all its solidity, almost fantastical.

Each hilltop on the map is indicated by a small circle, every one exactly in position if you line them up with The Wall. Other than these hills, the only things marked on my side of the barrier are the disappeared road through The Wall and the path up from the checkpoint to the olive grove. Between the junction of these two routes and the X, he has marked a series of complex squares, dots and squiggles. However much I stare, none of these makes any sense. The only way to understand them would be to go.

Three weeks after my disastrous delivery of food to Leila, the grounding ends. My ankle joint still aches, giving me a slight limp, but I can't wait any longer. I have a place to go, a job to do, a map to follow.

At midday, in summertime, the streets are almost empty. Everyone is at home, the shops are shuttered up for the long lunch break, and even the dogs go quiet. The middle of the day here is like the middle of the night: if you venture out, you'll probably see no one and no one will see you. That's when I set off, my shadow like a bobbing football between my feet as I walk through the blazing crush of sunlight. The map remains in my pocket while I cross the centre of town, and I clutch a tennis racket in my hand, carried as an explanation for my mum, or anyone else who might see, as to what I'm doing. I often play tennis against The Wall. In some ways it's the perfect tennis partner, except that it can't serve and it never loses.

I toss the racket from hand to hand, practising vertical spins and juggler-style rotations. I once saw a guy on TV pass his whole body through a stringless tennis racket. To do the last bit, he had to dislocate his own shoulders, then pop them back in again. It was disgusting, but impossible to look away.

I falter at the edge of town. The perimeter has the same feel as on the checkpoint road, the same strange leap from suburbia to wilderness. It always seemed unremarkable viewed from a car window, but on foot the abruptness of the transition feels creepy. You can actually see the

159

edge of the last lawn — see that it is just a few blades of grass, sitting on a skin of soil no deeper than my little finger, plonked on top of the grey-brown dusty earth that stretches out to the horizon. The sight of this edge makes the lawn, and all the other lawns, seem less like real grass, more like carpets that have been trucked in, rolled out and stamped down. It makes me imagine, fleetingly, the whole town as some kind of pop-up carpet that someone has unrolled on a hilltop for families like mine to live in.

I'm not supposed to go outside the town, but there's nothing to stop me. It's just assumed that no one will want to — least of all a boy, on his own, without so much as a handgun. No one can get through the checkpoint carrying a weapon, but even so, once they've crossed over it's possible for them to head in this direction, and if someone was determined enough to harm a person who strayed out of his safe areas, there were plenty of ways to do it. Beyond the edge of Amarias, if you weren't armed, you weren't safe. That's what we were always told.

But I no longer believe what I've been told, and I have a job to do, a promise to keep. In the last three weeks, barely an hour has passed without my thoughts spinning back to Leila's father, to that glimpse of the people crowded around his curled-up body, kicking him. I tell myself again and again that after I went down the tunnel, they must have stopped. It can't have been much longer before they decided they'd punished him enough. What, after all, had he done to them? He'd just walked into their alley.

You couldn't get killed for that. He had to be all right. He had to be back home now, with his family. That, surely, was the only possible outcome.

I don't usually pray unless I have to, because I know there's no point, I know there's nobody listening, but now, every day, I find myself asking for help from I-don't-know-who, begging no one in particular, muttering pointlessly into nothingness my plea for Leila's father to be safe.

I feel a faint breath of wind on my face. Inside town the air is cloyingly still, but out here, in the open, there's just enough breeze to cool the skin. Fine, invisible dust seems to dissolve itself into the sweat which oozes from my forehead and slips grittily towards my neck.

As my road joins up with the narrow route down to the checkpoint, I look back at Amarias, towards the newer parts of town where it has expanded outwards from the curved hilltop, like sauce oozing down a lump of ice cream. Our house was at the edge of town when we moved in; now there are hundreds of homes beyond it. The Wall is hidden from view behind the hillside. From here, the place looks almost normal.

In the distance, I can see the new road from Amarias to the city, fenced on both sides, rising up to bridge the valley floor before disappearing into a circle bored through the hillside. You'd think it was an express railway. Where it passes under a cluster of low, rickety houses, a concrete overhang leans out over the tarmac to stop people throwing stones at the traffic. For this road, you need a yellow number plate.

161

The tennis racket is sticky in my hand, heavier now than it seemed when I set off. I toss it into a gully. No one can see me now. I'll be able to pick it up on my way home.

My pulse accelerates as I draw the map from a back pocket and unfold it in the dazzling sunlight. The dusty sweat on my thumbs makes a brown smudge in each corner.

At the point where the two roads meet, a squiggle has been drawn along one side of the junction. I look to my left, into a ditch dotted with scrubby pockets of vegetation. It's dry now, but in rainy months this would be a stream. Straight away, the map's first puzzle is solved. The squiggle is the stream.

I walk on, the scuff of my trainers against the tarmac oddly loud amid this huge expanse of silence. Sidewinding snakes of dust skitter across the road in front of me, disappearing as soon as they've traversed the dark surface of the road. I'm thirsty now, wet from head to toe with sweat, my hair moist and flat against my scalp, but I brought no water.

Whether or not I'm right to ignore all the other warnings and threats that hang over the land around the town, I know I've been stupid to overlook this one. In heat as intense as this, without water you get weak fast. The second I realise my omission, I know I ought to turn back. But looking at the map, it seems as if I'm almost there. I have no idea if it's to scale, but this is where the detail intensifies, and I feel close to the marked turn-off from the road. He said there was a spring at the olive grove. If the directions are right, I'll get a drink sooner by carrying on than by returning.

Of course, I might get lost. I might never find the olive grove or the spring. By the time that happened, and with extra distance to cover, the journey home would be risky.

I should definitely turn round and head back, but I've waited three weeks for this chance, and there'll be another week of school before I get an opportunity to come back. I'm so close, having got past everything that might get in the way of a next attempt, it seems crazy to give up. Liev could choose to ground me again, and there's no way of predicting when and where security guards or soldiers might be stationed. Also, if anyone has seen me come this far, something will be done to stop me trying again. I simply can't let myself get this near, only to turn back just for a drink of water.

I look again at the map. The key intersection seems close. The road passes by a long rectangle, then runs alongside a short but emphatic zigzag. From there, a line diverges from the road, loops around the zigzag, and snakes between a series of circular scribbles before arriving at the X.

I give the town one last backwards glance, trying to commit to memory my distance from home, as a yardstick to tell me if I'm straying too far, then I turn and walk on, blinking sweat from my eyes, licking salty droplets from my top lip. After a few minutes, a low wall rises up alongside the road, enclosing a field the size of a five-a-side football pitch. The wall is made of dry rocks, held together only by the perfection with which the stones tessellate into one another. Outside this wall, the ground is rocky and uneven; inside is flat, unbroken soil, what looks like carefully tended farmland, except there's no crop, only thistles and patches of thorny, berry-laden weeds. The soil is packed down hard, and slatted with horizontal markings I recognise from the building site: bulldozer tracks, weathered down to faint grooves. One corner of the wall has been demolished, with piles of stones scattered across the ground, some pressed into the soil and squashed flush with the surface. The gap in the wall is roughly the width of a bulldozer. It is clear that the same thing happened to this field as to the house at the mouth of the tunnel.

I step off the road and crouch alongside the wall, touching the hot, rough stone with my palm. Someone spent weeks clearing the field to make this wall, lifting and carrying hundreds of rocks, a long time ago. The person who built this wall once put his hand on this very rock, exactly where I'm touching it now, maybe twenty years ago, maybe a thousand. Everything around here seems to be either brand new or very, very old.

I walk beside the wall, dragging my fingers against its uneven surface. At the furthest corner, near to the demolished section, is a heap of soil and rock, on top of which lies a single short coil of razor wire stretched between two iron rods. It looks like a bizarre attempt at a roadblock, pointless since there's nothing to stop you walking around the obstruction. Behind this barrier is a narrow footpath, heading uphill, away from the road, winding through a scatter of bushes.

My hand is trembling with excitement as I unfold the map once more. The rectangle, the zigzag, the line, the scribbles: the field, the razor wire, the footpath, the bushes. Unmistakable.

Forgetting my thirst and tiredness, forgetting everything, I break into a run, leaving the road, skirting the mound of earth, and darting between the bushes along the dry, compacted soil of the path.

Up ahead of me, standing out amid the dry, brown landscape, I can make out a patch of green. The sight of it wipes away all traces of tiredness and pushes me up the hill, as I sprint towards what I can now see is definitely an olive grove.

There are four terraces cut into the hillside, enclosed in another ancient-looking dry stone wall. The path leads me straight there, curving round one last thorn bush to a doorway-sized break in the wall: the entrance to Leila's family olive grove.

I skid to a halt, then stagger forwards and fall, breathless, on to my back. Giddy with exhaustion, I look around me at the thick, gnarled trunks of the olive trees, which look as if they must be older than the grandparents of the oldest person I'll ever meet. Despite the hugeness of the trunks, each tree has only a modest spread, with a canopy of narrow, dusty leaves casting dappled shade. The dazzling white sky shines through in shifting beams and flashes. I listen, with all the concentration you'd give a beautiful piece of music, to the only sound I can hear: the rustling of the not-quite-still air through the olive leaves.

I can't remember the last time I felt anything as good as this — the joy of being alone, quiet, in a secret place, surrounded by emptiness, with no one knowing where I am, and no possibility of being found or told what to do. I inhale a stream of hot air deep into my lungs, relishing its crisp, dry scent. This is the smell of freedom.

Remembering my thirst, I sit up and look around me. A square of land is enclosed by a waist-high stone wall, and is planted with twenty or so trees, in four almost-straight rows. The ground between the trunks is bare and neat, with no rocks and only a few small weeds. Faint circles in the soil are just visible around the base of each tree, as if a while ago the soil has been thinly ploughed.

At the back of this field is another stone wall, stronger-looking than the others, and higher. It's constructed into the side of the hill, and forms the lower edge of the next terrace up, which is a crescent shape, following the curve of the land. The trees up there look different.

A reflected beam of sunlight, one short flash, draws my attention to a thread of water at the edge of the field. I stand and walk towards it, finding a tiny crack in the rock, from which a trickle of water is steadily flowing. A series of grooves has been chiselled into the rocky hillside, channelling this water towards a man-made pool that has been dug out of the ground. From there, a thin stream of overflow runs out and spreads into a tiny delta of trickles that descend the hillside.

The water looks almost black in this stone hollow, but when I cup my hands and lift out a handful, it comes up looking clear. I rinse my face and tip the rest over my head, the cold wetness in my hair sending a shiver of bliss down my spine. I raise a second scoop to my lips and sip. The water is sweet, cool and delicious, tasting of nothing and everything, better than any I have ever drunk. I gulp down handful after handful until my stomach feels bloated, sloshing audibly as I stand.

I feel immediately stronger, and begin to explore the fields. The six trees on the second terrace up are smaller and straighter, dotted with tiny green fruit, no bigger than a marble. These must be lemon trees. Almost like some kind of clue, the waxy leaves are the shape of ripe lemon: oval with pointed ends. Above this are two further terraces, roughly the same size, also planted with six lemon trees, but it's clear that Leila's father is concentrating his energies on the lowest terrace. The trees on the top terrace are all dead and leafless, with the soil given up to the encroachment of thorn bushes. The middle terrace seems semi-abandoned, the trees limp and unhappy in cracked, weedy soil.

Under a plastic tarpaulin I find a spade, a gardening fork, a few other tools I can't identify, and a bucket. I take the bucket and set to work watering the lemon trees. I give one bucket to each tree on the lowest terrace, the parched soil sucking down the water like a hungry man would

167

gobble a meal. By the time I've watered these first six trees, the pool is empty. The trickle from the spring is so feeble, it will take a long time — a day, possibly two or three — for the pool to be full again. This explains the state of the upper terraces. For each visit, it was only possible to water one terrace; with a limited number of visits, the higher trees had to go unwatered. It looks as if he gave up on the top terrace first.

I walk up to the next terrace and examine it more closely. The weeds that have grown are thorny and well rooted. Though the trees haven't declined as badly as the ones above, it looks as if they are struggling to survive. Perhaps it's only recently that his permits were reduced to once a month. Perhaps he'd been keeping this field going using more frequent visits, but had recently given up on it to save the trees below.

I can't remember what he told me about the upper levels. I'm not sure if he wants me to work on this terrace as well as the one below. I don't know if the olive trees really need no water at all. Then it strikes me that it doesn't matter what he's asked me to do. It doesn't even matter what I want to do. I suddenly understand that this grove, from top to bottom, has presented itself to me as a duty. If I can look after this land, my labour and sweat might perhaps atone for what I have done. However injured he may be, however often the soldiers turn him back at the checkpoint, however cut off he is from his fields, I can keep these trees alive. I have found one small thing that I can do.

On Fridays, school is only a half-day. Friday afternoons are the time for sport and games and visiting friends, but not for me. Not any more. Every week, now, I hurry straight to the olive grove. After school on Monday or Tuesday I sometimes sneak out there, too, just to do an hour or so of work and put on a little extra water.

From the bottom of the understairs cupboard, I have dug out and taken Liev's winter gloves, which are made of brown leather. I've never actually seen him wear them, so it's unlikely they'll be missed. They feel big on my hands, with floppy ends at the tip of each finger, as if I need one more joint to fill them, but they're perfect for pulling out weeds and taking on thorn bushes.

Watering the trees of the lower and middle terraces is now just the start. It's laborious and surprisingly tiring to fill and carry the heavy bucket so many times, but once I work out a good system, with half a bucket for each tree, I can get this done reasonably fast. After emptying the pool I don't rest, but pull on my gloves and set to work at restoring the ground of the middle terrace to look as neat and clear as the one below.

The weed that has the firmest hold is a bush with thorns as long as matchsticks. It's impossible to touch them without gloves, and even with them you have to grip carefully, laying the thorns flat to avoid drawing blood. The tallest bushes reach my thigh and take hours to hack out of the dense, dry soil.

Today, Friday 2 June, I'm almost skipping with excitement as I hurry towards the grove. It's the first Friday of the month, the day Leila's father gets his pass. This is only my fifth visit to the grove, but I've already transformed the middle terrace, restoring it to something approaching the condition of the one below, spending more time there in three weeks than Leila's father would be allowed in several months. And today, he'll see for the first time what I've done.

As soon as I'm outside Amarias I toss aside the tennis racket I carry as a cover story and hurry on, wondering if Leila's father has been expecting me to keep my word, wondering if he's on his way at this moment, perhaps in line at the checkpoint, anticipating thirsty trees and cracked, dry soil. Or perhaps he could be there already, staring open-mouthed at his watered, weeded terraces.

It seems unlikely that he'd have much faith in me or my promise. Even in his most optimistic moments, he surely never hoped for anything like what he'll find today, when he arrives and sees all the work I've done on his fields. My heart twinkles and aches with pride as I try to imagine his reaction.

A darker, mirroring pleasure glows inside me at the thought that Liev will never know, and

170

how angry he'd be if he did. It gives me an extra thrill that I've done the work wearing his gloves, as if an enemy ghoul has taken possession of his hands and used them to perform the work of his most hated foe.

The first thing I do on arrival at the grove is always the same. I pause at the entrance, touch the wall with each hand, then cross the bottom field and kneel in front of the cistern. I cup my palms together and tip the first handful of water over my head, letting it drip wherever it wants to go, staying as still as I can, with my eyes shut, as it spills over my face, down my neck, and trickles to my torso and back. The second handful I drink, drawing the cool sweetness deep into my body, feeling it relieve the hot clench of the sun, which on the journey out often feels like a fist around a sponge, squeezing moisture from my body. No drink was ever better than this first handful from Leila's family spring.

I sometimes think of all the people who might have drunk here. For the last few months it was perhaps only me and Leila's father, but a hundred years, a thousand years, five thousand years, is the blink of an eye to a leaky rock. Drinking from this spring I feel myself joining a thread of people, linked together through unimaginable chasms of time, who have all knelt here, drunk here, tasted this taste, enjoyed it, been kept alive by it. If the bulldozers ever get here, that will be it. The rock will shift, the trickle will stop, the thread will snap.

I water the bottom terrace, then sit under a tree and wait, listening to the sounds of the leaves and insects. I watch a lizard squat on the side of the wall, dead still yet also tensed with life like a coiled spring. With a silent twitch, it disappears in an instant through a crack in the rocks no thicker than a key.

After a while, I walk up to examine the middle terrace. The bushes have all gone, but there's still a dense scattering of weeds. I amble among the trees, gently touching each trunk, enjoying the roughness of the bark against the soft pads of my fingertips. This terrace looks good, but there's still more work to do, though today I'm too excited about the arrival of Leila's father to get on with the weeding. There'll be plenty of time for that later, and before I can carry on, I need a little encouragement, or at least acknowledgement. I need to know I'm on the right track.

As the hours dribble slowly by, and it becomes clear that Leila's father isn't coming, my excitement curdles and sours. All the worst thoughts I've been keeping at bay over the last few weeks come creeping back.

Perhaps he's been stopped at the checkpoint. I cling to the hope that this is the reason for his absence, but I can no longer ignore what I saw in the alley. His curled-up body. The kicks landing in frenzied pounds on his back and head. I've tried to make myself believe the attack ended when my view of it ended, when I jumped down into the tunnel, but I know that if it had continued, he would have come to serious harm.

This was the day of his pass, and he hasn't come. Either the soldiers refused him at the checkpoint, or he was unable to attempt the journey. I can't pretend to myself any more. I can no longer shut out the idea that he is still, three weeks later, too injured to come, too weak to tend his land, perhaps even still in hospital, or dead.

The acid prick of tears stings my eyeballs, but I fight them back. I will not cry. Not today. I run down to the bottom field and yank at the tarpaulin. Wedged under the handle of the spade are Liev's gloves. I pull them on and clench my fists, feeling the dry, hot leather crackle under my joints. At my feet lies a spade and a heavy, rusted pickaxe. I haul the axe on to my shoulder and climb to the top terrace.

I haven't been up here since my exploration on the first day. It's narrower than the lower terraces, without any shade. Six straggly trunks sprout from the soil like tombstones, the branches blackening from the tips. A landslip has pushed out part of the perimeter wall, and the ground is strewn with stones and well-established thorn bushes. The largest one is a shoulder-high ball of dry, brown spikes, dotted with dark berries. I step towards it, swinging the axe, launching blindly into it with all my might. My first swing makes only a glancing contact with the main branch, and a clump of thorns tears a gash in my forearm, but I swing again, just as wild and hard. I slash and slash, not so much digging up the bush as smashing it to pieces. All sense of place and time, all sense of who I am and what I'm doing evaporates as I attack the bush, destroying every branch, fighting it, killing it.

Only when I find myself standing over a cracked stump, surrounded by shards of wood and thorns, do I come to my senses.

I drop the axe, toss my gloves aside and fall to the ground, flopping on to my back, looking up through the leafless branches of the dead trees at the rich blue sky, criss-crossed by two not-quite-parallel vapour trails. With the warm soil pressing into my wet back and thorny wood chips pricking at my skin, I try to imagine myself on one of those planes, flying away, shooting through the borderless sky. I imagine looking down from the aeroplane window at this faraway patch of land, seeing a boy on his back, next to a smashed-up bush, alongside a dropped axe and a pair of gloves. I imagine turning away from the window, towards a man in the next seat. He's sipping from a heavy glass. He smiles at me. It's my father.

Much later, I stand and look at the mess around me. I have to get home. I'm hungry, tired and in despair. I'll clear up on my next visit.

I climb straight into the shower before anyone can see the scratches on my arms. The steaming water drumming against my aching shoulders is hypnotically pleasurable. As the hot jets pummel my skin, I feel as if I can sense my muscles digesting the wild bout of axe-swinging, recovering and building up, readying themselves for the next test.

I stand dripping on the bathmat and examine my arms. With the dried blood washed away, the scratches aren't too visible. I run a finger along the small, raised wounds, then give my forearm a squeeze, clenching my fist. It feels hard, and ripples under my touch as I wriggle my fingers. My hands, too, look different: wider, with a bulge at the base of my thumb and rough fingertips. In the steamed-up mirror I look at my hazy outline, still skinny, but less so — as if my hands, arms and shoulders are leading me towards a new shape.

When I come out of the bathroom wrapped in a towel, Liev's standing there in the corridor, as if he's waiting for me.

'I need to talk to you. Man to man,' he says. I try not to roll my eyes, but I think my eyeballs do it anyway, on their own.

'What?'

'I think of you as a man now, do you realise that?'

'I need to get dressed.'

'Come in here. I have something important to say.'

Liev grips my arm and leads me back into the bathroom. He locks the door, puts the toilet lid down, and sits. With an open palm, he indicates that he wants me to take a seat on the edge of the bath.

The room is still steamy from the shower and I'm almost naked and this is possibly the strangest thing Liev has ever done. I stand there, looking down at him, and wonder if he's finally lost it. I almost tell him that if he needs the toilet we can talk later, somewhere else, but I get the feeling he'd take it the wrong way. I sit, tucking the towel firmly around myself.

'I think you know what this is about,' he says.

The sound of the whirring fan fills the room. I have no idea what to say, but Liev doesn't wait for a response. 'In a word,' he continues, 'responsibility.'

'OK. One word. That was easy.' I stand and take a step to the door.

'Sitsitsit,' says Liev, not shouting, not even cross. 'Please.'

He smiles at me, a look so strange and unfamiliar it somehow makes me step back and sit. I can almost see the effort in his straining cheek muscles.

'I didn't get you in here to argue,' he says. 'I just want to talk to you about your mother.'

'Mum?'

'Yes.'

'What about her?'

176

'She's a brave woman. You understand what she's been through, don't you?'

I shrug.

'You understand what grief does to a person, and how her faith has helped her through?'

'I know about grief,' I snap. 'I know about that.'

'Of course you do. Of course. In many ways you are a very mature young man. But in other ways ... I think you need to consider her feelings. I think you need to understand what you are doing to her.'

'What *I'm* doing to her?'

'You're hurting her very much.'

'What are you talking about?'

'I understand exactly what you're going through, Joshua ... '

'No you don't ... '

' ... how at your age the body goes through a lot of changes, and a man begins to feel differently towards his mother ... ' I'm beginning to think it's lucky we're in the bathroom, because any minute now I might puke. ' ... but I think it's time you considered taking her feelings into account.'

'What feelings? This is really sick. I have to get dressed.'

I stand again, but Liev gets up quicker than me and blocks my path to the doorway. We are suddenly too close, locked in this room, him fully clothed, me almost naked. The fan clicks itself off and the room fills with an eerie silence.

'You know exactly what I'm talking about,' he says. 'You want to be a grown-up? Great. Be a grown-up. Face up to what you're doing.'

'I'm not doing anything!'

'Do you need me to spell it out?

'Spell what out?'

'The secrecy, the lying, the sneaking off, the shutting her out, the disrespect. Treating this house like a hotel, and her as your servant. Is that clear enough for you?'

'Oh, it's me that treats her like a servant?'

'I'm not here to argue, Joshua. I've said my piece.' He swivels and sidesteps away from the door.

I know I ought to fight back, tell him what I really think of him, tell him all the ways he's crushed my mother and sucked the life out of our family, but there's something about him that makes it impossible to say the truth. If I had my clothes on maybe I'd give it a try, but like this, wearing only a towel, I can't face up to him.

I unlock the door and walk away.

We eat dinner in near silence, Liev and Mum alternating between falsely chirpy attempts to draw me into conversation and equally strained efforts to talk to one another as if I'm not there. I wear a long-sleeved top, so Mum doesn't see the scratches. I could have a leg missing and Liev wouldn't notice. He makes a couple of barbed compliments about how fast I'm growing up, which are his version of a nudge in the back, a reminder to act on what he said to me, but I don't even look at him.

Later, I lie rigidly awake in bed, trying to think my way towards a dream of that aeroplane, sitting there next to my dad, but the dream never comes and the clarity of the vision dissolves.

For a week, I think I've given up on the olive grove. For a week, I try to banish the place and the people who own it from my thoughts. But then it's Friday again, and school ends, and there's only one place I want to go.

As I walk out of Amarias, I notice that my pace is faster than usual. I'm in a hurry. I can see the top terrace in my mind's eye, exactly as I left it: the axe not even returned to the tarpaulin, the shards of wood everywhere, the gloves tossed down any old how.

The first thing will be to clear up. Get all the mess out of the grove. I'll then need the axe again to dig out the stump. When I've done that, I'll start on the next bush. Then, when I've done the bushes, I'll fix the collapsed wall. I'll work even harder than before, and I'll go there every Friday, and eventually he'll come. In time, he'll recover and he'll come. He'll come and he'll see my work, and his heart will lift with joy and surprise, and something between us that appears utterly unfixable will, in that moment, seem a little less broken.

I can't bring the trees back to life, but I can repair the terrace. I can get it looking how it would have looked before The Wall cut the grove off from its owner. Maybe I could even plant new trees. It was supposed to be possible to take cuttings from plants to grow new ones — I knew that — and if I did enough research, maybe I'd be able to find out how to take a branch from one of the lower trees and grow it on the top terrace. Or, better still, since there wasn't enough water for lemons, perhaps I could take a cutting from one of the olive trees. Even if it took years to produce a crop, even if its chances of survival were small, that didn't mean the effort was pointless. Those big old trees had been planted by someone, once. Planting a tree was never futile. To grow a tree was a gesture of belief on a timescale longer than a human lifespan, but that was how Leila's dad talked about the grove. He said the land was his father's and his father's father's and he was looking after it for his sons. If I planted a new tree, there might be no olives for him, but he'd know it was for his son, and his son's son. Or maybe even for Leila and her children. It was worth trying just for that, to show that I understood what he said, understood what this land meant to him, and wanted, in some minuscule way, to resist the theft of it.

Just as his olive trees predated The Wall by perhaps hundreds of years, one day in the future The Wall might be demolished, but a tree I planted could still be there, tended by a descendant of Leila's father, someone who'd have no idea who had put the tree into the soil, someone who might not know there was ever a time when this land was walled off. This unborn person would pick my olives, taste them on his tongue. He'd share them with his family; cook with the oil; perhaps take a cutting and grow another tree.

I wouldn't give up. I would clear the top terrace, and in the straggly shade of the dead trees, I would plant. However long it took, one day Leila's father, or her brother, or Leila herself would come, and they'd see, and they'd understand.

I start going to the olive grove almost every day after school, and it takes me three weeks to clear the top field of thorn bushes. Hacking down the branches proves to be the easy bit. Every one has a dense clump of roots that grip the hard, dry soil with amazing tenacity. Pulling at the stump is pointless; levering with the axe loosens it but does nothing to get the thing out of the ground. The only way is to dig a hole all the way round and go under where the roots are thin enough to split with a spade, hacking at the thicker ones with the axe. Each bush leaves behind a trench big enough to bury a dog.

If I only wanted the field to look good I could just cut off the stumps at ground level, but I know that to replant the terrace it's important to get out all the roots. When I refill the holes there's never enough soil, and I'm left with strange indentations, but I use the tarpaulin to drag in extra soil from outside the grove and flatten out the ground. I search carefully to source the best soil, but away from the spring the ground is so rocky it isn't easy to find anything at all.

I Google olive-tree planting, and the results are disheartening. It is possible to grow a tree from a cutting, but the procedure is technical and complicated. A cutting will only grow roots if it's dipped in a hormone powder or some kind

181

of special acid. You then have to plant it in something called rooting media, monitor the temperature, and keep the leaves wet with a misting machine. Even then it takes more than two months for enough roots to grow to let you plant it outdoors. There's no way I'd be able to do that. The time wasn't a problem, but it would be impossible to get hold of that equipment, and even if I could, there was nowhere to grow the cuttings without Mum and Liev noticing.

But one sentence on the same web page catches my eye. Apparently you can't grow a tree from the pip of an olive you get in a jar, because the brine kills the seed, and even without the brine very few seeds grow. But over long periods of time, a mature tree drops olives which rot down and produce seedlings. The page has a picture of one of these seedlings.

I blow up the image until this small picture fills the whole screen. I stare and stare at it, committing the exact look of the plant to memory. Young trees, it turns out, need frequent irrigation, but that's not a problem. I can do it. If I can find just one of these seedlings, anywhere at the grove, I can plant an olive tree.

After uprooting the thorn bushes and before dealing with the other weeds, I crawl over every centimetre of the olive grove looking for one of these seedlings. I spend an entire afternoon inching back and forth on my hands and knees, hunting for a baby tree.

When I've looked over the whole field with no success, I do it again, more carefully. Still nothing. I'm disappointed, but not surprised.

The field has been weeded and ploughed by Leila's father, and over the last weeks I've kept up the weeding myself, zapping anything that might take water from the trees.

I search the perimeter, right up to the cracks in the wall, hunting for any tiny plant that might have been overlooked, but there's nothing. My plan, already, seems to have failed. Then, as I lean on the wall, looking out over the dry ground, a flash of green catches my eye. Where the overspill from the irrigation pool drains out, a tiny delta of greenery is clinging to the hillside.

I leap over the wall, my heart pounding. I throw myself on to the ground and begin to search meticulously through the leaves, stalks and stubbly little walnuts of grass. When, in a rocky crack, my eye lights on a stem no thicker than a worm, topped by two minuscule leaves, I can barely believe what I am seeing.

For a few moments I stare at it in silence, mentally flicking from this seedling in front of me to the picture I memorised, then my screams can hold themselves in no longer. I leap into the air, toss my head backwards, and yell for sheer joy, dancing around the plant, flailing my arms and legs, whooping and shouting and screaming until my throat gives up on me. I have found one! I can dig it up, transplant it, water it, care for it, grow it! My work clearing the field has not been for nothing. And when Leila's father eventually comes, I'll guide him through the perfectly tended olive grove and the lower two terraces of watered lemon trees, then, just when he's beginning to get over his surprise, I'll be able to take him up to the top field and show him my sapling — our sapling.

With trembling hands I run for the spade, but falter as I pick it up. All that crawling around looking for the seedling has warped my sense of scale. The spade in my hands feels implausibly vast. This is not the right tool for digging something tiny and fragile out of a rocky crevice, and there's no room for error.

I have to wait. The seedling has survived this long, it isn't going to die overnight. I have to come back with a trowel. I can take the one Mum uses for the front garden. I'll be able to return it before she notices. Or maybe even that might be too large and clumsy. I decide I'll also bring a spoon and a knife. This job isn't farming, it's surgery.

I prepare the hole first: no bigger than my fist, dug into the loose soil where I removed a bush, central on the top terrace, with some shade from above. I pre-water it, and leave a full bottle by the side of the hole alongside a small heap of dark, composty earth taken from our front garden and brought out in a plastic bag hidden in my pocket.

The seedling has a slightly bent stalk, from growing sideways out of the slope then upwards towards the light. It is rooted right up against one edge of a crack in the rock, so the whole thing can't be dug out in a complete ball of soil.

I take the knife — one of Liev's steak knives — and cut along the surface of the rock, prising away the soil. I then saw a circle not much bigger than a tennis ball and lever in the trowel as deep as it will go. Pinching my fingers around the tiny stem to hold it in its soil, I press downwards and, with a twist, free it from the rock. It comes loose at the first attempt, and I slowly stand, holding my precious cargo with both hands.

I don't want to risk clambering over the wall, so I walk the long way round to the entrance and carefully climb the steps, one by one, taking care not to slip or stumble.

Kneeling at the fresh, neat hole, I edge the olive seedling into its new home, pushing a few crumbs of soil underneath to raise it to the

185

correct height. Bit by bit, I gently press soil around it with my fingertips.

With a bottle full to the brim, I can't get the nozzle low enough to the ground without risking a gush that might harm the plant, so I pour single handfuls into my left hand and tip them at the base of the stem, watching each one puddle and disappear before adding more.

When I've finished I just stare at it, in the way a new parent might gaze at their sleeping baby. Nothing I've achieved in life has ever made me as happy as this two-leaved stalk. It's not quite vertical, but that doesn't matter. It will straighten up in time, and even if it remains crooked, I don't care. To me, as long as it stays alive, it will always be perfect.

'I'm going to look after you,' I say. 'I promise.'

The words just come out. I know it's stupid to talk to plants, but I don't care. This is my place. No one can see me or hear me. I can do what I want. If I feel like talking to my tree, I'll talk to my tree.

With my seedling in the ground, safely transplanted, I find myself daydreaming about the olive grove more often than ever. During the school day I have to fight to keep my attention on the books in front of me. My mind constantly drifts off, back to the field, back to my tree and to the tasks I hope to complete before the first Friday of July, when Leila's father might visit.

That date is burned into my mind. I can't stop thinking about it, hoping he comes, imagining all the different reactions he might have to the work I've done on his fields. In all but one version, he's delighted. The fantasy reaction that scares me is one where he becomes angry, accuses me of trying to take over his land, and I can't explain myself.

It will be four weeks since his last pass, seven weeks since the attack. Even more frightening than a negative reaction is the possibility that he doesn't come at all. If there's no visit this time, he must be in dire trouble.

★   ★   ★

When the day comes I more or less sprint out of school and head straight for the grove. I've now weeded the top field so thoroughly that the only living thing in the ground is my seedling, sitting in a meticulously nurtured bed of moist, dark soil, its two leaves rinsed and glistening.

After clearing and weeding the terrace, the last remaining job was the collapsed wall. For a while I thought maybe I'd be able to rebuild it, but when I saw how intricately constructed the walls were, and discovered how hard it was to get the stones to fit together, I realised this was beyond me. Instead, I picked a corner of the field and carried the rocks over there one by one to make a neat stack. This took a whole afternoon, and left me so stiff and sore that for a few days I moved like an old man.

But as I hurry out on this terrifying and thrilling Friday, I notice that my suppleness has returned. I can stride fast, my legs pumping smoothly against the ground. The walk to the grove, which once seemed like an arduous trek, now feels easy, even in the heat of high summer.

I want to give the pile of stones a quick tidy and check that the soil under the rock fall is clear and smooth, but other than that, I'm ready for Leila's father's visit. Liev's gloves have fallen apart, but it doesn't matter. My hands are tough now, tanned and strong: worker's hands, man's hands. The rest of me feels different, too. My clothes are tighter than they were, around my thighs, shoulders and chest. I have changed the grove and the grove is changing me.

The longer I spend there, the more protective and proud I feel of my fields. I've taken to pacing over each of the terraces, usually in bare feet, for the simple pleasure of feeling the soil against my skin. I walk slowly and soundlessly, examining every tree, listening to the sounds of the wind and the wildlife — the occasional squeaks and rustles of lizards and mice, the ratcheting of the crickets, perhaps the scurry and flap of a surprised bird, and always, in the background, the trickle of spring water replenishing the pond.

An hour can easily pass watching a line of ants bustle to and fro, seeing how they react to the miniature catastrophe of a stick scraped across their route. Time behaves differently at the grove. I can start to strip a leaf back to its veins, tearing out each tiny segment of flesh one by one, and by the time I finish, the perimeter wall might be casting an extra foot of shade across the ground. What this means in hours and minutes, I don't seem to care. I spend a large chunk of one whole afternoon gathering handspan-sized sticks and building a tiny pyramid, a little wigwam, held up only by perfect balance. At the grove, there's nothing to do and everything to do. I'm never bored.

As the amount of upkeep and restoration work decreases, I continue to spend as much time there as ever. I just want to be at the olive grove. When I have the choice, why would I go anywhere else?

I never vary my method of watering the trees. Each tree gets a precise amount, half a bucket. I give them their water in two pours, each one distributed in a careful 'O' all the way around. As I wait for the first helping to soak into the soil, I put one hand on the trunk and say, 'I bring you water. I bring you water.' I don't know why I do it this way. It's a system that simply evolved, but now feels like some kind of sacred ritual from

189

which I can't deviate. I never feel calmer or more content than during the watering of the trees.

I always finish with a handful or two for my seedling, then, without saying anything, I touch each trunk on the top terrace. There's no point watering them, but those dead trees are still part of the grove, so I feel they should be included in the ceremony. I love those trees no less than the ones below. The way they are dead, but still there, reminds me of my father. In the grove, I feel his presence more strongly than anywhere. I'm a long walk from the town, a long walk from any other human beings, but I never feel alone. Sometimes I press myself close against the tallest of the dead trees, feeling the rough bark against my cheek.

I hurry into the grove, thinking Leila's father might be there already, but he isn't. I make a few final preparations and pace through the terraces, trying to calm down, to prepare myself for his arrival, but slowly, as the afternoon sun thickens the air, I feel my excitement souring, and my restless energy draining away.

By mid afternoon I've more or less given up hope, and I'm half asleep, leaning heavily against an olive tree, when I begin to think I might be hearing the sound of footsteps. I jump to my feet and run up to the top level. From there, I can just see down to the razor wire at the turn-off to the grove. Intermittent sections of road alongside the empty, walled field are visible, and sure enough, flickering in and out of vision is the head of a man in a black-and-white headscarf. I can't make out the face, and the figure looks somehow older than I remember Leila's father — slower and more stooped — but my heart immediately begins to pound with hope and excitement. It has to be him.

I leap to my feet and run down to greet him, but after only a few steps I realise that I want to see his true, honest reaction to the appearance of his fields. There will be plenty of time later for everything else. The most important thing is just to watch his face as he walks in and sees my work.

I turn back to the top terrace and lie down on my belly, choosing a spot where I'll be invisible from below. My heart is beating with such insistent thuds that I can feel it moving inside me, like a tiny, trapped animal, as I listen to the slow, shuffling approach of the man. I can tell by the scrape of his feet in the dust that he's wearing sandals.

When he walks through the entrance to the grove, I see for the first time that he isn't alone. He is leaning on the arm of a smaller figure who wasn't visible above the height of the wall: Leila. But more surprising than the presence of Leila is the sight of her father, when he pulls down his headscarf in the shade of the grove. It is him, and it isn't him. He looks like a different man. One cheek is covered by a purple and yellow bruise which spreads all the way to his jaw, and his nose is hidden behind a white plaster bridge. Both lips look swollen by a diagonal scar which cuts across his mouth, and a stripe the width of a hand has been shaved along one side of his head. Stubbly tufts of hair have begun to grow back inside the stripe, which is ridged with surgical stitches.

Tears prickle at my eyes and begin to seep down my cheeks. I wipe them away roughly with the base of my thumb, trying not to sniff, hoping to remain unobserved a little longer.

As if by some strange telepathy, at the same moment Leila's father makes an identical movement with his hand, brushing a tear from his cheek. He looks stunned, his body seeming to vibrate with shock, or perhaps disbelief. He staggers forwards and Leila rushes to help him, but he waves her away. She steps back to the entrance of the grove and hovers awkwardly, looking more anxious than pleased.

Without making a sound, I watch as he examines his trees one by one, poking a finger into the moist soil at their base, putting a hand tenderly on each trunk as you might pat a loyal dog. He inspects every tree closely, from the soil up to the leaves, inching across his land, climbing slowly from terrace to terrace. He's close to me now, so close I can hear his breathing, but still he doesn't notice me looking down from above. Leila watches him intently, but doesn't move from her position by the entrance.

When he's inspected every tree, he slumps to the ground like a marathon runner crossing the finish line, utterly spent. I almost rush down and show myself but something tells me to wait a little longer, something in the way he's holding his body, as if he's fighting an invisible force.

A moment later he isn't fighting any more, and his chest begins to surge and heave with sobs, the kind that burst through when you've been holding back with all your strength, until the moment when the pressure is too much, and your defences crack, and it all just floods out. I recognise the feeling, but I've never seen it take over anyone else, and never even knew it could happen to an adult.

Leila walks up the steps and sits next to him, but she doesn't speak and doesn't touch him.

I watch, and wait until he's finished. When enough time has passed for me to pretend I haven't witnessed his tears, I stand and walk down to where he's sitting.

As I approach in my bare feet, they both stare at me with pure bafflement on their features. I can think of nothing to say, and neither, it seems, can they. I hold out my water bottle. Tentatively, reluctantly almost, he takes the bottle and drinks.

He stands, struggling to his feet without taking his eyes off me, and opens his mouth. No sound comes out, and he closes it again.

'Come,' I say. 'Follow me.'

Leila stares, her jaw slack, her eyes wide.

'Come,' I say to her.

She takes her father's arm, and I lead them towards the top terrace. He looks more confused than ever as he struggles behind me up the loose stone steps. When he sees the cleared field, he freezes. I walk ahead and squat on my haunches, showing them my tiny seedling, sitting in its moist circle of rich soil. He stumbles towards me, bends stiffly, and reaches out to touch the underside of a leaf with his little finger.

After gazing for a while at this baby tree, we stand and stare at one another. I am smiling now, but his bruised face seems poised between puzzlement and suspicion.

'Why?' he says, after a long silence.

I shrug and almost begin to laugh, as I realise that even though I've imagined this moment hundreds of times, rehearsing endless variations, it has never occurred to me to think of an answer to this question.

I shake my head vacantly, trying to fight the grin that is spreading across my face.

'Tell me why,' he insists, a hint of anger entering his voice.

'For you,' I say.

'For me?'

'You saved me. And I saw what they did to you.'

'You saw?'

'I wanted to turn back, but . . . I ran away. I'm sorry. It was my fault. I — ' A second ago I was almost dancing with pride and excitement, now a quite different feeling seems to leap up and grab me by the throat. Without any warning, tears spring from my eyes and my throat tightens, cutting off any further attempt to speak, but it's a strange sensation, because I don't feel upset. The joy of being here with Leila and her father, showing them my work, is still singing in my veins, except some more powerful force has now swept through, and I realise that it is relief. Only now, seeing Leila's father safe and alive, can I face the depth of my terror at what might have happened to him. If he hadn't survived, his

194

death would have been my fault. Only standing in front of him, looking him in the eye, knowing he is all right, do I realise that I have been carrying around a cold sense of dread for weeks, locked away inside me, a lethal poison in a fragile bottle.

He looks at me, watching me cry, and I sense that he understands what I'm thinking. I don't notice Leila go or come back, but she appears beside me, holding out the water bottle, which is full to the brim and glistening with droplets from the spring. I drink, and the flow of tears subsides.

Leila's father reaches out and touches me on the cheek, with a strange and particular gesture, laying the back of his four fingers against my face and brushing my cheekbone twice with his thumb.

'Good,' he says. Just that.

To drink is good? To cry is good? What you have done in my olive grove is good? You are good? I have no idea which of these he means, but this is his only comment on my work.

We spend the next hour in the grove together. He teaches me how to prune the olive trees, pointing out the importance of cutting back the young stems that sprout near the base of each trunk. 'For good shape,' he keeps saying, and I nod as if I understand. He shows me a particular pattern to plough into the soil around each tree for maximum water absorption, and demonstrates, as if it is of particular importance, a procedure using a rusty metal hook, which keeps the spring unblocked and ensures a steady flow of water. When this is done, we sit, all three in a row, leaning against a shaded wall. He produces two apples from his pocket and hands me one. I try to refuse — I can get home quickly and eat as much as I want — but every refusal just makes him more adamant, so I take it and eat half. It's the best apple I have ever tasted, crisp and sweet, but I hand an uneaten half back, and he reluctantly accepts it, handing the gnawed hemisphere on to Leila.

He tells me he thought there would be lots of work to do, and he's too ill to do it all himself, which is why he brought Leila. He says it would be impossible to get a pass for any of his sons, but Leila is a good worker.

'It's strange,' he says, sucking a fragment of apple from between his teeth, 'just to sit and relax.'

'It's a beautiful place,' I say.

'Yes. Of course,' he replies.

After she finishes her apple, Leila begins a long and impassioned speech in her language. I can't understand any of the words, but I can tell that she's asking her father for something — begging him — and that he refuses and refuses, but she keeps on going, and eventually he gives way.

She kisses him on his unbruised cheek and jumps to her feet.

'Come,' she says. 'I want to show you something.'

I stand, brushing the dust from my trousers. 'What is it?'

'A place.'

'Where?'

'A secret place. I used to go there all the time. My mother took me.'

'Your mother?'

'Yes. Before The Wall we came together, all of us, and my brothers would help with the work, but I was too small, so my mother used to take me to this place.'

'Where is it?'

'Just follow me.'

She turns on her heel and walks out of the grove, almost running. Just outside the entrance, she picks out a thin path so overgrown I've never even noticed it was there. She rushes forwards, twisting her body this way and that to dodge between the thorny branches that have grown across it. I squeeze into my shoes and follow, scratching my legs in the effort to keep up.

A high rocky outcrop looms over the grove, and as we emerge from the patch of bushes into steep, barren, yellow-grey land, sparsely dotted with weeds and cacti, she picks out a route skirting upwards along the bottom of the rock face. She goes too fast for me to stay alongside her, and the path is narrow, so we don't speak. I just follow her, up and up, watching the agile and deft placement of her feet on the loose, stony ground, stepping where she steps and keeping close.

I'm sweaty and out of breath when we emerge on a smooth rocky plateau, not much bigger than a dining table, sheltered by a jagged overhang.

Leila stands on the lip of the precipice, looking

out at the view below, of the olive grove, the road to Amarias, The Wall, and miles and miles of land, stretching to a shimmering horizon.

'I can't believe it. I can't believe it,' she says, drinking in deep lungfuls of air. I stand, watching her, not knowing what to say. She's right in front of me but feels far away, lost in private thoughts. Eventually, she turns. Her face is glowing with happiness, a huge grin spread across her features. Until this moment she has always appeared to be a serious, watchful person, but it suddenly seems as if this girl smiling at me now is perhaps the real her.

'What can't you believe?' I say.

'That I'm here again.'

'Because you usually have to work?'

'Work where?'

'At the olive grove.'

'No — I hardly ever get to our grove, either. I only got the permit because my father is sick.'

'Oh.'

'And even if I do get to the grove, I'm never allowed up here. It's too dangerous.'

I look down at the lethal drop. 'But you came here when you were small?'

'It was safe then.'

'What do you mean?'

'Amarias was just starting. Your people stayed near their homes. There weren't so many guns.'

With a dizzying mental swerve, I realise what she means. The danger isn't the rock face. It's the people from Amarias.

'Could you come here with your father or your brothers?' I ask.

She shakes her head. 'If you meet the wrong person out here, it's not safe.'

'But it's OK with me?'

'You want me to thank you?' she snaps, almost snarling out the words.

'No!' I say, as quickly as I can. 'Not at all. I'm just trying to understand. I mean, I should thank you. For bringing me here. It's beautiful.'

She nods. 'Come.'

She sits on the ground, her legs poking outwards into thin air, and pats the rock next to her. I edge forwards, trying not to show my fear of the drop, and sit alongside her. She looks out at the view, devouring it with her eyes. I want to just stare at her, at her mysterious, pristine, beautiful face, but I know I can't, so I sit as she sits, balancing myself with my hands planted behind me, staring outwards at the land, my body humming with awareness of the thin barrier of air between us.

A delicious, comfortable silence keeps us company.

'You used to come here all the time?' I say, after a while.

'Yes. Before The Wall.'

'And now?'

'It's been more than a year.'

'Since you went to the olive grove?'

'Since I went anywhere. It's too difficult.'

'You haven't gone anywhere? You haven't left your town?' I know the astonishment in my voice is rude, insensitive, ignorant, but the words tumble out, shrill and gormless, before I can censor myself.

'Let's not talk about it,' she says, throwing me a quick, acid glance. There's a flash of emotion in her eyes I've never seen before, a spark of something wild and furious, but under control.

'Sorry,' I say, hoping we can get back the friendly silence of just a few moments earlier, but it seems to have slipped away. The fact of who I am and where I live is fizzing and crackling between us, impossible to ignore.

'You must be very angry,' I say.

She doesn't look at me. Her voice is flat as she says, 'If you were angry all the time it would kill you. And if you were never angry, that would kill you, too. You have to have somewhere to put it, and you have to know when to let it out. As long as you are in control, it's OK. You have to keep control.'

I can't think of any answer, except to mumble, 'I couldn't do that.'

'You'd learn. I'm not special. There's no choice. But let's not talk about it today. Not today. Not here.'

She spins back from the ledge and stands. I stand, too, and watch as she closes her eyes, turns her face to the sky, and breathes, deep and long, over and over, pulling the air into her lungs like rare and delicious chocolate to be tasted and savoured, one mouthful at a time.

While her eyes are shut, I can stare at her without embarrassment. It's her lips that pull hardest at my gaze: the curve of them where they meet; their soft, moist redness; the gap between them where they are slightly parted, showing a glimpse of tooth. As I stare at her mouth, my

200

heartbeat accelerates. We are alone. I could take a single step and kiss her. I could taste those lips with mine. I could breathe her air, touch her, stroke her skin and smell her hair and kiss her perfect mouth; and I sense, in an overpowering instant, that she'd let me, that perhaps she might even want it.

Her eyes snap open and she turns towards me as if she knows what I'm thinking. For an instant, we seem to float free of the rock, upwards from the land, the two of us utterly alone, loosening ourselves from everything around us.

She licks her top lip and speaks, her voice slightly hoarse, as if it has been hours since she last made a sound. 'We should go,' she says, but she doesn't step back or begin to walk.

'OK,' I say. 'If you like.'

'My father will be worried.'

'OK.'

'It was lovely to come here,' she says.

'I know. Thank you for bringing me.'

She nods, turns, and leads me back to the olive grove.

As soon as we get there, Leila's father points at his watch and indicates that it's time to leave. He mutters some harsh words at Leila, but she only shrugs. It's clear that we stayed longer than we were supposed to, and that he's cross about it, and that Leila doesn't really care.

We walk back towards Amarias together, but as soon as the town comes into view, Leila's father stops and shoos me away.

'Not safe,' he says. 'You go ahead.'

He responds to my goodbye with nothing more than a nod. I look at Leila, and it seems excruciating that now, because her father is there, I will have to leave without kissing her. I had my chance, and it passed, and perhaps it will never come again.

'Bye,' I say.

'Bye. Be careful,' she says.

'And you.'

'Go,' says her father. 'Hurry.'

I do as I'm told and walk on. Every time I turn round to check on them, they haven't moved. Even when they're far away, out of earshot, I can see them just standing there, patient and immobile, waiting for me to disappear.

Only as I walk into Amarias do I realise I still haven't asked his name.

During July the situation becomes more tense. Liev refuses to switch on the TV news because he says it's all exaggerated, and he doesn't buy newspapers. I see headlines, though, and hear snippets here and there on the radio. Even if you hid yourself away completely, it wouldn't be possible to miss talk of the crackdown. In Amarias you can hear it with your own ears, every night, coming over The Wall: sporadic bursts of gunfire; the squeak and rumble of tank tracks; helicopter blades hacking through the sky. Sometimes there are other, more mysterious sounds: glass shattering, shouts, falling masonry, sudden revving of diesel engines, the odd explosion.

I know Leila's father will want to visit his olive grove on the first Friday of August, but as the crackdown goes on I begin to fear he might not make it. There's talk of a curfew. The checkpoint is likely to be either closed or restricted. He survived the attack in the alleyway, but every time I hear an explosion or a gunshot, I know there's a chance Leila's family have been harmed.

When the day comes I'm just as excited and fearful as the month before, even though there's nothing new to show him other than two fresh leaves unfurling on my baby tree. I've kept everything at the grove in immaculate condition, sneaking away from home as often as I can, more for the simple pleasure of being at the grove than because there's any particular work that needs to be done. Any weed that dares show itself above ground is immediately and ruthlessly eliminated. My bedroom is messier than ever, but those terraces are as tidy as an operating theatre.

★　★　★

After watering the trees and checking the ground for new weeds I sit and wait, my head spinning the same questions round and round, like a washing machine. Will he come? Will Leila come? Would we be able to take another walk together? Would we go to the same place? Might I get another chance to kiss her?

But just like last time I wait and wait, and no one comes, and my nervous anticipation gives way to boredom. After an hour or two I lie on the ground and watch a drone, high above, beetling to and fro across the sky like an industrious insect. My eyelids begin to feel heavy, drooping in long, slow blinks.

I try to fight off the sleepiness, but eventually cave in and find myself enveloped by a dream both comforting and sinister. My father is in the cages at the checkpoint, waiting his turn near the front of a long line of people. He looks bored but resolute as he inches forwards among the crush of bodies. He's wearing his army uniform. It is drenched in blood, but when his turn comes to go through the turnstile, he's waved on without a second glance. He walks to a window of thick

204

bulletproof glass and hands his papers through a slot. On the other side, in full uniform, is my mother. She skims her eyes over the pass, glances at Dad, and expressionlessly nods him through as if she doesn't recognise him. Then he's on the road to the olive grove, squinting into the hot, white sunlight. The blood seems to be coming from a chest wound, and it has run down the left side of his body. One leg is clean, the other is soaked through, entirely red. His left foot squelches as he walks. Behind him is a trail of red, left-only footprints, widely spaced, snaking back down the road towards the checkpoint.

He seems to be unbothered by his wound, and walks purposefully along the route to the olive grove. At the razor wire he turns off the road and up the path, but instead of going around the obstruction he lifts his bloody leg high into the air, plants a foot on top of the wire and steps casually through, unharmed. At a steady pace he climbs up to the grove, where he finds me sleeping under a tree. Without speaking he shakes me gently by the shoulder, then more roughly as my body wobbles and flops, not responding. His expression darkens and his shakes grow more forceful, turning into angry, painful yanks at my arm, and now I seem to be begging him to stop, yelling at the top of my voice, but he won't. Then my eyes open, the sun's glare dazzling me with blinding force. I can see, or half-see, but the dream doesn't seem to stop. Someone really is tugging my arm. Arrows of genuine pain are shooting up through my shoulder. Against the bright sky, it takes a moment to recognise the face that's looming above me. It is Liev.

'What are you doing here?' he snaps.

'I —'

'Get up.'

Without waiting for me to do it myself, he pulls me on to my feet, wrenching my shoulder with an audible crack. He holds his face so close to mine that I can feel the warmth of his breath on my lips. His features are glistening with greasy sweat and twisted into a hot, red knot of rage.

'WHY ARE YOU HERE? IS THIS WHERE YOU'VE BEEN COMING?' he shouts, barely waiting for an answer, just piling straight on, taking my silence as assent. 'All these weeks, all the secrecy and slipping away and lying to your mother, so you can come here and sleep under a tree like a peasant?'

I look down at the soil and say nothing. My feet are bare, toe to toe with Liev's black leather shoes, which are freshly polished, but coated with dust and sand.

'ANSWER ME!'

I don't move and don't speak.

'Where are your shoes? Who do you think you are?'

I look up into his eyes, which I had always thought were grey, but out here, in the sunlight, they seem green. His pupils are tiny dots, a full stop in the middle of each eyeball. For a moment I think I might, in this place, find the strength to defy him, but he stares me down with a gaze of such vibrant, blazing intensity that I sense he might lose control. At moments like this, one to one, away from my mother, I can see how much he hates me. If he unleashed himself on me out here, if he allowed himself to hurt me, I have no idea how far he would go, and whether he'd be able to stop.

'WHERE ARE YOUR SHOES?'

I point at the entrance to the grove. Neatly, side by side on the path, are my trainers.

'Put them on and come home at once. This nonsense is over.'

I walk through the gateway to fetch my shoes, and as I bend to pick them up a flicker of movement at the corner of my eye makes me glance down the path. Leila and her father are approaching, moments away from entering Liev's field of vision.

I freeze, frantically scanning my brain for a way to turn them back without alerting my stepfather. Leila smiles and waves at me. I give her a small shake of the head. She either doesn't see or doesn't understand, and carries on walking towards me.

I shake my head again, more clearly. She halts, stopping her father with a gentle tug, but it's too late.

'What are you doing?' barks Liev.

I turn and attempt a casual shrug. 'Putting my shoes on,' I say, squatting down to block the narrow exit from the grove.

Liev rushes towards me, barges me aside, and runs down the path towards Leila and her father, who are now walking briskly away. Liev darts ahead and stops him with a hand on the shoulder. 'Who are you?' he snaps. 'Why are you here?'

Leila's father doesn't answer. He looks infinitely weary. After a long silence, he speaks in his quiet, heavily accented voice. 'This is my olive grove.'

'Oh, it's yours, is it?' says Liev, with heavy sarcasm.

'It is. It is mine, and it was my father's and his father's.'

'We'll see about that,' says Liev. 'Where's your pass?'

'I've been through the checkpoint. I've already shown my pass.'

'Are you refusing to show your pass?'

'I have shown my pass.'

'This is the last time I will ask you,' says Liev, his right hand moving to his belt, where it undoes the popper on the leather holster which holds the gun he wears when he ventures outside Amarias.

Leila's father reaches into a pocket and hands over his pass. Liev holds it contemptuously between thumb and forefinger, as if to minimise the transmission of germs, and examines the text. Leila's father snatches a quick glance in my direction. I give an apologetic shrug, which meets with no response. Leila just looks at the ground, as if she's trying to make herself invisible. Her face seems terrified and calm at the same time.

'You are responsible for these fields?' says Liev.

'Yes,' says Leila's father.

'Does anyone help you?'

There's a momentary pause before he answers. 'No,' he says.

'No one? You come once a month and you look after the grove on your own.'

'Yes.'

'Does my son help you?'

Leila's father blinks. 'I do not employ anyone else to work here.'

'Does he help you?'

'How can I know what happens when I'm not here? You must ask him.'

Liev swivels towards me. 'Do you work for this man?'

'No!'

'Do you help him?'

'No!'

'Why are you here? Why have you been coming here? To sleep?'

'I just came here. I found it and I liked it. Sometimes I put some water on the trees. He hasn't asked me to do anything.'

'You know that if he is employing illegal labour here, this land can be confiscated. I've seen you coming home with soil under your fingernails. I knew you were up to something.'

Leila's father speaks up, his voice thin and high. 'I haven't employed him. I've never paid him anything. I didn't even know he was here!'

'So what's this?' says Liev, brandishing a piece of paper out of his back pocket. I recognise it instantly. It is the map Leila's father drew for me, which I'd stashed at the bottom of my wardrobe. 'I'll tell you what it is,' continues Liev. 'It's Exhibit A, that's what it is. And the next time you're going to see it is in court.'

'Leave him alone!' I shout, my voice filled as much with anger towards Liev as towards myself, for not having thrown away the evidence. 'He hasn't done anything!'

Liev grabs me by the T-shirt and pushes me hard against the wall of the grove. A sharp stone jabs into my spine and my neck snaps backwards. However angry you get with Liev, he can always outdo you. 'Don't you DARE tell me what I can and can't do,' he says, his voice icy and crisp. 'You don't understand anything here. You have no idea what you've done.'

'I haven't done anything! I've just watered some trees.'

'Those aren't just trees, Joshua. Nothing here is only a tree. Just because you feel cosy and secure in the home I've made for you, that doesn't mean we're safe. This is a war zone. We are surrounded by people who hate us and want to take our land and kill us, and every tree and rock that belongs to our enemies is a potential launchpad for a missile that can kill you or me or your mother. Or take out your entire school with every single child still in it. Hundreds of people are plotting to get us, right now, this minute and every minute. Do you understand me?'

With this, he lets go of me and takes a step back. His cheeks are flushed and his breath is short. Two off-white curls of foamy spittle have settled in the corners of his mouth.

I pull the fabric of my T-shirt into shape, push my shoulders back, and stand up straight. For once, I'm not going to let him bully me into silence. Leila and her father are watching. I have to be strong.

'It's not a launchpad,' I say. 'It's an olive grove.'

'If that's all you see here, then you are blind,' he says. 'You see hills and fields? Fine. You're very lucky. Because what I see all around us is a battlefield, and anything that isn't ours is an enemy outpost.'

'If that's what you think, then why did you bring us here?'

'To do the Lord's work! He gave this land to our people, and no one is willing to fight for it except us! We've been in exile for two thousand years and only now are we fighting back, taking what is ours. If you can't take pride in that, you're a weakling and a traitor.' His eyes are sparkling now, radiant with passion. 'Do you still not understand what this is for? How long we've waited? Can you not even see that at long last, after all this time, we're winning! Bit by bit, we're winning! And if it takes another thousand years, and we have to fight inch by inch, so be it.'

'You can't fight for a thousand years. You'll be dead.'

'The next generations will carry on the fight.'

'I'm the next generation. And I think you're crazy.'

His lips pucker into a thin crease as he takes three long, slow breaths through his nose. The skin around my eyes tenses, a minuscule flinch that I try to suppress.

'You think you can disrespect me like this? You think you can carry on saying these things?'

I shrug.

'You think you're smarter than me?' he barks, jabbing me hard in the chest with his index finger.

I shrug again, lowering my face to the ground.

A shuffling sound emanates from below, as Leila's father begins to edge away. Liev swivels and grabs his arm. 'What is it you want here?' he says. 'What are you playing at?'

Leila's father holds his gaze. 'What is it *you* want?'

'I want you to leave my son alone.'

'I'm not your son,' I say.

Liev spins on his heel and raises a hand above his head. In the fraction of a second before his fist comes down to strike me, I see Leila's father's arm stretch forwards to block the blow, then withdraw again as he changes his mind. Liev's knuckles strike me between the corner of my mouth and my jaw, knocking me off balance. I stagger and fall to my knees in the dust. When I dizzily raise my head, Liev isn't even facing in my direction, but is squaring up to Leila's father.

'This path is closed. You've seen the razor wire.'

'These are my fields.'

'This access route is deauthorised by military order. You know that as well as I do.'

'I own those fields.'

'If I ever see you anywhere near this path or my son again, I'll have you arrested.'

I scramble back on to my feet.

'I'm not your son,' I say.

Liev turns to face me. His eyes are wild and

red. 'Are you *trying* to provoke me? Do you have any idea what I've done for you and your mother? Do you know where you'd be right now if it wasn't for me?'

'Not here, that's for sure.'

'Are you mocking me? How dare you mock me? After everything I've done for you.'

'You've done nothing for me!' I shout. 'I hate it here! I wish you'd left us alone!'

'You have no idea how much damage you've done.'

'I haven't done anything wrong.'

'You were sent to hurt me. You don't even know what a destructive force you are. Everything you touch — '

'I haven't done anything!'

'Why do you think you don't have any brothers and sisters?'

'What's that got to do with anything?'

'If you weren't so selfish, you'd know.'

'What are you talking about?'

'I'm not saying any more.'

'What do you mean?'

'You are a very confused young man. One day you'll realise . . . '

'Realise what?'

'What you've done to me and your mother. The damage you've caused. WHERE DO YOU THINK YOU ARE GOING?' Liev pushes me aside and barges towards Leila's father, who has quietly walked around us and into his olive grove.

'I have work to do.'

'I told you to leave!' shouts Liev.

'I don't think you did.'

'Well I'm telling you now.'

'Under whose authority?'

'Mine.'

'I have a pass. I'm only allowed here once a month.'

'I'm telling you to leave.'

'I'm afraid I can't do that.'

'You can't?'

'I have work to do.'

With that, Leila's father turns away and walks into the olive grove. He takes a hoe from under his tarpaulin and begins to work the soil.

Liev follows him into the grove, pulling the gun from its holster. He raises it fast and points it at Leila's father.

'You love to try our patience, don't you? You just can't resist pushing everything to the brink.'

Leila's father ignores him.

'OK, big guy,' Liev says. 'This is your last warning. I'm telling you to leave now.'

You can hear the click as he undoes the safety catch on his gun.

Leila's father doesn't even look up. His work doesn't quicken or slow down. With his back to Liev, he carries on turning the soil. Leila still hasn't moved from her spot on the path.

'There really is only one language you people understand, isn't there?' says Liev. His hand is trembling now, the gun jiggling at the end of his stiff, tense arm.

I know I ought to intervene, but my body refuses to move.

The air seems to thicken as Leila's father

214

continues to turn the soil, with Liev's pistol trained at his head. The gun tracks his movements as he works slowly back and forth. High above, the drone is still buzzing away. I sense that an invisible thread between the two men is being pulled tighter and tighter. Any second, it will snap.

With a swift movement, Liev's arm swivels towards the nearest tree. The report from the gun hammers through my skull as Liev's bullet tears a fist-sized lump out of the trunk, exposing ragged splinters of pale wood. This sight unlocks my paralysed muscles. I leap at Liev, but he pivots out of the way, brushing me aside before spinning back into position and burying another bullet into the tree.

I spring forwards again, this time not at Liev, but towards the tree. I flatten myself against the wounded trunk, and stare down the barrel of Liev's gun.

His hand is steady now, his nerves seemingly calmed by having fired off his first two shots.

'Get out of the way, Joshua,' he says. 'This is none of your business.'

'I'm not moving.'

Liev lets out a forced chuckle. 'Er . . . I think you are.'

'Mum knows you followed me here, doesn't she?'

'Yes.'

'So you can't touch me. If I get hurt — '

Liev chews at his tongue for a second, thrown momentarily off balance. Then the smile returns to his face. 'There's plenty more trees, Joshua.

215

You going to stand in front of all of them? Mr hippy tree-lover. Which tree are you going to hug now?'

He turns and fires another bullet into the tree next to me. If he'd missed the trunk, the bullet would have hit Leila's father, who is staring at us, motionless, his hoe gripped loosely in his hands. He flinches as the trunk in front of him shatters and splits, but he doesn't move away.

At that moment, a new anger seems to lift me in the way air lifts an aeroplane. I feel strong and clear-headed as I step towards Liev, along the sight-line of his gun, and shout at him with an indignant fury that blows every last drop of fear out of my body. 'ONE MORE BULLET!' I say. 'You shoot one more bullet, and I'm not going home. Just watch me. I'm going out there, up into those hills, right now. If I hear one gunshot, I'm not coming down. And whatever happens to me, you'll have to explain to Mum.'

'You stay up there, the jackals will get you. You couldn't last one night.'

'I know,' I say.

I hold his gaze, not flinching from the rage that seems to be buzzing through his body like an electric current. For once, I square up to him and hold my ground. Before my courage fails me — before Liev can see I have the slightest doubt in my mind — I turn and run, not even stopping to collect my shoes, out of the grove and upwards. I glance quickly at Leila as I flee. Her eyes are glassy with tears, staring towards me expressionlessly, as if she doesn't know who I am or what I'm doing.

I take Leila's path, pushing myself through the thicket of branches, desperate to get up and away before Liev chases after me. Thorns tear at my skin and rocks jab into the soles of my feet, but I don't let myself pause. Running with all my might over the loose, stony soil, I force myself upwards, heading for Leila's secret plateau.

I can't see Liev behind me, but that doesn't mean he isn't following, so when I see a slope rising up from Leila's path with a good supply of jagged rocks, I decide to take it. It looks climbable, but steep enough to put off Liev. I speedily clamber up, my mind filled with nothing more than footholds and handholds as step by step I haul myself skywards. I feel no pain or tiredness, only a glowing hum of concentration as I work at the task of getting up the rock face.

It's more of a surprise than a relief when suddenly there's no further to climb. I find myself on a plateau of brown rock, the size of a couple of parking spaces, so smooth and clear it seems as if it has been swept. I must have bypassed Leila's overhang and reached the peak. A powerful wind from the coast buffets and nudges my body, flapping the cuffs of my trouser legs.

I can see the whole of my town and Leila's town. From up here it looks like a single place, surrounded by countryside but divided by a wall — one half neat, new, spacious; the other cramped, higgledy-piggledy, old.

It's strange to see Amarias, which from the inside felt like a whole universe, shrunk to this: just a blotch of red-roofed buildings surrounded on all sides by land that goes on and on, fading into the heat haze. And like a thick grey scar, alongside the town, The Wall. Up close it's the height that surprises you; from here, it's the length. I'd never seen so much of it all at once, or taken in its superhuman scale and ambition, like a piece of concrete geology.

Leila's grove, not far below, is out of sight from the hilltop. Liev can't see me and I can't see him. For a long time I hear his voice, piping weakly upwards towards the summit, calling my name, going through various cycles of tone: angry, pleading, threatening, reconciliatory, really angry, eye-poppingly livid. He tries them all.

I pick up a handful of stones and throw them in the general direction of his voice. I know they won't hit him, but it's satisfying to try — to be, for once, the one on the attack.

As my heart rate settles, the sting and throb from my gashed flesh begins to come through, quietly at first, then louder and louder. Thorns have ripped several cuts into my calves and thighs, slashing through my trousers and flesh. I sit and look at the soles of my feet. They are tougher now than they used to be, but are blotched with muddy patches of fresh blood. The skin is too caked with dust to see exactly what has happened, and since there's nothing I can do, I decide not to investigate further. Up here, pain doesn't feel quite so painful.

After a while the calling stops and the hillside goes quiet. I hear no more gunfire.

Tentatively, I shuffle to the ledge of the plateau

and let my legs dangle out. A stone skitters downwards, sending up puffs of dust as it dances against the rock face, before coming to rest silently, far below.

Looking out at The Wall I think of my mother, of the scar across her front, and Liev's accusation rings again in my ears. Since she married him, I've seen no more of her body than her face, arms and feet. Not for several years have I seen the scar.

A memory comes back to me, one of the few I still have from when I was small, living in the house by the sea. It is of me and her and my father, all crammed into the bath together, a jumble of limbs jostling for space, all of us laughing and squealing. The bath started as Dad's, but I asked to get in with him, then Mum said it looked like fun and she climbed in, too, raising the water level almost to the brim. I remember asking about the scar, and her soft voice telling me that I got stuck during my birth, so the doctors cut through her tummy to get me out. She let me feel. I ran my index finger gently along the line of it from one end to the other. It was raised up a little from the rest of her skin in a little ridge, strangely hard under my fingertip, almost like plastic. She said I could touch it only once, because it felt strange for her, numb and ticklish at the same time.

The whole thing is clear in my head, including how the atmosphere changed after I mentioned the scar. In the silence after I touched it, I asked if it hurt when they cut her. She put a finger under my chin and looked me straight in the eye.

She told me she was given medicine that got rid of all pain, so the only feeling she had was pure happiness. She said it as if she was trying to persuade me of something she didn't expect me to believe. Dad was weirdly quiet and still.

Only very gradually, year by year, did it become apparent that, unlike my friends, I was never going to have a sibling. By the time I realised, I also understood that it was forbidden to ask why. There were secret hospital consultations; panicked, extended disappearances into the bathroom; and bedridden, teary days with no convincing explanation. I know things happened, but they all went wrong, and there was never a baby.

It hadn't occurred to me that just by being born I could have harmed my mother, but a knife had slit her open to get me out. Someone had gouged into her and pushed a hand through her flesh to pull me into the world. While I was taking my first breaths, the doctors must have been crouched over her, stopping the bleeding, sewing her up, leaving a scar that never went away.

Was this the damage I'd caused, on the first day of my life, before my eyes even opened? Could something have gone wrong with the operation? Did this cut, which saved me, wipe out my brothers and sisters?

She never blamed me. She put a finger under my chin and looked me in the eye and told me in her most serious voice that the only thing she felt was happiness. I could see how much she wanted to convince me. But perhaps the real effort was to convince herself.

220

High up on the peak, I feel as if I'm tingling with life at the same time as being almost half-asleep, detached from reality, in an elevated bubble that is mine and mine alone. Time seems to have both slowed down and speeded up, giving me the sensation that I can track the sun's movement, minute by minute, as it reddens and slips towards the horizon.

Pools of darkness settle into the valley bottoms beneath me, as if night is something that leaks upwards from the earth. Pinpricks of electric light appear on the hilltops, glittering weakly as far as I can see in all directions. The wind slackens and the air cools, nipping at the bare skin of my arms. As the sky begins to take on a pink tint, I force myself on to my feet, rolling down my sleeves against the cold. It's hard to part from the view of this just-starting sunset, but I know that to climb down in darkness would be crazy.

As soon as I lower myself from the plateau, the light changes. Just a short way below, it is far darker than at the summit. I have less time than I thought.

Finding footholds on the way up was easy — I could pick out crevices and ledges as I climbed past them — but going down, even simple parts of the climb become tricky and frightening. Again and again I have to clutch desperately at the rock, holding my weight on one trembling leg while I scrabble blindly with pointed toes in search of support. Twice, a rock gives way underfoot, jolting me into mid-air, leaving me dangling from my arms, kicking out to regain some grip on the rock face. All the way down, my heart thunders with fear. I climbed up with barely a worry crossing my mind; now I need all my self-control to force my mind away from the idea that one slip could break my legs.

I'm a long way from the nearest street lamp. When it gets dark here, it will get pitch dark. If I'm not on the road by the time that happens, I'll be lost. It will just be me and the darkness and the jackals, all night. I have no idea where I'd go, or how I'd hide myself. Perhaps I'd have to fumble my way towards a corner of the olive grove, up against a wall so nothing could get me from behind. I wonder what it would be like to peer out into pitch darkness, waiting for a wild animal to leap out and get you — a wild animal with eyes that watch your every move even as you gaze out blindly into the night.

I don't pause for long enough to feel even a moment of relief as I reach the bottom of the rock face, but turn and run through the grey half-light, skidding downwards over the dusty soil, swerving through the boulders and weeds. As my legs begin to weaken, my thigh muscles take on an alarming jellyish looseness. When I'm beginning to wonder how much further I can run, the olive grove comes into view ahead, visible against the grey-pink sky as a silhouette whose shape I recognise instantly.

Climbing up the hill in bare feet was painful enough, but going down is worse, particularly at speed. Every footstep is heavier, and it's almost impossible now to guide my feet on to smooth or soft soil. With every footfall a spark of pain shoots up my leg, as stones jar against my lacerated skin. For each deliberate step, two or three after it are wild staggers to recover my balance. I know I'm taking it too fast, but the lower I get, the darker the air becomes. In the distance I hear a high canine wail. Or maybe it isn't so distant. I can't tell. On and on I run, stumbling over the loose soil, until the thicket near the entrance to the grove slows me to a walk. I drag myself as quickly as I can through the thorns, ignoring the needles scraping against my flesh, and stop at the olive grove wall.

I can make out a pattern of dim light interrupted by the vertical black lines of the tree trunks. I can't see what damage has been done, and don't have time to go and check, but I know the grove well enough to tell from one glimpse that nothing has been chopped down.

I remember exactly where I left my shoes, and kneel to retrieve them. They aren't there.

I fumble around on all fours, searching both sides of the wall, but there's nothing. My shoes have gone. Liev, I realise, has taken them. I stand again, feeling a bubble of loathing rise up and burst inside me, spreading a hot, poisonous glow across my chest.

My throat is still gulping down air in thin, wheezy gasps. I tap the olive grove wall with my hand, hoping it might transmit me good luck, and walk on, my scratched feet reluctantly placing themselves one in front of the other as I hurry down the path through the soupy darkness. I don't dare slow down, but at this speed I end up veering and dodging in sudden, panicked lurches, as bushes and rocks loom up out of the black air barely an arm's length in front of me. Not far ahead, invisible, directly in my path, is a coil of razor wire. Rushing blindly towards it feels like one of those nightmares where your legs carry you towards a cliff edge.

A sliver of moon is hanging in the sky somewhere above Amarias, too thin to give off any useful light. Sensing I'm close to the wire, imagining what the coil of blades will do to my flesh if I fall into it, I force myself to slow down.

A sudden softness underfoot alerts me to the mound blocking the path. I stop dead. Inches from my nose I can just make out, like some evil version of a bird's nest, the tangle of sharpened steel.

Navigating more from memory than by the glimmer of moonlight, I pick out a route around the wire and on to the road. Turning my body to the right, I know I'm pointing towards home. I can make out the shape of the town, a cluster of orange spots flickering through the gloom like embers, but around me I can't see as far as my own feet.

The jackals are calling louder now, more than one of them, closer than before. Perhaps they can smell me, and sense that I'm afraid. Maybe they're watching me already, waiting for a moment of weakness, drooling into the thirsty soil.

I pick up a handful of stones to use as ammunition in case I hear any suspicious noises. I toss one ahead of me, just because it's almost impossible to hold a stone and not throw it. There's an eerie moment of silence, as if the stone has simply vanished, then I hear it land with a distant skitter. In this darkness, throwing a stone feels more like dropping one down a well.

The shimmer of Amarias street lamps tells me which direction to walk, but though the road is more or less straight, there's nothing I can see to help keep me on it. There are ditches and gullies on either side I could fall into, and occasional signposts which, if I veer off course, would announce themselves to me with a smack in the face.

The feel of the tarmac under my stinging feet is the only sensory information I can rely on. I shuffle to the edge of the road and feel with my toes for the drop at the side where the tarmac ends. Having felt this marker I can visualise my position, and I begin to walk slowly forwards.

I soon come up with a system. Ten steps, then a shuffle sideways to feel for the edge of the road, then one sidestep back on to the tarmac followed by ten more forwards steps.

As the lights from the town approach, the way in front of me gradually becomes clearer, and I allow myself more steps before each check, until a faint orange glow seeps into the air around me, revealing the tarmac under my feet. I break into a run, sprinting in desperate staggers towards home.

With my feet cut and my clothes torn, haunted

by the fear of being lost in a wilderness where I could be attacked by wild animals, the suddenness of the transition into Amarias is stranger than ever. As soon as I reach the first streetlight, the cars and buildings and gardens all seem to behave as if I am instantly back in the heart of safety and cosiness. With a single step, I appear to have hauled myself from extreme danger to absolute security.

Looking outwards towards the grove I can see nothing whatsoever, only purest blackness. I turn and run through the town.

As soon as I'm through the door, my mother leaps at me. 'Oh, my God! Joshua! What happened to you? Where have you been? What's happened?'

She shrieks a volley of questions, staring in horror, while I stand in the hallway with my back against the door, catching my breath, both feet bleeding silently into the rug.

When she notices the blood, she takes my arm, leads me to the bathroom, and sits me down. As she strips me to my underwear, her panic seems to subside. She stops shouting questions, raises my feet on to a towel on her lap, and concentrates on cleaning my cuts with disinfectant and cotton wool. She does this in silence, with immense care, while I sit limply on the edge of the bath, feeling dazed and spent. I only realise she's finished when she appears in the doorway with my pyjamas.

'I'm hungry,' I say.

'Put these on and come to the kitchen.'

I have two sandwiches and a whole carton of

orange juice inside me before she asks again what happened.

'Where's Liev?' I say.

Her shoulders slump, as if my question is somehow predictably disappointing.

'He's here,' she answers. 'In the living room.'

'Well, hasn't he told you what happened?'

'He told me you had an argument. He said you've been doing stupid things, associating with dangerous people and sneaking out to fields that don't belong to us and doing God knows what with God knows who.'

'There you go, then,' I say sarcastically. 'There's your answer.'

'That's not an answer!'

'What, you don't believe him?'

'Yes, I believe him, but I need to know more. I need to know what you've been up to. And where you went tonight. And why you're cut to pieces.'

'It was Liev.'

'Liev? He didn't do this to you.'

'Oh, so you believe him, but you don't believe me.'

'Not when you're lying.'

'I'm not lying!'

'Liev sent you out all evening? Liev cut you?'

'Yes. Effectively.'

Liev's voice booms out from the doorway. 'You see what he's like? A born liar! I don't know what else we can do with him!'

'He pulled a gun on me!'

'Ach!' Liev swats the air in front of him.

'He threatened me, and he threatened a man

I've been helping. I've been learning about trees — how to grow lemons and olives — I haven't done anything wrong, but Liev came out with a gun and he nearly killed us.'

'He's crazy!' says Liev. 'Your son is crazy!'

'Why are you saying these things?' says my mother, her words strangled and desperate, as if she's pleading with me.

'I had to run up into the hills to escape him. To stop him shooting. Then it got dark and the bushes cut me on the way down. He stole my shoes so I had to walk all the way back barefoot.'

My mother kneels on the floor beside me and takes my hand. Her eyes are filled with tears. I can see that she's trying to speak, but can't get the words out. Eventually, in a trembling voice, she says, 'Why are you doing this? I'm trying my best for you. Why are you determined to make things so hard?'

'What are you talking about?'

'Why do you have to be like this?'

'Like what?'

Her voice drops to a whisper. 'Why do you hate him so much?'

I snatch my hand away. 'I've just told you!'

'What has he ever done to you?'

'I TOLD YOU. I'VE JUST TOLD YOU!'

'Do you know where we'd be without him? Do you know what he's done for us? Who do you think pays for our food? How do you think we've got a roof over our heads?'

'WHY WON'T YOU LISTEN TO ME?'

'He's your father now, and he loves you, and there's no way back to the life we had before.

228

That's over. You have to accept what we have. Trying to destroy it and make everything impossible for me is just selfish and stupid and it has to stop. I've had enough.'

'You're blind! You're totally blind!'

'STOP IT!' she snaps. 'I said I've had enough. It's time for you to grow up, and begin to think about other people. Do you understand? I've reached my limit.'

'Which other people?'

'Your family! The people who are trying to look after you!'

'And no one else?'

'Stop arguing! Go to your room and think about what I've said. This behaviour can't go on.'

'You're such a hypocrite.'

I stand up from the table, the back of my knees sending my chair clattering to the floor. As I walk away, Liev steps into the room and pulls Mum into an embrace.

My bedroom door slams behind me, and I slump to the floor.

Part Four

For the first half of August we always go on holiday, to the same boring resort as every year, where Liev lolls by the pool in his knicker-trunks, and Mum flops out next to him reading and snoozing, as if her do-nothing, stay-at-home life has somehow exhausted her. I'm farmed out on daily watersport sessions, which I usually love — just being away from Amarias and out on the water all day is enough to make it the highlight of my year — but this time I can't relax. It's the hottest, driest month of the summer. The grove needs me more than ever, and I can't be there.

After we get back, Mum and Liev are all over me like prison warders. This time they work together, watching everything I do, making me account for every minute out of the house. If I try to go anywhere alone, one of them comes with me. Their final attempt to fix me — to make me grow up — seems to be to treat me as if I'm three years old. When I point this out to them, they don't see the joke.

I don't get a chance to visit the olive grove until the first Friday of term. As I hurry out of Amarias, straight from school, my head spins with visions of what I might see when I get there. Liev and I haven't talked about it, but I know he might have contacted the army and told them about the illegal use of a closed access route. The evidence was right there, in the watered trees and weeded ground. At any point since my last visit, the bulldozers could have been sent.

Beside the junction with the checkpoint road, I spot my tennis racket lying abandoned on the ground. I'd forgotten all about it until I see the familiar shape, covered in a skin of dust, unmoved for a whole month. I make a mental note to reclaim it on the way home.

The first thing I do after rounding the razor wire is to look at the ground, examining it for bulldozer tracks. The soil is unharmed. I sprint up the path, my heart pounding with hope and dread.

The grove is still there, undamaged apart from the two bullet-scarred trunks.

The soles of my feet are still too sore for me to remove my shoes, but it feels strange to walk into the grove without the sensation of soil against skin. In that place, having my feet encased in leather and rubber seems somehow unnatural and cumbersome, like a heavy coat on a hot day.

The ground is parched and cracked, covered in a scattering of dry leaves. In July, when I went regularly, hardly any leaves fell, but now the trees are shedding heavily. I don't know if this is normal or is some kind of thirst-induced crisis management. I water as best I can, carefully sharing out the precious liquid, and rake up the leaves. Only then do I climb to the top terrace.

My seedling is dead.

It stands there in the cracked soil, nothing more than a short-branched twig with four small leaves at its base, a laughably tiny catastrophe. All my effort and excitement and hope has produced only this. Could any failure possibly be more ludicrous, more insignificant?

I know I can't allow myself any sorrow or regret. What will it make me, standing in this semi-confiscated olive grove, living among thousands of people who suffered like Leila's family suffered, if I give way to even a moment's grief over this trivial little death? To shed one tear for what was no more than a twig would be an outrage of self-indulgence. I cannot allow myself to feel anything.

I pick up one of the tiny dry leaves. It is crisp and brittle, snapping as I fold it in two. Without knowing why, I step forwards and grind my heel into the stem, squashing the shoot flat, twisting my ankle until the flimsy white roots pop out from underground.

Feeling a numb regret settle into my belly, I trudge down to the lowest terrace and examine the two trees that were shot. Each bullet has taken out a chunk as big as an orange. The splintered wood inside the trunk is pale and jagged, a fresh-looking wound, as if the shots were fired a minute rather than a month ago. There is an eerie nakedness to these trees now. They both seem to be surviving — there's no sign above of any dying branches — but it's as if their solidity has been undermined. They now look vulnerable, mortal, somehow temporary.

I sit, leaning against my favourite tree, and wait. It is the first Friday of September. Where before I might have fallen asleep, today I feel wide awake, uncomfortable and tense. Something has changed in the atmosphere of the grove. The air seems to thrum with an unsettling electricity I've never before felt out in these fields, so far from The Wall. Part of my reason for coming here, again and again throughout the summer, was to escape this exact buzz of tension, which I now sense has crept outwards to this patch of land and poisoned its air.

Today the grove doesn't feel like a haven, away from the soldiers and guns and watchtowers and checkpoints, it feels like the front line of a secret war. Sitting here, exactly where I've sat calm and undisturbed so many times before, I imagine a set of crosshairs lining up over my body, watching me, taking aim. Liev was right. This spot was not just an olive grove. It was a slumbering battlefield.

I stand, I pace, I weed. I stare out at the road, straining my ears for the sound of footsteps, but the sun begins to sink, the air cools, and nothing happens and no one comes.

Eventually, I wash all traces of soil from my hands in the thin trickle of the spring, pick my fingernails clean with a twig, and walk back to Amarias, straight to David's house. My plan was to phone home from his place and ask if I could stay longer, in the hope this would convince Liev and Mum I'd been there all along, but looking at David's front door, I falter. I can't do it. I don't want to see him. I have nothing to say to him, and I don't have the strength to pretend.

I turn away and walk home, my feet dragging against the concrete. I'll say nothing about where I've been. If they want to punish me, they can punish me. I hardly care any more.

Liev is waiting for me as I walk in. He's sitting in his favourite armchair with a leather-bound book on his lap, but by the time I've got through the door, his eyes are already on me.

'Where were you?' he says.

I shrug, and walk towards my room. 'Out,' I mumble.

'DON'T WALK AWAY FROM ME! Where were you?'

I stop, almost out of sight through the doorway. 'At David's,' I say, in a tone of voice that even to me sounds barely convincing.

'Are you lying?'

I shrug.

'I really hope you're not lying,' he says, raising a hand in the air with one finger pointing at the ceiling and the others curled inwards. He has a whole range of gestures like this, which he thinks make him look precise and clever.

I shrug again.

'So if I call David's mother, she'll tell me you left five minutes ago?'

'Call who you like, I don't care.'

While I'm walking away, Mum says, 'You stay put, I'll call her.'

As I lie on my bed, staring up at the ceiling, I can hear the muffled rise and fall of her voice through the wall as she speaks to David's mother on the phone. I listen as carefully as I can, but I can't make out what she's saying. They seem to talk on and on for ages, far longer than it should take for her to find out what she wants to know, and as I strain my ears to pull some kind of meaning from the soft rise and fall of her speech, it occurs to me that these would have been the first sounds I ever heard, in the womb. Even now, it's almost a comforting sound, despite knowing my mother is talking to someone who's exposing me as a liar, revealing a lie for which Liev will have to invent a whole new level of punishment.

Moments after I hear her hang up the phone, the door of my room opens a crack and my mother's face appears in a shaft of light. She looks at me, I look at her, and for a long while neither of us moves or speaks. The sound of Liev coughing breaks the silence. She purses her lips regretfully and gives a slight shake of the head.

I feel my eyes prick with tears, which I try to blink away. Mum slips into the room, sits beside me on the bed, and kisses my forehead.

'Are you hungry?' she says.

I nod.

She kisses me again and walks out. I hear another muffled conversation, this time between her and Liev, then she reappears with a sandwich on a tray and a tall glass of iced orange juice. I drink down the juice in one go, with Mum watching me until I've swallowed the last drop.

I wait and wait for Liev to appear. The longer he leaves it, the more certain I become that the waiting is an extra element of his punishment. He's torturing me by letting me stew in anticipation of what he's going to do, both of us knowing it will have to be something more severe than anything he's inflicted on me before. I almost go out to confront him, to demand that he get started.

The next thing I hear is Mum calling out that dinner's ready. We sit round the table eating, and Liev still says not one word about my absence. The mysterious thing is, he doesn't even seem angry. I know he has a pseudo-nice act he sometimes puts on just before switching into punishment mode — a routine he thinks gives added dramatic effect — but he isn't much of an actor. This is something else.

I try to catch Mum's eye, but she avoids my gaze until one swift moment, as she stands to clear the soup away, when we look at one another, and a twinkle seems to pass across her features, accompanied by the barest fraction of a smirk.

She's lied. She's covered for me. I want to jump out of my chair right then and hug her.

'You sure you don't want the rest of that soup?' she says.

I look down at my bowl, at the soup I've barely touched, and realise that I'm ravenous.

'Maybe I'll finish it off,' I say, tucking in with my heavy spoon. 'It's delicious,' I say, looking her pointedly in the eye. 'Thank you.'

'I'm pleased you like it,' she says, brushing my cheek with a fleeting, tender stroke from the back of her index finger.

Liev leans back in his chair, making the legs creak, and says he wants seconds. Mum takes his bowl and scurries away to the kitchen.

* * *

For a week, I can't stop worrying about Leila and her father. Had Liev really scared them away? After all his struggles over so many years, could Leila's father really have given up on his olive grove just because of something Liev said to him? Or had something else happened to keep them away?

One crisp, bright morning that should have been like any other September day, before I'm even fully awake, I get my answer in the most surprising and horrible way.

Never before did a day start like this. One moment I'm asleep, the next my head is flailing around in the air, flopping up and down against the pillow. Something has grabbed me by both arms, a pincer clamped on to each bicep, and this thing, or person, is violently shaking me. The curtains have been drawn and dazzling light is flooding over me, revealing only a confusing silhouette. My brain and eyes take a moment to comprehend what is happening, but when they adjust, I see above me — of course — the irate, bearded face of my stepfather.

'Wake up! Wake up!' he shouts. 'You traitor! You liar! Wake up!'

'I . . . I'm awake!' I stammer. 'What's happened?'

'THIS!' he shouts.

Hovering in the doorway, her arms folded nervously around herself, is Mum. She hands Liev a piece of paper, which he brandishes in my face.

'What is it?' I ask.

'WHAT IS IT? YOU'RE TRYING TO TELL ME YOU DON'T KNOW WHAT THIS IS?' A shaft of sunlight briefly illuminates the spittle spraying out of his mouth.

'What is it?' I repeat.

'Let him see,' says Mum.

'A LETTER. THAT'S WHAT IT IS!' shouts Liev.

'What letter?'

'YOU'RE TELLING ME YOU DON'T KNOW WHAT LETTER?'

'Let him read it.'

'A letter for who?' I ask.

Liev stares at me, breathing like an angry horse, his nostrils flaring. His mouth is screwed up tight, and for an instant I think he might spit in my face. He shoves the letter into my hand.

I'm still wearing only a pair of underpants; they're both fully dressed. I feel naked and defenceless, but it's clear they aren't willing to postpone the discussion of this letter while I fetch some clothes. My mouth is parched, drained of all moisture by the shock of this terrifying wake-up, my tongue so dry it seems to stick against the roof of my mouth. I look across at Mum, but her face is closed and hard. I don't dare ask for a drink. Sitting up straight and pulling the sheet around me, I put the letter on my knee and begin to read.

The paper is thin and waxy, traversed by lines hand-ruled in red biro. The words are written with blue ink, in small but gently bulbous handwriting. Every letter perches with meticulous accuracy exactly on the line; nothing is crossed out or corrected. I've never seen anything handwritten with such care, and I realise immediately who it's from.

Dear Joshua,

Thank you so much for everything you have done in our olive grove. You are a good person and your work has made my father very happy or maybe I should say it has made him less sad.

You know what happened to him that day he helped you back to the tunnel. He lost a lot of blood and he got better but not completely and his blood pressure is very high. There are few medicines here but the doctors have told him he must take aspirin every day to keep it low.

After the last visit his blood pressure is worse and since the crackdown the shops here are almost empty. There is no aspirin left in the town but the soldiers won't let us leave. He is getting worse and worse every day and now it is very serious.

I hate to ask you but I am worried that my father might die and you are the only person who can help. Please please please get some aspirin and bring it to us.

I hope you understand. I am sorry. This letter is a secret.

Love,
Leila
xxxxx

I count her five kisses then immediately read the whole thing again, the paper trembling in my hands. After two readings, I still stare down at the page, unable to speak. The content of the letter is bad enough, but the fact of it getting into Liev's hands means something else entirely, something I cannot yet grasp.

243

'WELL?' says Liev.

I drag my eyes up from the page, which has softened between my sweat-coated fingers. 'Well what?' I ask. I have no idea what to say, or how to defend myself.

'This is not the day to play smart,' says Liev, the veins in his temple bulging like forked lightning. 'If you don't explain this letter to me *right* now, if you give me any nonsense, I'm warning you, you *will* regret it.'

I flinch in the glare of his wild eyes. He's bigger than me, and stronger than me, and angry enough to do just about anything. The only way to save myself would be to run away, but he has me trapped. There's no escape from this room until I've accounted for the letter and suffered the consequences. No lie or excuse can save me. I'm cornered. All I can do now is tell the truth.

My tongue feels loose and heavy as I whisper my confession. 'I went through a tunnel. I met a girl. She helped me get back.'

It's just a short string of words. A few seconds on my lips. But I know that by letting them out, I have lit a fuse.

'What? You went through a tunnel? To the other side of the wall? YOU WENT THROUGH A TUNNEL?'

I nod.

'What are you talking about?'

'I found a tunnel.'

'Do you think this is funny? Do you think I'm joking around?'

'I'm telling you what happened.'

'What's wrong with you? Why can you never tell the truth?'

'I'm not lying.'

'If there was a tunnel the army would know about it, and if the army knew about it, there wouldn't be any more tunnel.'

'I'm not lying.'

'*There are no tunnels!*'

'OK, there are no tunnels,' I say, shrugging, my voice flat.

He turns to Mum. A heavy, still silence fills the room as they stare at one another in some kind of mute conference.

Liev snaps back to face me. 'Where?' he barks. 'Where is it?'

I shrug, feeling a knot of dread tighten in my stomach.

'WHERE'S THE TUNNEL?'

I pull the sheet up to my chin as I shake my head. With sudden, brutal force, he rips the bedding away, grabs me, hoists me into the air and rams me against the wall. The back of my head bashes against the plaster. He holds me pinioned, legs dangling, one hand pressing into my chest, the other around my throat.

'I'M LOSING PATIENCE HERE, AND I'M NOT GOING TO ASK YOU AGAIN. WHERE IS THAT TUNNEL?'

I try to shake my head, but his grip is too firm and I can't move. The ball of his thumb is against my windpipe, choking me.

'You're messing around with the wrong guy,' he says, 'and I'm not in a patient mood.'

Mum's voice rises up from a corner of the

room. 'Let go of him. He can't breathe.'

'Sure I'll let go of him, when he tells me where the tunnel is.'

'He can't speak. Let go of his neck.'

Liev changes his grip, lowering me until my feet reach the mattress and I can support my own weight. His fingers spider upwards to squeeze me by the jaw, pressing so hard I can feel my teeth cutting the inside skin of my cheeks.

'DO YOU KNOW WHAT THOSE TUNNELS ARE? DO YOU KNOW WHAT THEY'RE FOR? TERRORISTS! PEOPLE WHO WANT TO KILL US! YOU AND ME AND YOUR MOTHER AND EVERYONE LIKE US! THEY WANT US OFF THE FACE OF THE EARTH AND THEY WILL DO *ANYTHING* TO KILL US! THEY HAVE NO MORALS! THEY WILL STOP AT NOTHING! AND YOU THINK YOU CAN KEEP A TUNNEL SECRET FROM ME? ARE YOU CRAZY? DO YOU THINK I'M AN IDIOT?' He pulls me towards him then gives my body a shove, banging my head against the wall. 'WHERE'S THE TUNNEL?'

I can feel the salty tang of blood pooling in my mouth. I roll a puddle on to my tongue and spit it into his face. Crimson dots splatter across his cheeks and forehead. He blinks to clear his vision and tightens his grip on my jaw.

He leans me towards him and bashes my head once more against the wall. 'WHERE'S THE TUNNEL?'

Then again, harder, my skull resounding

against the plaster with a hollow thud. 'WHERE'S THE TUNNEL?'

The next impact knocks a picture off its hook: Rafael Nadal holding the US Open trophy, beaming a carefree smile towards an admiring crowd. I cut it out of a magazine myself and bought the frame with my own money. It skids downwards, shattering against the foot of my bed.

I'm dizzy now, with prickles of whiteness dancing at the fringes of my vision, and can barely see beyond Liev's blood-speckled face. I can hear my mother saying something — a burble of words that sounds like a plea, getting louder and louder — but the world seems to have shrunk away to just me and Liev and the wall, and the rhythm with which he's thumping my head against it, thud after thud after thud, until I realise that my mother is between us now, yelling, prising us apart, one of her hands pressed into Liev's face, her nails digging into the flesh under his eyeballs, then I'm back down on the bed, crumpled on to the mattress, vaguely feeling shards of glass nipping at my legs, and my mother is screaming louder than I have ever heard anyone scream, pushing Liev out of the room and slamming the door.

Perhaps I then fall asleep. Maybe for just one second, maybe for several minutes, because the next thing is a feeling something like waking up, and I'm still on the bed, and my mother is stroking my hair and telling me that she loves me, and she isn't going to let anyone hurt me.

My head is booming as if it's still being

rhythmically struck with something hard and flat. I don't move, and I don't want her to move. I just lie there, feeling limp and empty and confused, letting her stroke me. It feels good to have her around and above me, comforting me like a child, as if I'm still that small boy who needed only his mother's presence for the world to feel safe.

I can't remember her ever stepping in to protect me from Liev. Today she intervened, but too late. He's finally done to me what he always wanted to do.

Maybe I fall asleep again, I'm not sure, but I feel a little less strange, a little less dizzy, the next time I open my eyes. My head is on a pillow and Mum's perched on the edge of the mattress, sitting how she usually sits, folded in on herself with her elbows tucked into her sides and her knees and ankles pressed together. The sheet feels smooth again, cleared of broken glass. A cup of water is waiting for me. I raise myself on to my elbows and gulp it down.

She takes the empty cup and kisses me on the forehead. 'Are you OK?' she whispers.

I nod, and with her little finger she brushes a wisp of loose hair away from my eyes, repeating the movement several times, even though it takes only one flick to move the hair. She hasn't shown tenderness like this towards me for years, not in all the time we've lived in Amarias, not since she met Liev and seemed to harden inside. This gentle hand on my face, stroking my skin, feels like a hot bath, like a slice of cake, like the deepest sleep.

Liev's presence always fills the house, even when he isn't there. Alone with my mother, at this moment, I feel a rare sensation of him receding to a great distance. She dug her nails into the skin of his face and shoved him out of the room. For the first time ever, she stood up to him, and protected me.

I reach for her hand, not wanting to speak, or do anything to disturb the moment, but hoping to let her know that I'm grateful, and I love her. She interlaces her fingers with mine, wrapping herself around my palm, and squeezes.

An intense thought seems to be hovering on her lips, struggling to fight its way into words. I wonder if this morning, seeing what Liev did to me, she at last saw through him. I wonder if she finally understands that his hands are in fact around both our throats all the time; that his beloved Amarias is a brutal, suffocating lie; that we have to escape. We could pack one suitcase and be out of there that very day. I'd be happy to lose everything we owned if she would just agree to get up, together, and walk out. It would take only a moment to make the decision. We wouldn't even need to tell him. We could hop on a bus as if we were going on a shopping trip, with nothing but a toothbrush, and just never come back. We could go into hiding, and even if he tracked us down, he wouldn't be able to force us to return, not if we stood up to him together.

'Joshua?' she says.

'Yes,' I say, thinking yes, *just say it, say we can go, say we can run away.* I squeeze her hand as hard as I can, willing her on.

She squeezes back. 'I need to know. Where's the tunnel?'

I look up, scrutinising her face. Her eyes are filled with compassion and love, but I feel as if she's pulled back her hand and slapped me. Liev throttled me in front of her. She saw how much he relished hurting me, how far he was willing to go, but her loyalties haven't budged. I can't even trust her strokes and kisses. She wants information, just like him. He tried his interrogation technique, now she's trying hers.

In this instant, I realise that she will never leave him, whatever he does to me. We will never leave Amarias.

'Where's the tunnel?' she repeats 'You have to tell me.'

I roll on to my side, towards the wall, pulling my knees up to my chest.

'You have to tell someone, and don't you think it's easiest if it's me?'

'Is that a threat? What are you going to do to me?'

'We have to tell the army. We don't have a choice.'

'Yes, you do.'

'Just tell me where it is. If you do, I can protect you.'

'From what? From who?'

'Tell me, Joshua.'

'I can't.'

'Why not?'

'Because it's not mine, and everything I do just destroys things and makes everything worse for people who don't deserve it, and I can't live with myself if I do it again.'

'You can't go through that tunnel. Never again. You have to forget about the letter. Put it out of your head. These people are trying to manipulate you. They are very clever and they will do anything to get what they want. Whatever they've made you think, whatever they've done to you to get you on their side, you are just their tool, and they will crush you as soon as they've finished with you. That's not going to happen. You are never going to see any of them ever again. Do you understand?'

I stare at her, not nodding or shaking my head, trying to freeze the muscles of my face into a wall of secrecy.

'You know what my job is?' she says. 'Over and above anything else I've ever done.'

'What?'

'It's keeping you safe. You're my only child, and if anything happens to you, my life won't be worth living.'

'If you want to keep me safe, get me away from Liev.'

'He feels the same as me. He just wants us all to be safe. That's why he's so angry about the tunnel. Nothing is more important to him than the safety of this community.'

'Have you forgotten what he did to me? You were right here! You saw it!'

She gives a slow blink, as if her eyelids can wipe away irrelevant distractions. 'It seems like you've done some stupid, dangerous things, and I can't let that carry on. I just can't.'

'It's my life,' I say. 'You can only decide what I

251

do for so long. In the end it's up to me.'

'Maybe. But while you're in my house, you're my responsibility.'

'I'm my own responsibility.'

'A bomb could come through that tunnel today! Today!' she says, her voice lifting to a high, strangled thread. 'Every hour that tunnel exists is an hour that we are in mortal danger! You can't be this stubborn! You can't! Liev's going crazy out there! He's acting like he wants to kill you! You have to be sensible!'

'If I tell you, you'll send the army in.'

'I don't know what's going to happen, but we have to tell the authorities. For the sake of ourselves and our neighbours. For all our people. We have to protect our own people.'

'And who are our own people?'

'All of us who live here!'

'All of us?'

'Yes!'

'On both sides of The Wall?'

'When are you going to stop this nonsense? You know perfectly well who our people are. It's you and me and people like us. Our friends.'

'But I have friends on the other side of The Wall. And there are people on this side of The Wall I hate. There's someone living in this house who I hate. So who are my people? You tell me.'

'When are you going to stop this?'

'There's only one person who wants to kill me, and he's married to you. You said it yourself.'

'What's happened to you? How can you be so cruel and divisive? When did you become this

252

person? I . . . I . . . I feel like I've lost you. You're my only child and I . . . I've lost you. Who *are* you?'

Her sobs start slowly but gather momentum, until it begins to seem as if she won't be able to stop. I pass her tissue after tissue, horrified and embarrassed, while a series of retches and convulsions pass through her body. Even the death of my father didn't do this to her. Or if it did, she never let me see.

By the time she finishes weeping, a soggy mound of crumpled paper almost covers her feet. She blows her nose and looks at me with reddened eyes, which have shrunk back behind puffy, swollen eyelids.

'I won't let anything bad happen to you,' she says, her voice snotty and moist. 'I promise.'

'It's a bit late for you to say that, isn't it?'

'I can't help you if you're lying to me all the time — if you're living in my house but sneaking around and tricking us and hiding yourself away. It's still my job to look after you, but I can only protect you if you're honest with me.'

I shrug.

'And I have to know you're on our side.'

'Whose side? Who's us, anyway?'

'Just tell me where the tunnel is. You only have to tell me. It can be our secret.'

She gently rolls me towards her and leans close to my face. 'Just whisper it once in my ear.'

I never thought tears had a scent, but I can smell them on her, wafting towards me in thick, sweet waves.

'Our secret?' I say.

We're nose to nose. She nods, not flinching from my gaze, willing me to be stupid enough to trust her.

A question springs to the tip of my tongue. I want to ask her if she is dead. *Are you both dead — you and Dad?* These seven words sit behind my lips, ready to blast out, an insult for her insult, a slap for her slap.

I press my mouth close to her ear. A strand of tear-moistened hair brushes my cheek. She is utterly still, her body rigid with anticipation.

'I have to ask you something,' I say.

'What?'

It's as if I don't even choose the question. The question chooses me, popping out of my mouth before I even know what I'm going to say. 'Did something happen when I was born? Something bad?'

'What do you mean?'

'When they cut me out. Were you hurt?'

A barely perceptible flinch scampers across her face, then the skin around her mouth tightens into a clenched smile. 'Of course not. It's a simple operation. They do it all the time.'

'But did something go wrong?'

'Why are you asking me this?'

'I need to know.'

'You mustn't worry. Why are you — ?'

'Liev said I damaged you.'

'He didn't mean it like that. You're confused.'

'I know what he said and I know what he meant.'

She puts a hand on my chest, above my heart.

254

'You're the only child I ever wanted,' she says. 'The only one.'

Another lie. Her eyes fill with tears, then empty again, as if by sheer willpower she's sucked the liquid back into her head.

'OK?' she says.

I shrug.

'You believe me.' She phrases it more as a statement than a question, so I don't answer.

'Now it's my turn,' she says. 'Where's the tunnel?'

I barely have enough saliva in my mouth to form the words as I whisper, 'The building site with the blue hoardings. Round the corner from the bakery.'

She nods and kisses me once, swiftly, on the lips. For a moment we breathe one another's breath, as if there's no distance at all between us. 'I love you,' she says. 'Nobody's going to hurt you.'

She slips off the bed and begins to pick up the mound of tissues at her feet, but with only two or three in her hands she stands upright, remembering there are more important things to do, and walks to the door.

'You don't have to go to school today,' she says, half-turned towards me in the doorway. 'After what happened. I'll say you're sick.'

'No,' I say, 'I'm fine. I want to go.'

'Are you sure?'

'Is Liev still here?'

'Yes.'

'I'm going to school,' I say. 'I'd rather be at school.'

She lets out a disappointed sigh, and walks out.

Now I have to move fast. I throw the sheet back and jump out of bed. The room sways and tips, my weak, rubbery legs crumpling under my weight, slumping me downwards in a slow-motion topple on to my knees.

I take a few breaths and pull myself up, using the bedstead to support me, but part of my brain seems to think I'm still lying down, with a conflicting voice telling me I'm vertical but floating. I know I ought to get back into bed, give myself a few hours for the booms and throbs in my head to subside, but there's too much to do, and no time to waste.

I dress as fast as I can and grab my piggy bank from the windowsill. It's in the shape of the Empire State Building, sent by my uncle for a birthday, years ago, and is supposed to look like it's made of bronze, but the surface has worn away at the corners to show the white plastic underneath.

I prise out the cork, pull free a couple of notes that are jammed in the opening, and coins cascade on to my desk. I shove the whole lot into my pockets — all the money I have — and walk as fast as I can to the front door, skipping breakfast, not wanting to stay a moment longer under the same roof as Liev. I sense from the feel of the house that he's already left, but there's nothing to be gained by checking, so I try to slip away unseen.

I'm several steps into the front garden when Mum comes after me, holding out my backpack.

'Your schoolbag,' she says.

'Oh, yes. Of course,' I reply, taking the bag, pretending I want it, pretending I'm going to school.

She kisses me and turns towards the house.

'Bye, Mum,' I say, regretting immediately that I didn't kiss her back, wondering, as I walk away, if I will ever see her again.

Hot, dry air, blown straight from the desert, tingles in my throat. A wind from the south usually leaves the car dusted with a film of sand, but our driveway is empty. Liev has gone.

I stop and breathe. Each dose of fresh oxygen, sweeping in from far away, soothes my head and steadies my balance. Every puff I exhale will be in another country by the end of the day.

There's no time to indulge my weak legs and lingering dizziness. I break into a run, but stop myself after a few strides and revert to a brisk walk. I have to move fast, but calmly. It's important that I don't draw attention to myself.

The white security car glides past me. I don't let myself catch the driver's eye. They can't be watching me yet. The car passes by and recedes from view. It's too early to get suspicious, but just the idea of being followed makes it hard to walk naturally, hard to know where to look, what to do with my arms, how fast to go.

I head for the nearest chemist, stopping twice to tighten my shoelaces, using the crouch to look around me in all directions. As far as I can tell, I'm alone.

A bell over the chemist's door chimes as I walk in, making me jump. The man at the till looks up from his paperwork, frowning. I smile, but he returns to his work without acknowledging me.

258

The shop smells of boiled sweets and swimming pool.

I find the shelf with painkillers, a bewildering array of brands in almost identical packets showing silhouettes of body parts dotted with orange and red circles, rings of pain drawn to look like targets. The pictures remind me I still have a headache myself, but these aren't for me.

Confused by the breadth of choice, I contemplate buying a selection, then remember Leila specifically asked for aspirin. There are six packets. I scoop them into my hands and carry the unwieldy pile to the till.

The shopkeeper continues writing for a few seconds after I drop the pills on to the counter, then looks up and eyes me sceptically over his frameless glasses. His bald pate is glistening in the strip lights. 'Are these all for you?' he says.

I nod.

A frown remains grooved into his forehead. He makes no move to pick up and scan the aspirin. I hear myself gabbling, 'It's for a school project. Chemistry. I was sent out to get them for an experiment.'

'The school doesn't buy its own materials?'

'It . . . I don't know . . . the teacher just asked me.'

'I can't sell them to you.'

'I'm not lying.'

'I never said you were lying,' he says, in a crowing tone which seems to imply that he's just proved I am. 'It's the law.'

'I'm old enough!'

'Nothing to do with your age. Only one packet

259

of aspirin to be sold at a time. To anyone. It's the rules. People do stupid things.'

I'm not sure whether or not to believe him, but there seems to be little point in attempting to argue him round. I shove five packets aside and pay for the remaining one. He takes my money with limp, reluctant fingers and hands me the box of pills, seemingly disappointed to find the pleasure of thwarting me coming to an end.

I clatter out through the glass doors, pinging his bell as loudly as I can. Back in the fresh air, I walk briskly out of the chemist's field of vision before pausing to calculate an alternative plan. I can think of one other chemist, three grocery stores, a petrol station and two newsagent's. All of those probably sell aspirin. One pack from each place will make eight. With a better cover story I might be able to get two at each shop, which would push me up to a decent tally of pills.

I plot a route on my mental map of Amarias and set off, soon finding myself at a newsagent's. I buy a chocolate bar, and as I am paying say, casually, as if it's an afterthought, 'Oh, Mum asked me to get a couple of packs of aspirin.'

The guy reaches behind him and hands them over without a moment's hesitation, barely glancing at me, or the pills, or my money.

The woman at the till of the first grocery store says she isn't allowed to sell two packs, but when I tell her my Mum has flu and I've taken the day off school to nurse her because my father is dead, she takes pity on me and changes her mind.

I'm up to eleven packs, with two more shops to go, when my route takes me towards the building site with the blue hoardings, round the corner from the bakery.

I already know what I'll see. I know what my mother will have done. 'It can be our secret. Whisper it once in my ear,' she said, stroking me, kissing me, lying to my face.

The soldiers are exactly where I expected to find them, two bored-looking conscripts only a few years older than me, their guns slung casually over their shoulders. They're guarding the entrance to the building site, which looks like it has been smashed open with a bulldozer or a tank. As I get close, I can make out a set of track marks on the flattened wood.

They acted fast. I approach the soldiers, wondering how quickly they searched, and if they've realised yet that I directed them to the wrong building site.

When I look in, I'm surprised to see only three men ambling disinterestedly around the site. Maybe they didn't really believe Liev's warnings. Perhaps they have alerts like this all the time.

I turn to the soldiers on guard duty and ask what's happening.

'Anti-terrorism operation,' one of them mutters.

'Did you find anything?'

'Not here. I think they got something up the road. A tunnel.'

His words hit me with the force of a punch in the stomach. How had I been so stupid? Why had I directed my mother to the wrong building site when there were only two in the town? If they drew a blank at one, they'd of course search the other. I could have sent them way out of Amarias. I could have chosen anywhere.

I turn and run, sprinting towards the tunnel, and from the end of the block I can already hear the noise. Army trucks have closed the road at both ends, and a bulldozer is audibly crushing something. Two jeeps carrying important-looking, grey-haired soldiers turn up just as I arrive, and I watch from the taped-off end of the street as they hurry out of their vehicle and through the flattened gates into the site. The soldiers here look tense and alert, their guns pointed to the ground but gripped in both hands.

I push through the gathering of onlookers and try to get the attention of the soldier manning the roadblock, but he won't speak to me. I shout as loudly as I can, but he alternates between ignoring the whole crowd and insisting we move on, behaving as if dealing with civilians is an embarrassingly menial chore he doesn't want to be seen doing.

As I watch, I feel all hope drain out of me. My only way to help Leila and her father is gone. I have the aspirin, but I'm trapped on this side of The Wall. The tunnel has been found, and will be guarded, then sealed. I'll never get through the checkpoint on my own, and there's no other way through. Posting the aspirin might have been possible, but Leila had written no return address on the letter, probably for fear it might be intercepted. Even if I did know where to send the pills, it seems unlikely the parcel would be delivered unsearched and intact.

A further truckload of soldiers arrives, accompanied by a lorry stacked with green metal crates, as large as coffins. The soldiers unload the crates at speed and carry them over the crushed gates towards the tunnel. I gaze at the efficient swirl of activity, asking myself again and again what I should do now. Could I really just give up? Could I possibly go home and carry on with my life, pretending I'd never met Leila and her family, pretending my stepfather hadn't almost throttled me, pretending there was even a shred of trust left between me and my mother?

The soldiers stand aside as a helicopter arrives and hovers overhead, sending up waves of dust. I turn, cowering from the flying grit, and walk. I have no plan. I don't know where I'm going. I'm just walking away.

I stumble on, my mind empty of all thought, until I realise I've walked out of town, on to the forbidden road to the olive grove. My tennis racket is still in the dust beside the junction, now almost perfectly camouflaged.

As I hurry onwards along this familiar strip of tarmac, away from Amarias, towards the hills, my head begins to clear.

I examine the soil at the start of the footpath. Still no bulldozer tracks, but for how much longer? Liev was already suspicious of the olive grove, of my visits here and my relationship with the owner of the land. Using me as the link, he's bound to have reported a connection between this place and the tunnel.

I run up the path, kick off my shoes and throw myself on to the ground, lying flat on my back with arms and legs stretched out. Above me, tiny green olives not much bigger than peanuts are hanging from the branches. I stand, reach up, and pluck one. It's dry, hard, slightly rubbery, nothing at all like the plump, juicy globes you buy in jars. I lift it to my lips and take a nibble. Spears of bitterness spike my tongue. I spit out the shard of flesh, toss away the remainder of the olive, and hurry towards the spring. A scoop of cool, fresh water, gathered up in my cupped hands, soothes my mouth. I tip a second handful on to my bruised head. Droplets trickle deliciously down my spine as I pull myself on to the wall and sit on the rickety stones, looking back at Amarias.

What now?

The idea of returning home and simply carrying on is intolerable. I can't go back to that house. I can't pretend for one more day, one more meal, one more minute, that I feel anything towards Liev except hatred. As for my mother, I no longer know what to think. Everything between us feels suddenly clearer and also more confusing. Today another bond snapped, another barrier went up. I am less of a son to her, now, than I was this morning; and she is less of a mother.

I look up at a solitary puff of cloud hovering far away, one lonely wisp hanging weightless in a vast expanse of blue. A pressure in my chest seems to ease, a knot loosens, as a plan, out of nowhere, drifts into my mind.

Year after year I've been waiting for my mother to take me away, and it's clear now this is never going to happen. The only way I'm ever going to leave is if I do it myself. As I gaze across the scrubland towards Amarias, I see for the first time that running away shouldn't frighten me. There's no reason to fear setting off on my own, because if I were to stay, if I were to go back home, I'd be no less alone. My mother has cut me loose. From now on, whatever I do, wherever I go, I'm alone. There's nothing left tying me to my home. I'm free to run.

If I manage to get back to my village by the sea, there are people who might remember me. Perhaps someone would take me in — a family who'd been our friends when Dad was alive — or I could seek out a charity that gives protection from violent parents. I've seen adverts for emergency phone numbers. My mouth is cut and my head is bruised. My neck is red with strangulation marks. I won't even have to lie. My stepfather attacked me. If I turn myself in, describe what was done to me, I'll be given a bed somewhere. I'll be looked after, housed, fed. All I have to do is run away.

The longer I wait, the less visible my injuries will become, and the harder it will be to prove what Liev did. I have to act fast, but one thing stops me jumping on the next bus. I can't throw away my stack of aspirin. I can't abandon Leila's father without making an attempt to deliver the medicine.

With the tunnel in the hands of the army, there's now only one way to get beyond The

Wall. In normal circumstances it isn't anything I'd even contemplate, but I can think of no other method, and I know that if I don't try something, I won't be able to leave with a clear conscience. I won't be able to leave at all. It's far riskier than anything I've attempted before, and can't be tried until after dark, but it's the only plan I have.

I decide I'll make one attempt at the delivery, tonight, then I'll run away to the place where I was born. I can hide out at the grove for the rest of the day, then around the time the school bell goes, I'll head home like a good boy, eat a family meal without looking at Liev or letting him anger me, then go obediently to bed. I'll seem chastened and placid. I'll do my homework. Everything will be perfectly ordinary, apart from a chime in my head, reminding me each passing second that everything I do, I'm doing for the last time.

Before leaving the grove, I touch every tree, silently willing each one to survive and grow. After putting on my shoes, I walk back for a final look and pluck twenty olives, one from each tree on the lowest terrace. I slip them into my trouser pocket, turn, and hurry away, not looking back.

I nestle my fingertips among the clutch of olives as I walk down the path, around the razor wire, and on to the road.

At the fork, I glance down towards my tennis racket and decide to leave it there. I no longer feel it's mine. The boy who used to own it — who used to play tennis against The Wall without even wondering what was on the other side — no longer exists. Besides, I can't take it with me. I can't take anything with me.

Approaching Amarias, I begin to hear the roar and crunch of the anti-tunnel operation. A couple of muffled explosions reverberate in the air, but it's impossible to identify them as near by or far away, underground or overground, this side or the other side of The Wall. A clattering roar, quiet at first, grows in volume as I get close to the edge of town, but only when the source of the noise comes into view do I realise it's moving towards me. It pulls out suddenly between the last two houses, as wide as the entire road, crunching and squeaking against the tarmac: a vast, armoured bulldozer.

The enormous machine bears down on me, shuddering the earth under my feet. Moments later we are directly in front of one another, me heading into Amarias, it driving out, towards the olive grove.

I stop walking, but don't step aside. I can't be certain where the bulldozer is going, but I can guess. A useless, helpless rage fizzes inside me, obliterating rational thought, freezing me to the spot as the towering vehicle, with a scornful mechanical sigh, brakes.

A soldier with a cigarette drooping from his mouth opens his fortified cabin and shouts at me to get out of the way. I look up at him, ignoring his order, not moving.

He shouts again, twice more, making threats I can barely hear, then with a casual swat of his hand he closes his door and revs the engine. The rumble of the diesel pistons seems impossibly loud yet strangely distant. For a moment, I seem to float free from myself, as if I'm not in the road, looking up at the bulldozer, but watching from one side, seeing myself block the path of this colossal machine, wondering what I'll do next.

The bulldozer inches towards me at the speed of an idle stroll, until the scoop touches the bones of my shin. I snap to attention and step back, then back again. The bulldozer accelerates steadily.

Now I'm walking backwards as fast as I can, and the bulldozer is still increasing its speed. If I keep going, sooner or later I'll slip and fall under the tracks.

I jump aside.

The bulldozer gives a gloating roar, exhales a black belch into the air, and accelerates away. I stare for a while, following its squeaky progress across the valley, then realise I can't watch. I don't want to see; I don't want to know. If I leave immediately I'll be able to cling to the hope that the bulldozer went elsewhere. The only image I'll have in my head will be of the olive grove as it is now, as it was for Leila and her father, and his father, and his father before that. I don't ever want to see it any other way. And whatever that machine does, in my pocket I have twenty olives, twenty seeds.

I turn and run home, for the last time.

The only part of the evening when I can't avoid Liev is dinner time. I come to the table at the last possible moment. It's roast chicken, Mum's idea of my favourite meal. This cooked dead bird, sitting on the table in a puddle of its own melted skin, is the closest I'm going to get to an apology.

I know how I'm supposed to react. I can see the scene in Mum's head: nothing said, no mention of what Liev did to me, just smiles and nods and hearty appetites showing that the nastiness is behind us, over, forgotten. My little rebellion has been dealt with; the tunnel has been sealed; the town is safe again.

I don't look at her, and ask for breast even though I prefer leg. I know they were talking about the tunnel before I appeared — I could hear them as I came down the stairs — but now I'm in the room, nobody seems to know what to say or where to look. I catch them both snatching furtive glances at the marks on my neck, but neither of them asks if it is still sore, or refers to what happened.

The first words to come out of anyone's mouth are Liev complimenting Mum on the meal and asking her for seconds. She hasn't even half finished her own food, but she gets up and serves him another portion.

'Why don't you just give him twice as much in

the first place?' I say. It's the last time I'll ever eat with him, so I figure this is my chance to say what I've been thinking for years.

'What?' says Mum.

'He eats two platefuls every time, so why don't you just heap it all on at the start? Just give him one massive mound of food so we can see how much he eats.'

'What are you talking about?'

'Forget it.' I put my head down and cut a mouthful of meat.

Mum looks at Liev, her mouth half open. Out of the corner of my eye, I see him give her a small shake of the head. Even for him, it seems like the fight we had in the morning is enough for one day.

Nobody says another word until dessert. It's chocolate cake, another of Mum's treats, the same recipe she's used for every one of my birthdays, as long as I can remember. She's not particularly good at baking, and it isn't much of a cake, but I savour every mouthful, knowing I'll never eat it again, knowing my next birthday will be the first one without it.

I try to lock away a precise record of the flavour, so wherever I end up, whenever I need it, I'll be able to serve myself a fantasy slice. When I look up from my empty plate, Mum's staring at me, smiling a pleased-with-herself smile. I didn't notice her watching me eat, but from the look of contented relief on her face I can tell she thinks the cake has done the trick. As usual, she doesn't notice what's right in front of her. Show her black, and if she wants to see white, she'll see white.

I stand up from the table, thank her for the meal and walk away, not even glancing back for a last look at Liev.

* * *

Lying in bed, I think through my plan again and again, examining it for flaws, rehearsing every element in advance. One of my worries had been that I might fall asleep, but as the clock nudges towards midnight I feel as if I've never been more alert, or more alive.

It feels strange to be the only person awake in the house. The dark seems darker, the quiet quieter. I get up and begin to pack, gently tipping out my schoolbag on to the floor: textbooks, pens, half-filled exercise books, a calculator, all now redundant. In among the pile are eleven packs of aspirin. I fish them out and return them to the backpack, along with my identity papers, one change of clothes and a toothbrush. I need to be light on my feet, and nothing else is essential.

I hoist the bag on to my shoulders and look around the room, which I realise I'll never see again. Knowing I'm leaving, I find myself looking at it through fresh eyes, as if this were the bedroom of a stranger. It's a surprise to realise, setting off almost empty-handed, how little there is here that I expect to miss. A ceiling-high shelving unit is crammed with games, toys, magazines, books and gadgets, most of which have been untouched for months or even years. Piles and piles of stuff — my precious possessions — and now I'm walking away from every last thing, realising that none of it, in fact, is precious at all. I spot three swimming medals clumped into a dusty, forgotten heap, won for some tiny achievement so many years ago I can't even remember it. When I look along the shelves at each individual object, almost everything seems to belong to a person who no longer exists.

The wall above my bed, apart from a rectangle of space where Rafael Nadal used to hang, is covered with pictures of footballers and tennis players, fists clenched and teeth bared in moments of triumph, crisply frozen against ranks of blurred faces, smudges of awe and adulation. The glow of purpose in their eyes, the focus and determination, is what I need to find inside myself. The task I'm about to undertake is my own private Grand Slam final, the prize nothing more than getting away from Liev, out of Amarias.

I take a last look around the room in search of one thing I might miss. My eye falls on the bedsheet, its pattern of red-and-white lines so familiar it has become almost invisible. I have no idea where my next bed will be. What will it look like? How will it feel to be in a room with no personal objects, no history, everything institutional and unfamiliar?

My stomach lurches at the thought of Mum entering in the morning and finding my bed empty. Until now, I haven't visualised this moment, imagined her terror and grief.

To disappear without a note, without the slightest warning or explanation, seems too cruel. There isn't time now to compose anything careful, so I grab a piece of paper and scrawl.

Mum
   I can't live in a house with Liev any longer. I can't live in Amarias. I have decided to go. I love you.
J
xxx

I read it three times. Seeing those bald words in ink, my departure seems shockingly definitive and brutal. It strikes me, for the first time, how they'll interpret my escape. To them, it will look like vengeance.

I try to think of something I can add to the letter, explaining that I'm only trying to save myself, not to attack them, but no words come to mind. Nothing I can say will lessen the wound I'm inflicting on my mother.

I've tried everything to persuade her to leave, with no success. She insists on remaining in a place that I despise, and I can't live there any longer, purely to spare her. I'm not dying, I'm only leaving. If she wants to come and find me, she can. She doesn't have to live without me, she just has to choose: me or Liev. This doesn't need to be written down. She'll understand.

With trembling hands I put the note on my pillow, pulling the sheet into place and flattening out the creases. From the doorway I look back at the bed, at what my mother will see in the morning. The sight of it reminds me of my father's grave.

I turn away and creep through the house. My footsteps seem louder than normal, the stairs creaky where they've never creaked before. The latch on the front door clicks like a snapped stick as I release the lock, but none of this seems to rouse Liev or my mother. Glancing back towards the living room, listening out for footsteps, all I can hear is the slow rasp of Liev's snoring.

Sparks of fear, relief and excitement tingle in my veins as I slip out of the house and down the street. I walk on, feeling conspicuous even though there's no one around to see me. The drag and skid of my trainers on the paving stones is the only sound. Darkness seems to press in against the streetlight, squashing it onto orange pools around the base of each lamp-post. A bat darts past me through the cool night air, quiet as a falling leaf.

I know the route to the checkpoint well. It's only a twenty-minute walk. My plan is to climb the outcrop overlooking the gateway, which should give me a view of where the tanks and personnel carriers assemble before crossing over to enforce the night curfew. I'm hoping to spot a pattern in the movement of each type of vehicle.

As I clamber up the rock face to my observation point, I think again of the bat that flitted past me outside my house. Never before have I seen one so close, or glimpsed that distinctive silhouette which flashed before me as it flew in front of the street lamp. For a moment this seems like a sinister omen, then I decide it has the opposite meaning. This is how I have to move: silent, quick, invisible.

On the other side of The Wall, I know the soldiers only step out of their trucks and tanks if they have to. Here, at their last stop before they cross, things are different. They are safe here, and their guard is down. They stand around chatting and smoking, with that cocky calm that seems to come over people when they are off duty but carrying a gun.

I watch closely to get a sense of how the operation works: where the soldiers go before they cross; how they move from vehicle to vehicle; where they congregate when they're relaxing.

My goal is to get on top of one of the personnel carriers when no one is watching. Using the high wheels and thick metal bars across the outside of the truck, it will be easy enough to climb up. The challenge is to do it without being seen.

Despite the apparent calm of the soldiers, I know this is no game. Those guns are real guns, loaded with live ammunition, and if they see anything suspicious they won't hesitate to shoot. For one of the people from the other side it would be suicidal even to try, but if the soldiers see me, they'll know I'm one of them, and I feel pretty certain they won't pull the trigger. They'll think I'm just a kid pulling some prank. I have a cover story ready about how I'm so desperate to be a soldier I can't wait for my military service, and am climbing on a truck to find out for myself what really happens on patrol.

At worst I could be arrested, or even imprisoned, but they wouldn't fire at one of their own. Whatever they catch me doing, I surely won't be shot by a soldier from my own army. I know I'm taking a risk, a risk it's impossible to calculate, but I have to do it. I can't run off to the coast without attempting to deliver Leila's father his medicine. If I simply flee I'll never find out if he survives, and I sense that I might spend the rest of my life worrying that I had a hand in his death.

The military assembly point is lit up by four floodlights which illuminate a square of land with an intense white glow. Each convoy seems to pause here on the way in and on the way out. I focus my attention on the last personnel carrier at the back of the line waiting to cross. It's just outside the lit area, and as it's the final vehicle in the convoy there'll be no one behind it to see me. If I keep low as the truck crosses the checkpoint, after that I'll be more or less hidden from view.

From what I've seen, I guess that the soldiers will spend a few more minutes chatting, gathered around their supply area, then they'll be heading back to their vehicles and starting the next patrol. The right kind of truck is in the right place, out of the light, unobserved. This is my moment.

I scamper down the escarpment, taking care not to dislodge any loose stones, and scurry towards the personnel carrier, moving in a wide arc, as far out of the light as I can manage. I roll my foot from heel to toe with each step, trying to walk as quickly and as soundlessly as I can. My backpack seems to rustle and thump as I move, until I reach behind and squash it into my shoulder blades with a bent arm.

A windowless storage hut gives me temporary cover, a chance to pause and catch my breath before making one final dash for the truck. I peep around the side, watching the soldiers' casual banter. A couple of them stub out their cigarettes, crushing them with a heel into the dust. This means their break is coming to an end. I have to hurry.

Only twenty or thirty metres remain between me and the truck, but there's nothing more to hide behind, and it seems much lighter down here than it appeared from above. The longer I wait, the higher the risk, but for a while my legs won't move. The signal telling them to run seems to fade away before getting to my muscles. Then I'm off, my heartbeat booming in my ears as I race at top speed towards the truck.

I don't turn to see if I'm being watched, I just run with my head down, skidding to a halt on the darker side of the personnel carrier, hidden from view behind a tyre. I squat on all fours and look under the truck, towards the cluster of soldiers. I can see only their legs. No one is yet walking towards the convoy.

Standing upright, I pull myself swiftly on to the wheel arch then clamber upwards until I'm on top of the truck. As soon as I'm up there I flatten myself against the cool, dusty metal of the roof. I've worked out that in this position I won't be visible from ground level. The roof of these trucks is too high, or at least I always thought it was too high, but now I'm in position, the ground feels closer than I was expecting. I try to reassure myself that no one will look upwards, but as my confidence in my invisibility wanes, so too does my certainty that if they find me they won't hurt me. If they hear a noise, or see some movement near their vehicle, how closely will they really look before they reach for their guns, how many fractions of a second will they wait before pulling the trigger?

I squash myself down as low as possible and lie there, my lungs filling and emptying as if I'm running a sprint, my breath refusing to settle. Pressed against the metal roof, with a chilly night wind blowing across my back, I begin to shiver, whether from cold or fear I don't know. I thought the soldiers were on their way, but it now seems a long wait, with no sounds of movement, no revving of engines, no audible issuing of orders, just a low murmur of chat with an occasional burst of laughter, and as I lie there, I feel as if I'm deflating — as if all hope is seeping out of me. I am on top of an army vehicle, surrounded by armed men who are trained to kill, stuck inside a plan that now seems little more than a child's fantasy.

I begin to thrash my head from side to side, looking for an escape route, wondering if I can jump down and run for it before it's too late, before I'm through to the other side of The Wall, but the soldiers' voices are getting louder. With one eye, I see a group of bobbing army helmets move in my direction. There's no way out now.

As they approach, their words become more distinct. One of the soldiers is being pushed around and mocked by the others — something about a girl, and what he either has or hasn't done with her. One of them lets out a high, squeaky laugh. The doors of the truck clang shut, but through the thin roof of the vehicle I still hear the rise and fall of the jokey conversation, without any longer being able to make out the words. The engine starts, juddering my head, chest, arms and thighs, rumbling through my body like a seismic tremor.

For minutes on end the truck sits there with the vibrations of the motor rattling my skeleton, until eventually the gears crunch and the truck sets off. We creep forwards, at the back of a short convoy, towards the checkpoint.

I keep my head down and hear the driver call something out to the two guys at the barrier, which slips upwards, glides past just above me, then clangs down back into place.

Beyond The Wall, buildings soon close in, looming above the truck. I feel less exposed now, as we snake through the narrow streets not much faster than you'd ride a bike. Once we're into the old town centre, all I have to do is get down.

There are no windows at the rear of the truck. If I hang from the back as we approach a corner, then jump free and run out of sight as the truck turns, no one should see me.

Shuffling to the back while the truck is moving will mask the sound of my movements, but is risky if the vehicle corners. I have a solid bar to grip at the front of the roof, but there's little else to hold on to further back, and the metal is slippery. If I pick the wrong moment, I could be thrown off the side.

The convoy stops and starts at regular intervals. During the next pause, I let go of the bar, swivel on my belly to face the back of the truck, and slither forwards as fast as I can. Before I've reached another handhold, the truck lurches into motion, sliding me left and right with every turn, rolling me from edge to edge. I don't dare kick to keep my balance because the soldiers inside might hear me. All I can do is flatten myself harder against the metal and hope that friction holds me in place. Then the brakes jam on, sending me skidding back to where I started. I freeze, wondering if they've heard my body slide around on their roof, and are about to jump out to capture me, but no doors open, so while the truck remains still I crawl again towards the rear doors.

I move faster this time and get my hand on to a protruding hinge, but when I begin to swing myself down, the truck jolts forwards. For an instant, my brain can't compute what has happened: why I can no longer sense any metal against my skin; why the sky doesn't appear to be in the correct position; why my body seems to be still, but in motion. Just as I begin to understand that I'm somersaulting through the air, I feel a sharp blow to my shoulder as I land in the dust. I sit up, groggily watching the truck pull away in front of me, then it stops and the rear lights go white.

I leap to my feet, ignoring the pain shooting

from my shoulder, and run down a side street. I hear the mechanical squeal of the personnel carrier reversing at speed, and realise this street will only shield me from view for a second or two longer. I need to hide, but the road is just a row of shuttered houses. I sprint towards a line of parked cars, take off my backpack and throw myself into the gutter, sliding under a tiny red Fiat, dragging the bag in behind me.

The truck screeches to a halt and I hear the sound of doors opening, followed by the clomp of several pairs of boots jumping on to tarmac. I lie as still as I can, wedged under the car. My nose is only millimetres from an oily puddle which stinks of old urine, but there's no space to lift my head any higher. The sweet, acrid stench fizzes in my nostrils like a tiny insect trying to drill towards my brain.

The voices of the soldiers move closer, encircling the car. One of them is claiming to have seen something, another is mocking him for being blind. I can see black boots ahead of me and on both sides of the Fiat.

The rasping sound of air pushing itself in and out of my panicked lungs is so loud it seems impossible the soldiers won't hear me, but the harder I try to control it, the noisier my breathing becomes.

An ear-splitting crack — a gunshot — rips through the air. Every muscle in my body jerks, jolting my head against the exhaust pipe of the car. A ringing in my ears momentarily blots out all sound, until a high-pitched wail, like a small child in intense pain, pierces through. The soldiers crouch down, taking up combat positions, and no one speaks. Then a burst of laughter fills the street.

Soon, the soldiers are walking around again, laughing and talking over one another. Another gunshot goes off, bringing the ongoing wailing to an end. The soldiers, now clumped together, strolling casually, walk back towards my hiding place. As they go around and past the car, I pick out a few snatches of conversation, all of which seem to be making fun of one particular soldier for his stupidity and bad eyesight. He has shot a dog.

The chatter recedes as the soldiers climb into their truck, still mocking the man who fired his gun, saying his difficulty telling dogs from humans explains a lot about his choice of girlfriends.

That dog, I realise, was shot in my place, and has saved me. Someone must have caught a glimpse of me jumping off the truck, or they wouldn't have stopped and searched the area. Without that animal explaining away the movement that was seen, they would have carried on searching, and it wouldn't have taken them long to find me. If I'd been running when I was spotted, I might have been shot.

The air fills with the noise of the personnel carrier's engine clattering into motion. I listen as it drives away, not moving a muscle or even withdrawing my nose from the puddle, until the sound of the truck has faded to nothing.

Pulling my bag after me, I roll out from under the car and dust myself down. I'm filthy. My

T-shirt is ripped and bloodstained at the shoulder. A searing ache makes it difficult to lift my right arm. The back of my head stings where I banged it against the underside of the car. I touch the sore spot gingerly, and my fingers come back smeared with oil and blood.

It's hard to put my backpack on again, but with a careful slide up my injured limb I just about manage, and stand next to the car wondering what to do next.

It's obvious I didn't think through my mission with enough care. I knew it would be dangerous, but I now feel this was a word I simply didn't comprehend. As I stand there, breaching the curfew on the wrong side of The Wall, bloodstained, shaken and sore, the fear that is clamped around me contains not a shred of excitement or thrill. A sickening dread squats in my stomach, paralysing me. I don't want to be there. Soldiers, patrolling this place with guns, really will shoot me without asking who I am first. In this curfew, any moving shadow is a target. It's madness for me to be here, risking my life to deliver a few boxes of aspirin. I have made a terrible miscalculation, but now there's no way back. Walking to the checkpoint and trying to turn myself in would be too risky. I no longer believe the soldiers would hold their fire long enough for me to explain who I am, or why I'm there.

My only option is to press on. I have to find my way to Leila's house without being seen by any military convoys. Once I get there, I'll be safe for the night.

I try to walk out of the side street without turning my head, but after a couple of steps I can't stop myself glancing backwards. In the middle of the road, a skinny mongrel with a patchy grey coat is lying in a pool of blood. His back is arched and his legs are splayed, as if he's in the middle of a joyful leap, but his eyes have a misty, alien coldness I've never seen before. It's the look of the dead, a look that freezes and hypnotises me, prolonging my glance into an intense, horrified stare.

I don't blink, I don't swallow, I don't move. My father, after he was shot, must have had eyes like this. He, too, lay in the street, in a puddle of congealing blood, with strangers looking at him in the way I'm staring at the mongrel. And this dog, of course, could have been me. With a worse place, or a panicked movement at the wrong time, I could have taken that very bullet, and now I'd have those lifeless eyes in my head, staring but not looking.

I've never tried to imagine myself dead before, and even now it feels almost impossible, but less impossible than it did an hour ago.

It's a while before I turn away from the dog and walk back towards the main road. At the corner I stop and peep out, looking in both directions for a convoy. The road is clear.

Keeping close to the walls, rushing from doorway to doorway so I'm never far from a hiding place, I scurry in the direction of the high street. Every few steps I take cover, pause, and look behind.

Nobody is on the streets. Moving on foot

through the town, it's clear the crackdown has caused havoc. Chunks of masonry are missing everywhere, with scaffolding poles wedged into gaps left by collapsed walls. One first-floor apartment, still fully furnished, gapes open where a shell has hit. Through the hole I can see a TV, a sofa, pictures still hanging on the wall.

A blue Peugeot is parked at a skewed angle, the front half squashed flat, the back curiously unharmed. I pass an office whose door is off its hinges, squashed and bent on the ground. Inside, filing cabinet after filing cabinet is open, with papers strewn over the floor like a thick snowfall. Two rows of four desks are still in place, every one supporting a computer with a smashed screen.

I walk on through the destruction, towards the high street. Here, telegraph poles have toppled, and what look like high-voltage wires are strewn across the ground. I can't tell if they're live, but I tread carefully. More cars have been flattened by passing tanks. Shards of glass glisten across the street, twinkling in the moonlight, crunching underfoot. Guessing as to the correct direction, I make for the flying cake bakery, still huddling in the shadows, pausing in shop-fronts, looking and listening for soldiers.

The first convoy to pass is audible long before it comes into view. I take cover in a burned-out shop while it passes. A waft of diesel fumes drifts towards me as the earth-shaking wheels trundle past. I wait, cowering behind the fire-scorched wall of the shop, until the sound and smell have subsided. A peek up the road confirms that the convoy has gone, and I set off again.

Just as I hear the rumble of the next convoy I spot the flying cake bakery, the distinctive sign still intact, but no longer illuminated. I take a few steps into an alleyway and conceal myself behind some bins as the trucks pass. Crouched in the stinking darkness, my thoughts turn again to the dead dog. On the other side of The Wall, a dog that skinny would have to be a stray, but here I'm not so sure. Did someone, asleep somewhere in this town, own that dog? Did they love it? How long would they spend looking for it, and would they ever find out what happened? Or perhaps, living here, it was easy to guess.

By the time my mind jolts itself out of this cascade of questions, the air is once again still and quiet. The convoy has passed. I inch out of the alleyway and scan the street in both directions, before heading back up the road, running this time, excited to know where I am, and confident that I have a sense of the spacing between the convoys. I turn off into the next side street, navigating now by a mixture of instinct and half-memory, rushing onwards through a network of narrow, empty streets.

Just when I'm beginning to think I might have gone the wrong way, I see a motorbike. The black motorbike I hid behind. And right next to it, up three steps, the green door with the round iron knocker. I run towards the house, elated, and knock.

There's no answer.

I bang again, five times. They can't be out. There's a curfew.

I push up the flap of the letterbox and call inside. 'Let me in! Let me in!'

Still no reply.

It had not even crossed my mind this might happen. I sink to my knees and feel a surge of dismay grip me. Could they have run away from the fighting? Might Leila's father already be dead?

Then I hear a rustling on the other side of the door, and a high, clear voice I instantly recognise. She makes a brief sound, just three syllables, but I can't understand them; the same three sounds, twice in a row; then three more, with a hesitant intonation, this time in my language: 'Who is it?'

'Josh. It's me. Joshua. Let me in.'

'Joshua? You've come?'

'I have the medicine. Let me in.'

After a burst of hurried chatter, I hear bolts and locks being drawn back. The door creaks open, and as soon as the gap is wide enough I push through and slump to the floor, my body drained of strength. Leila crouches over me, with a crowd of people I don't recognise close behind, all of them staring at me blearily through sleepy eyes.

'You have the medicine?' says Leila.

I'm still too breathless to speak, and simply nod, pushing the backpack off my shoulders and handing the whole thing over to her. She grabs it, looks inside and disappears, calling something to one of her brothers as she goes. He walks after her, then reappears with a chair, takes my arm and hoists me up, staring at my every move as I lower myself on to the seat. I stare back, too tired and overwhelmed to speak or even smile, as Leila's brothers form themselves into a silent arc in front of me.

I can hear something that sounds like an argument from the main room of the apartment, then Leila's father appears, supported on one side by his daughter, on the other by his wife. He looks ten years older than the last time I saw him, with sunken cheeks and dull, waxy skin. His mouth seems to have retreated into his skull.

The huddle of people around me parts at his approach. His eyes, beaming with furious intensity, lock with mine, and he shrugs away the two women who are gripping his arms. Without their support he looks precarious and frail, as if the slightest nudge would knock him over.

'You came,' he says, in a thin, breathy voice, his tongue clicking strangely in his mouth as he speaks.

I nod.

'You brought me the medicine.'

I nod again. 'As much as I could get. It's not a lot, but I did my best.'

One of his eyes becomes briefly shiny, as if a tear might be trying to form, but he blinks it away. 'Thank you,' he says.

I nod once more, a series of sharp, fast movements that push back a tearful swelling in my throat.

'How?' he says. 'The tunnel's been sealed. There's a curfew.'

'I hid.'

'You hid? Where?'

'An army truck.'

'You hid in an army truck?'

'On. On the roof. I jumped off after the checkpoint.'

He stares at me in disbelief, then a hubbub ripples through the room as this information is translated, debated and digested.

'Can I stay here tonight?' I ask.

This question seems to burst a bubble of tension, and a roar of laughter fills the room, rolling around from person to person, rising and falling, as the question is repeated in both languages, with Leila's mother and brothers making expansive gestures offering me all the space, all the food, all the time they have to offer.

I soon find myself swarmed upon, with my filthy T-shirt pulled off me, my wounds bathed, and clean clothes shoved over my head. An array of food appears on the dining table: a plate of flat, white bread cut into strips, a bowl of olives, a dish of yoghurt, plates of dried herbs and olive oil. Even though it's the middle of the night, everyone gathers round the table, chatting and picking at the food, as if my visit has turned into a strange, impromptu party.

When I say I'm tired, the food is whisked away and I'm given a mattress in the corner, next to Leila's eldest brother. Within minutes, the room transforms from excited bustle to dead silence.

I'm still not sure how I'll get out, or even where I'll go. The shooting of the dog has shaken my confidence. The idea that I can head off, alone, to look after myself, without a family, or even any friends, looks somehow different now, viewed from here.

I'm still desperate to get away from Amarias, but even this short distance from home, everything already seems more violent, more frightening, more hostile than I anticipated. I thought it would be all right to be alone, since I felt alone in my own house anyway, but I now see there are further degrees of aloneness I hadn't understood. I'll be cutting myself off from more than I'd anticipated, heading towards an isolation I now realise will be deeper than anything I can yet imagine.

Lying on this thin, musty mattress, surrounded by sleeping strangers, my shoulder and head pulsing out dull throbs of pain, I sense that I've perhaps used up my reserves of bravery. But could I go back? Could I really just turn round and go home, let myself into the house and tell Mum the letter was a joke?

I close my eyes and listen to the snoring and shuffling around me. In the distance, a convoy rumbles and clatters. I'm too tired to make any decisions. For now, I just have to sleep. Tomorrow I'll figure out what to do, where to go.

The house is strangely hushed when I wake. I open my eyes to a room full of people, all of them already out of bed, conversing tensely in low voices. The volume rises a little when they realise I've woken up, but a note of anxiety in the air doesn't lift. They are all around the table in the far corner of the room, some sitting, some standing. There aren't enough chairs for everyone to sit at once, nor is there enough space around the table, but everyone is nibbling at pieces of dry bread, which they dip into a plate of green herbs.

As I approach the table, one of the brothers stands and insists that I take his chair. I try to refuse, but everyone rounds on me with various noises on the spectrum between affectionate hospitality and offended outrage until I relent and take the free chair. The largest piece of bread is placed in front of me, along with a supply of herbs.

I start to eat, struggling to feign enjoyment of this meagre, spicy breakfast, but with each mouthful the flavour becomes a little less strange. Just as I'm beginning to think I might almost like it, Leila's father appears and is given the chair at the head of the table, next to mine. Before he's allowed to speak to me, Leila's mother insists that he translate her apologies that, because of the curfew, the bread isn't fresh.

She seems to go on and on, but this is the only translation I'm given.

When she stops talking and moves away, he says, after a strained pause, 'We want to know how you're getting back. The tunnel is gone.'

'I'm not,' I reply. The response falls from my mouth without any hesitation or doubt, without me even realising I'd made the decision to continue my escape. It's a new day. My determination has returned.

His eyes register a fleeting panic, as if he thinks I want to stay with his family for ever.

'I'm running away,' I say. 'Back to where I was born.'

This is the first time I've said it aloud. It feels good to hear the words, the simplicity of the explanation making the project seem less fantastical.

'How?'

'I don't know. I just have to get away from my stepfather.'

'The only way out is through the checkpoint.'

'Isn't there another way? A route to the bypass?'

'Only through the checkpoint. Every other road out of town is blocked.'

'But if I get through the checkpoint, there are buses?'

'Yes, of course.'

'To the city?'

'Yes.'

'Then from there, to anywhere?'

'Probably. But . . . ' His voice trails away, and he casts his eyes down to his hands. I notice that everyone in the room is rigidly still.

'What?' I ask.

'There's something I have to say.'

'Yes?'

He raises his head and looks at me with sad, heavy eyes. 'I'm grateful for what you've done,' he says, 'but the longer you stay . . . ' He seems to lose his thread for a moment, then swallows and goes on. 'If anyone saw you come in here, you are putting us in terrible danger.'

'Oh,' I say, unsure how to respond. A memory of the shocking, bitter tang of freshly picked olive flashes into my mind as I realise that despite what I've brought him, he wants me to leave.

'They will be looking for you,' he says. 'Your stepfather saw my identity papers. If they found you here . . . '

His voice trails away. He doesn't have to finish the sentence. 'You're right,' I say, standing up from my chair. 'I have to go.'

'We'd all be punished. They'd accuse us of kidnapping you.'

'I'll go. I understand.'

'I'm sorry, but it's not safe. They could tear down the house. They can do anything.'

'I know. I'm sorry. I didn't think.'

'Don't apologise,' he says, taking my hand, inviting me to help him up. His skin feels dry and brittle, like the flesh of a leaf. Eye to eye, still gripping my fingers, he repeats, 'Don't apologise. Leila will take you to the checkpoint.'

'It's OK,' I say. 'I can find it. I don't want to put her in danger.'

'You'll wear this,' he says, handing me the

headscarf Leila lent me on my first visit. 'This time you must keep it. No more coming back.'

'Thank you,' I say, taking the scarf, 'but I'll find my own way. I don't want anyone else to get hurt.'

'And we don't want you to get hurt,' says Leila. 'It's not close and there are no signs. You won't find it on your own.'

'If I find The Wall I can find the checkpoint, and I can't miss The Wall.'

'It's not so easy,' says Leila's father. 'Some parts are unsafe. You need a guide.'

'I don't want to risk it,' I say.

'I'm coming with you,' Leila insists. 'It's because of me you are here. I have to help you leave.'

'But — '

'I'm coming. Even if you say no, I'm coming. Now have a drink and let's go.'

She hands me a glass and holds my gaze as I drink.

'He will go ahead, he will go behind,' she says, pointing to two of her brothers. 'Early warning system.' The two brothers nod at me, then the elder of them turns and leaves, muttering something I don't understand to Leila before slipping out through the front door.

'Two minutes,' says Leila.

Her father reaches out a hand, and I extend mine, thinking he's going to shake it, but instead he grips my palm between his cold, desiccated fingers and rotates it, placing his other hand gently over my knuckles. 'Thank you,' he says, staring into my eyes, squeezing my one hand within his two.

'Thank *you*,' I reply.

'Now go,' he says, releasing me from his grip.

Leila arranges the scarf over my head, then leads me swiftly out of the house. In the doorway I smile and nod at her family. They each give me a small wave, but no one speaks.

The low sun casts elongated shadows across the street, but is already giving off intense heat and a dazzling glare. Leila sets a fast pace, wordlessly indicating that I should keep up without staying too close. She seems to want me a pace or two behind her, no more, no less.

We walk on, through a succession of unpaved streets, all of them puddled with stagnant water and criss-crossed by dangling loops of electric cable and laundry. The Wall occasionally comes into view, but we seem to veer away from it as often as towards it, our route never straight for more than a minute at a time. As far as we walk, the density of rough concrete structures never seems to diminish, with every square foot of land inhabited, buildings bulging and twisting to cram themselves into each available nook of land.

Leila doesn't look at me or speak for the entire walk, until we arrive at a flat area of empty bulldozed land. She stops, glances at me, and with a flick of her chin indicates a rubble-strewn field, as big as a football pitch, beyond which is the checkpoint, sealed by concrete slabs and reels of razor wire. Behind the roadblock are rows of metal cages leading into the corrugated-iron structure that is up against The Wall. A narrow strip of tarmac, empty for a short distance, leads towards a line of waiting people.

A dozen or so boys run across the field, shouting and throwing stones at an army jeep that is driving towards a shelter in front of the checkpoint. A few stones ping off the metal of the jeep, but the soldiers don't seem to care, and the boys aren't noticeably excited when they score a hit. Something about the confrontation has the feel of a weary ritual.

By the time I look back at Leila, she's already walking away. It seems impossible that this view of the back of her head might be the last I'll ever see of her, that she won't even say goodbye, but I know this must have been what she was told to do, and that to go after her would put her at risk. There's no way of knowing who's watching. No one could be allowed to see she was with me.

I stare at her slender form receding down the stark, bright street. At a junction just ahead, the two brothers are waiting for her. Neither of them appears to speak as she rejoins them, and they walk away immediately, disappearing from view. Leila's step falters. Instead of following her brothers, she stands there, in the middle of the road, motionless. In one quick movement, her head swivels to face mine. She blinks twice, but doesn't smile, or move, until, after a long stare, her index finger comes up to her lips, and she gives her fingertip a kiss. Without releasing me from her stare, she turns her finger towards me, pointing it skywards, and presses the fingertip subtly in my direction. Before I can respond, she turns with a quick scuffle of feet, raising a cushion-sized cloud of dust, and is gone.

I stare at the space where she stood, watching

the dust settle back to earth. My blood feels heavy and sluggish in my veins; my limbs doughy, thick and immovable. Leila has gone. Though she lives less than a mile from my home — or what used to be my home — I know I'll never see her again.

It strikes me that I don't know what to call the feeling that has grown between us. It was hardly what you could call a friendship. 'Affection' or 'tenderness' seems closer, but still wrong. Whatever the word might be, I sense that I want to hold on to it, keep it alive for as long as I can, though I know she has gone, for the last time.

It's dangerous to stand there doing nothing, drawing suspicious glances, but for a while I can't move. With a terrible effort, I eventually force myself to turn round and look again at the checkpoint. The jeep has disappeared from view, and the boys have formed into a huddle around a small fire of burning rubbish. Most of them are still holding stones which they toss idly from hand to hand.

A line of people snakes out across the dry, empty land, held back from the checkpoint by a solitary soldier. Some of them have umbrellas against the fierce sun, others rely on scarves and hats. There's no shade.

The crossing is obviously closed. I don't know why, or when it will open. I haven't thought about what I should do from here: join the queue and hope no one notices who I am, or walk towards the soldiers and tell them I belong on the other side?

After the previous night, I feel scared of the

army in a way I've never been afraid of them before, but I remind myself that it's no longer dark, and there's no curfew. Once I take my scarf off, they'll see who I am. If they're close enough to shoot, they're also close enough to see I'm not from this side. Their job is to protect people like me. If I walk towards them, they surely won't open fire.

I decide that approaching the soldiers is a safer option than taking my chances in the cramped, hot line, especially with the stone-throwing boys loitering close at hand. They remind me of the ones who chased me, and I don't want to risk being spotted as an outsider, as the enemy.

Skirting the edge of the cleared land, with my face wrapped in the scarf and my head turned away from the boys, I edge towards the checkpoint, attempting what I hope looks like a casual stroll. If I can reach the empty space between the waiting crowd and The Wall, I feel I might be safe.

The closer I get, the more I accelerate, but I'm still cutting across the stony land when a heart-stopping bang rings out, and a spot of soil in front of me spits up a spray of earth and stones. I stop, take off the headscarf, and raise my arms.

'IT'S ME!' I shout. 'I'M NOT FROM HERE! I'M FROM THE OTHER SIDE!'

No one at the checkpoint responds. I don't move.

Eventually I hear a shout, telling me to put my hands on my head. I do as I'm told and take one more step forwards. Immediately, another gunshot pierces the air. The bullet fizzes into a rock, and something flies up from the ground, whacking me in the chest. A yielding, melting sensation bursts hotly inside me. My legs begin to give way, but I don't dare stagger forwards in case this draws more fire from the checkpoint. Then I feel a sudden sharp pain in my back, as if I've been punched, or hit with a hammer, which for a moment is completely inexplicable. I don't know whether to stand or fall or run, or which direction I'd be able to go, even if my legs were capable of it. Then a stone flies over my shoulder, narrowly missing my head, and lands in front of me, soon followed by another one. I slump downwards and cower on the ground, realising that I'm being shot at from in front and stoned from behind.

The hail of stones continues. One hits me on the shoulder, and as I flinch, another crashes into my ear. A long, high note, like metal scraping against metal, fills my head, only to be drowned out by a new round of firing, this time from more than one gun: a fast, purposeful volley of shots. I press myself into the ground, flattening myself against the soil, but only when I hear a scream of pain some distance away do I notice that none of the bullets are striking near me. I raise my eyes and see a group of soldiers running out from the checkpoint, their guns wedged into their shoulders, firing towards the wasteland. The stone-throwing boys are now fleeing for cover, but before I can see if they're getting away, or who has been shot, my vision darkens and shrinks to two discs of light, like looking through binoculars. Slowly, these discs contract to nothing more than pinpricks of whiteness, as if I'm at the bottom of a hole which seems to be getting deeper and deeper, further and further from the light, just as the metallic shrieking fades, and the gunfire quietens to muffled pops, and the pain in my head and chest magically dwindles to nothing. The feeling is almost like dozing off, yet somehow more so. Every muscle in my body loosens and fails, disconnected by a wave of paralysis which plunges from my neck to my feet, as if a giant hand is wiping over me, erasing all sensation with a single sweep.

I flop on to my back, the tiniest of falls, but one which feels like a plummet into nothingness. For an instant my vision returns, showing me a flash of dazzling sky, a pristine dome of unbroken blue, before darkness floods in and the world slips away.

Part Five

Squares of white ceiling tiles stippled with black flecks, divided by a grey metal grid. Two tubes of light encased in a grooved plastic oblong. A low hum, like a computer or a fridge, and intermittent high beeps. White sheets, white walls and a white door with a circular window. Tubes, bottles, wires, needles. Stuff dripping into me, stuff dripping out. My hands, puffy and absent, far away at the end of my arms. My mother, half-asleep next to the bed. Then, in an instant, she's up on her feet, shouting something, almost screaming. I can see how loud it is by the veins popping out on her neck, but I can't hear what she's saying. It's as if I'm lying at the bottom of a swimming pool, looking up at her above the surface shouting inaudibly downwards into the water.

A fizz skids down my spine, something sucks and pops in my ears, and I hear her calling to me, calling for nurses and doctors, shouting that I've woken up. She repeats my name again and again and again, her eyes wild and fierce. After a while, I realise it's a question. She's asking if I can hear her.

I open my mouth but no sound comes out. My tongue and lips feel dry and numb, like tools I no longer know how to use. My head is wrapped in gauze that presses tightly against my chin.

I nod, two minuscule jerks of the head, blinking at her to show I understand. Tears gush from her swollen, bloodshot eyes. I can see she wants to hold me, pull me towards her, smother me, but with all the tubes and bandages there's no way in. She presses her face into my hand, or what looks like my hand, but I feel nothing. With my eyes, I trace the path of my arm from my wrist up to my shoulder, in the way you might check a gadget is plugged in. It is definitely my hand, and it isn't. She's squeezing my fingers, pressing her wet skin against my palm, but if I were looking the other way I'd have no idea it was even happening.

'You're back!' she keeps saying. 'You're back. You're safe. Don't ever leave us again. I won't let you leave us again.'

I look at her and wonder if I ought to be crying, too. I can't stop thinking about my hand. The thing at the end of my arm doesn't seem to be part of me any longer. I try to clench it. I try to clench the other one. Nothing happens.

A flurry of white-coated medical staff appear in the room, walking so fast they are almost running. They brush my mother aside and get to work on me. She steps to the foot of the bed, and there is Liev, waiting, his arms crossed over his chest. He reaches out and pulls her towards him, one hand spreading across her back, the other folding her head gently down into his neck. Her body shakes with sobs, and over her shoulder Liev looks at me, his lips curled into an expression that could be a smile, or could be something else entirely.

306

A week or so later, my hand gives a twitch. Within minutes, people I don't even recognise start arriving with elated expressions on their faces to congratulate me and prod me. One nurse even cries and nuzzles her soggy cheek against my arm, as if I'm some long-lost friend returned from the dead.

Mum's there every day, even though the hospital is miles from home, outside The Zone. It ought to be annoying, having her in my room all the time, but actually it's OK. She reads to me, changes the channel on the TV, keeps me company, and never tells me what to do. But maybe that's because I can't do anything.

After the twitch, a new nurse is assigned to me, some kind of physical therapist, who gives me exercises and monitors my progress, which everyone always tells me is 'wonderful', as if I'm somehow responsible for it. She brings a diagram of my body, which she marks with lines, ticks and crosses, showing me how I'm improving. Bit by bit, sensation creeps up my arms. After a while — I don't know how long — it's impossible to keep track of time in a hospital — I can sit up. Eventually, I'm given a wheelchair, which I learn to steer and propel.

Everyone acts optimistic and excited, as if this gradual, partial creeping back to how I was before is some astonishing superhuman flowering. It's like I'm the captain of an underdog World Cup team, from a tiny island no one's ever heard of, and I just keep on winning games, triumphing against all the odds, and getting closer and closer to the final. That's how everyone behaves, and I try my best to go along with it, even though I know — and everyone else knows — I'm just a paralysed kid slowly getting a little bit better.

No one ever gives me any bad news, but after a while it dawns on me that the therapist has stopped showing me her chart, and the bubble of excitement around me has deflated. Despite endless pummelling and stretching, my legs remain limp and useless.

Visitors now arrive in coats, so I know it must be winter. They walk into the room swathed in a tiny cloud of outsideness which takes a minute or two to dissipate in the hot, dead air of my room.

Liev comes once a week, on Friday afternoons, but I can see he doesn't want to be there. He spends the first five minutes trying to make conversation. I don't ignore him, but I don't exactly answer him, either. Around the five-minute mark, he gives a 'that's the best I can do' look to Mum, then he sits, and stays seated, not reading, not even looking out of the window, for fifty-five more minutes. Then he leaves. Each time he comes, he looks somehow smaller than the last time I saw him.

David also comes every week. At first he's even more reluctant and uncomfortable than

Liev, and there doesn't seem to be anything to talk about, but he starts bringing cards, and we just play, and he gives me a book so I can teach him new card games, and in the end I think it's David's visits that keep me going. Mum always hugs him when he leaves, which I don't think he likes.

Mum gets me a book of card skills, and my own pack, and pretty soon I'm a demon shuffler and magician. People love it when I do tricks. It gives them an excuse to be impressed by me, like when a toddler successfully uses a potty, and gets told they're a genius just for taking a piss.

One day, Mum brings my coat. I'm going home. There's nothing more the hospital can do for me. I have 'stabilised', which is a funny word to use for someone who can't stand up.

Most 'para' words are exciting: parachute, paranormal, paratrooper. Paraplegic is different. It's one of those words no one wants to say, or even hear. As I wheel myself out through the hospital, it's visible on people's faces that I have become this word, and people don't want to see me while at the same time finding it impossible not to stare. I quickly learn the pattern I know is going to follow me for a long time: the glance, the double-take, the appalled gaze with an expression moving from horror to pity, followed by a belated realisation that the polite thing is to look away.

Paranoid is another 'para' word. Maybe I'm a paranoid paraplegic, but I don't think so. The second I leave my ward and find myself among ordinary people, I realise that my life has crossed some invisible threshold to a new world, into a little bubble of disability that is going to envelop me for ever.

If I ever become a magician, I could bill myself as Joshua the Paranoid Paraplegic Prestidigitator.

Mum hardly talks to me as we drive back home, but not in a bad way. We've spent so much time together over the past few months, silence feels normal. It's exciting to see people out on the street, doing things, to see the world carrying on as normal, to remember that a hospital ward is just a room, not a universe.

The hills, at first, are blurry. My eyes can't adjust to anything far away. But I recognise Amarias when I see it, just the same, stretched from The Wall up to the hilltop, and down on the other side. The 'Welcome to Amarias' sign is still there, blocking the view of Leila's town, but with a hole in one corner where it took a hit during the crackdown.

David is waiting for me outside my house. I show him a trick, while Mum unfolds the wheelchair. He tries to push me inside, but I tell him I'd rather do it myself.

I'd never even noticed there was a step up to the front door, but I do now, because a metal ramp has been bolted on top of it.

Mum shows me to my new bedroom, on the ground floor, where the spare room used to be. I wheel myself in, and my chair just fits with barely a centimetre to spare, which seems lucky until I notice a tiny gap in the tiling at the threshold, and catch a whiff of fresh paint from the doorframe. I'm not sure if I'm supposed to

310

notice these adjustments to the house, whether I'll upset Mum if I'm grateful, or if I'm not.

David chats to me as we go into my room. Everything I own seems to have been brought down and arranged as closely as possible to how things were upstairs. He leads me to a pile of presents from other kids in our class. People I know never even liked me have bought welcome-home gifts. We unwrap a few, all board games or video games. He tries to act as if he can hardly contain his delight at the amount of fun these presents are going to bring us, and it's this — his attempt at optimism and excitement — that makes me want to cry, for the first time since I was shot.

I can see him sensing the atmosphere shift, and he's relieved when I tell him I'm tired, and he should go.

It's not just the doors and the bathroom and the light switches that have changed in my house. The biggest difference is Liev. Or, rather, Mum and Liev. He doesn't talk as much as he used to, and when he does, Mum rarely appears to listen. She no longer seems on the alert, poised to do what he asks. She doesn't wait on him, and she walks faster, stands more upright. I never see her pray, and I never hear her talk about her back.

Mostly, Liev and I ignore one another. Sometimes, out of curiosity, I'm slightly friendly to him, and he usually seems pleased. If I ask him to play cards with me, he always will.

I never hear them argue, I never hear Liev shout, but one morning Mum walks into my room with a strange look on her face, carrying a suitcase, and she begins packing my clothes. I can hardly believe what I'm seeing. I know immediately what this means, but I can't bring myself to ask, to check that it's really happening, in case I've got it wrong. I watch her every movement, the set of her jaw, the uncharacteristically hurried way she's folding my clothes, feeling more and more hopeful that I might be right, that the thing I've craved ever since we moved here could at last be materialising. Only after she's zipped the case shut does she look up.

'We're leaving,' she says. 'My bag is already in the car.'

She walks out with the luggage, then comes back for me. Liev stands in the living-room doorway, watching us go, but he doesn't speak, and Mum gives him nothing more than a curt 'goodbye', as if we're just popping out to the shops, but I know we aren't. I know this is it.

As she's stowing my wheelchair in the boot of the car he appears outside the house. He begins to shout at her that she's making a huge mistake, that she's betraying everything she really believes in, that she's being short-sighted and selfish, but Mum acts as if she can't even hear him. She climbs into her seat, shuts and locks the door, smiles at me, and we drive away.

She asks me if I want to say something to David, and at first I do, but as the car begins to slow outside his house, I realise that I have waited too long. I can't slow down now. I'll phone him. He can visit us. But right now, what I can't do is stop.

'Keep going,' I say. 'Just keep going.'

She understands — she understands exactly — and floors the accelerator, revving our sluggish, tinny engine. As we pass the 'Welcome to Amarias' sign, driving away for the last time, I roll down my window and whoop with all my might. Grinning, she rolls down hers and whoops along with me. Only when I feel as if my throat is giving way do I let my neck flop back against the headrest. A single tear is sitting, unwept, in the corner of her eye.

We let the wind buffet us as our car zooms

along the road out of the Occupied Zone, towards the sea. Mum's hair flaps everywhere, blowing over her face as she drives.

Her hair! Uncovered!

'Can you see?' I shout.

She smiles. 'Mostly.'

'How does it feel?'

She takes one hand off the wheel and leans her head right out of the window. Her hair streaks backwards in the onrushing wind. 'WONDER-FUL!'

I lean out, too, pulling myself up from the seat with my arms. The sun feels warm, high and generous, the air crisp with a gentle caress of spring. A grove of almond trees beside the road is shimmering with an explosion of pristine white blossom.

'I'M PROUD OF YOU!' she shouts.

We wind up our windows and fall back into our seats. That tear has broken free of her eye, and streaked backwards towards her ear.

'I'm proud of you,' she says again, switching her eyes from the road to me, for as long as it takes her to speak.

I've heard this so often, over every tiny increment of my recovery, that it has become meaningless, but this time she's saying something different. I can hear it in her voice.

'Why?' I ask.

'I've been asleep for almost five years. You woke me up.'

'What do you mean?'

I don't know why I'm asking. I know exactly what she means, but I want to hear more.

'You did a good thing,' she says.

'I tried.'

'Yes,' she says. 'And that's why I'm proud of you.'

'It didn't turn out very well.'

'I'm not saying I'm pleased you did it. I'm not saying it wasn't stupid.'

'Thanks.'

'I'm not saying I don't wish you'd talked to me instead . . . '

'I couldn't!'

'I know. And that's why I'm to blame.'

'You're not. It wasn't your fault.'

'You don't have to say that,' she says. More tears are flowing, now. Vertical ones. The diagonal streak was a one-off. I don't want her to cry, not today, not on the day of our escape. I want her to be happy.

'I wonder what it would look like to cry upside down,' I say.

She glances away from the road and looks at me for a moment, shocked and puzzled, then suddenly she's laughing, with her head rocking backwards, laughing and crying at the same time. The sound of it is as delicious as the most beautiful music I've ever heard.

'Your father was crazy, too,' she says. 'I never knew what he was going to come up with, either.'

'Shall we stop, and you can do a handstand. I'll hold your ankles.'

I can picture it. The little saloon in a deserted, stony lay-by; the boy in a wheelchair, holding the legs of a middle-aged woman executing a handstand, weeping, tears dribbling through her eyebrows into her long black hair.

She laughs again, still crying, still driving, zooming us towards the sea.

This is where I come to think. It might seem weird to spend so much time in a car park, but I can wheel myself here, and it has the view I want, of nothing but water, like the one from the bay window in the house where I was a child. If I get my chair in the right spot, I can look out at a pure blue world.

Someone else lives in that house now, and we couldn't afford it anyway. We're in a similar town, a few miles up the coast, in a tiny flat with boxy rooms and no view other than the back of the neighbouring apartment block. Even though it's half the size of our house in Amarias, it feels twice as big because there's no Liev. I never realised how much space he took up. Not his body, but his presence. Liev's demands and moods, or just the idea that he was always watching, squeezed me and Mum outwards to the fringes of that house, her into the kitchen, me into my bedroom. Here, all the space is ours, without any rooms you have to avoid because of the conversation you'll be drawn into if you enter.

For a while, being here was perfect. To be away from Liev, from Amarias, from the Occupied Zone was like recovering from a disease — a disease you've had for so long you can't even remember what it's like to feel healthy. Perhaps that's a strange thing to think for someone stuck in a wheelchair, but that's how it felt: like a miraculous recovery.

Mum even managed to get me into a normal school, where all the kids were so helpful it made me feel extra paranoid. Everyone was friendly and polite and hurried to help me through doors and fetched anything I asked for, and they smiled and smiled and smiled, but I could feel their relief when I moved away.

I'm like a hero and an ogre, rolled into one. A Herogre: a semi-mythical legless creature who propels himself on giant wheels and will eat you alive if you are ever caught not smiling at him. The legend of the Herogre is that he was created by a magic bouncing bullet sent as a punishment into the spine of a boy who went where he was told not to go, and tried to help people he was told not to help.

As people got more used to me, the Herogre thing diminished, and life began to seem normal; normal in the way Amarias had seemed normal before I found the tunnel and saw what was on the other side of The Wall. Here, there's no Wall, there are no soldiers — except off-duty ones visiting home — and this version of normal seems like how I imagine normality in other countries.

But when I come to this car park, and look out at the sea from this beautiful clifftop near the centre of my tranquil, prosperous town, I find myself thinking a shameful thought that I could never share with my mother. I begged and begged her to release us from Amarias, and finally she brought us here, and I can hardly even confess it to myself, but I don't feel as if I have escaped at all. This place no longer seems how it was before we left for the Occupied Zone, because back then I barely even knew what The Zone was, and once you know something, you can never unknow it.

I have left Amarias, but I now realise Amarias will never leave me. I hated that place because it felt like a huge lie, but this place doesn't feel so different. The Zone is less than an hour away. Leila and her family and millions like her are just as close. The off-duty soldiers, sitting around in cafés, sipping cappuccinos, will be going back there at the end of their leave, to man the checkpoints and police The Wall, and keep their tanks and planes in readiness for the next crackdown, but we are all supposed to behave as if The Zone is far away, in another world, out of sight beyond the horizon. The lie here is different, but more convincing, easier to fall for.

Perhaps that's why I'm drawn to this spot: partly because the view reminds me of how I felt when I was small; partly because I know that out there, over the sea, there are other countries beyond the reach of this lie, where perhaps I could forget what I want to forget. I'd go if I could. But, of course, there is another wall, a different kind of wall, around those places. With my passport I could visit, but I couldn't stay.

It's summer again now. It must be dry in Leila's olive grove. I still have the seeds, which I will plant if we ever get a garden. Every tree, leaf and stone of that grove is fixed in my head. I can take myself on imaginary walks through the terraces whenever I want. The only way I can walk at all is like this, in my own head, so that's where I always go. I do it again and again, keeping the place alive in my memory, making sure nothing fades. I touch the bark of every trunk; I lie down on the hot, dry soil; I water the thirsty trees and drink from the spring; I weed and prune in shifting sunlight which twinkles and flashes through the chattering leaves. I sit, awake in this car park, imagining myself sleeping there, in the olive grove. But I can never blot out the vision of that bulldozer trundling towards it. I know the walls might be down, the spring blocked, the trees gone.

I turn my chair away from the sea, and face back towards the hills. A gust of wind blasts from the cliff just as I take my brake off, nudging me into motion, and like a fleeting waft of a familiar smell, a vision comes to me of what is going to happen in the years ahead. For the first time since I was shot — for the first time in my life — I suddenly realise where I am going. I know what I will do. I understand, at last, that my goal should not be to forget, but to remember.

My arms feel strong as I wheel myself home, my body pulsing with a vigour I had almost forgotten it could contain. I don't know when it will happen, or how it will happen, or what exactly I will do, but I feel driven by a new sense of purpose. I will work. I will focus everything on work, and I'll learn whatever skills are needed to be of use, and I will go back to The Zone. When there is something I can do, I will return, not to Amarias, but to Leila's town, perhaps even to

320

look for Leila herself.

I tried to help and I failed, but I can try again, and I can keep trying, and if I fail again I can try once more. With this realisation, I immediately feel renewed, fortified, blessed, knowing that even if I spend my whole life failing, I will be failing at something I believe in; I will be fully alive and fully me. If the alternative is to do nothing, to forget, there is no alternative at all. How can I possibly forget when I sit, all day every day, in a wheeled reminder of the soldiers, and The Wall, and the people who are supposed to be invisible?

The wind is still at my back as I hurry home, and for a moment I almost twist round to check that it really is only the wind, but I know there's nothing to see, so I don't turn, hoping that by not looking I might hold on to the sensation for a few more seconds of someone behind me, a fatherly presence, helping me along.

Author's Note

The town of Amarias is fictional. Although it draws on many elements of Israeli settlements in the West Bank, it should not be taken as an accurate representation of any specific place. The checkpoint outside Amarias is based on Qalandia checkpoint.

Readers seeking a non-fiction portrait of the West Bank, and of how the occupation and 'security wall' have changed the lives of the people who live there, should read *Palestinian Walks* by Raja Shehadeh and *Against the Wall*, a collection of essays edited by Michael Sorkin, in particular 'Hollow Land: The Barrier Archipelago and the Impossible Politics of Separation' by Eyal Weizman.

A fascinating insight into life inside the settlements can be found in *Forty Years in the Wilderness: Inside Israel's West Bank Settlements* by Josh Freedman Berthoud and Seth Freedman.

When the Birds Stopped Singing by Raja Shehadeh and *Sharon and My Mother-in-Law* by Suad Amity provide vivid and contrasting accounts of life in Ramallah under curfew.

I would like to thank all the above authors, whose work was extremely useful in researching this book.

Fifteen per cent of the author's royalties from the English language edition of this book will be donated to Playgrounds for Palestine (www.playgroundsforpalestine.org), a charity which constructs playgrounds for children in Palestinian towns and refugee camps.

Acknowledgements

This novel owes a great debt to Alexandra Pringle, the consummate editor. It could not have been written without my participation in the Palestine Festival of Literature, for which I would like to thank Ahdaf Soueif and the Palfest Committee. My thanks also to: Felicity Rubinstein, Daniel Chalfen, Anna Steadman, Emily Sweet, Fred Schlomka, Yahav Zohar, Raja Shehadeh, the four families in the West Bank who offered me their hospitality during my research, Adam, John and Susan Sutcliffe, and, above all, more than ever, Maggie O'Farrell.

Other titles published by
The House of Ulverscroft:

THE DRESSMAKER

Kate Alcott

Tess, an aspiring seamstress, is stunned at her luck when the famous designer Lady Lucile Duff Gordon hires her to be a personal maid on the Titanic's maiden voyage. When disaster strikes, Tess is one of the last people allowed on a lifeboat — her employer also survives. On dry land, savage rumours begin to circulate: did Lady Duff Gordon save herself at the expense of others? Tess's dream of becoming a skilled dressmaker is within her grasp but now she is faced with a terrible choice. Suddenly she finds herself torn between loyalty to the fiery woman who could help her realise her ambitions and the devastating truth that her mentor may not be all she seems.

INVISIBLE

Carla Buckley

Growing up in the small town of Black Bear, Dana and her older sister Julie are inseparable — until a devastating secret compels Dana to flee from home. Years later, when she receives the news that Julie is seriously ill, Dana knows that it is time to return. But she arrives too late . . . Julie has left behind a shattered teenage daughter and a mystery — what killed Julie may be killing others too. Dana struggles to uncover the truth, but no one wants to hear it, including her niece, who won't forgive her aunt's long absence. Dana left her hometown to protect her secrets, but Black Bear has a secret of its own — one that could tear apart Dana's life, her family and the town itself . . .

BEFORE SHE WAS MINE

Kate Long

Freya's two mothers couldn't be more different: Liv, her adoptive mother, is earthy and no-nonsense, whereas Freya's birth mother Melody is still apt to find herself thrown out of Topshop for bad behaviour. Hard as it has been for Freya to try to reconcile her two families, it has been harder for her mothers. Proud of her mature and sensible adoptive daughter, Liv fears Melody's restless influence. Meanwhile, forced to give up her baby when she was just a teenager herself, Melody now craves Freya's love and acceptance — but only really knows how to have fun. When tragedy strikes, can they finally let go of the past and pull together in order to withstand the toughest challenge life could throw at them?